DISCOVER AND READ
OTHER GARY D. HILLARD BOOKS

Books Available NOW!

<u>Bett's Best</u>
Book One in the Bett's Trilogy

Betts is a quiet and curious seven-year old already bruised and battered by the chaos in her life. After a short life of abuse and neglect, a whirlwind of failed foster homes and a locked psychiatric unit, Betts finds herself in a kinship placement with her shy uncle Ames, a wounded vet who has retreated to a tiny cabin on Bear Hill, trying to keep his own demons from the Sand Wars at bay. Zoey is the young and hopeful social worker who believed in this placement, and who falls in love, first with Betts, then with Ames. Family, school, and friendship are all hard, as Betts slowly learns to trust those around her, and the magic of the Vermont woods.

FOUR Books Coming SOON!

Bett's Becoming
Book Two in the Bett's Trilogy

Eleven-year old Betts is now living with, and fighting with her best friend, Cara. Their teacher might be a witch, the therapist has a talking cat, and Betts' anger spills over at school, bloodying a bully and threatening Betts' place there. Cara's mother is missing, then horribly found, and Cara has to fight to stay in the cabin on Bear Hill. Families are lost, and then found, and love finds a way to heal and hold the people in Bett's life.

Bett's Belonging
Book Three in the Bett's Trilogy

Teen-aged Betts finds her strength, her art and finally, her own romantic love. Betts also finds new dangers in the world around her, and tries to save the next girl. Betts works on building some walls, and breaking others down, trying to find a balance between safety and connection.

Road Trip

Two girls on the run, Stella, 13, a warrior, and an expert on running, and Brandy, 15, who can no longer stay with her mother. A hardened foster kid helps an older girl run away, trying to get all the way from Chelsea, Vermont, to Albuquerque, New Mexico. Breaking and entering, car theft, and assault and murder are worse than anything Brandy has ever thought to do, but she finds herself happier than she has ever been, and Stella discovers something worth fighting for.

The Fosters of Camp Algonquin

Six hard-scrabble foster kids are sent to wealthy Camp Algonquin for the second session of the summer, under the distracted eye of the counselor, a soon-to-turn-18 foster child who is aging out of the system. The Fosters, as they are called by the rest of the camp, are there as an experiment by the well-meaning board of Camp Algonquin, who wanted to do something kind for children in need. Strangers become family up in Cabin 17, and Camp Algonquin gets more than they bargained for.

THE
BUCKMAN
KIDS

By

Gary D. Hillard

ISBN Amazon Print Version
9781655151279

Independently Published

Bear Hill Books, LLC
1182 Bear Hill Road
Randolph, VT 05060

540.355.5341
gdhillard@yahoo.com

Dedicated to the families

who care about other people's children,

and to faith, hope and love.

It's going to be good.

Spelling List. Test on Friday

Backside
Bale
Baptist
Bar
Barn
Barre
Bass
Bathtub
Bear Hill
Beating
Beauty
Beaver
Beech
Belief
Betrayal
Bible
Biscuit
Bless
Blond
Blood
Book
Boot
Bridge
Brookfield
Brush
Brother
Buckman
Bunny
Burial
Bus

THE BUCKMAN KIDS

CHAPTER ONE

The Buckmans moved onto our hill on April twenty-fourth, of nineteen sixty-six. I know that's right, because of the old beech tree on the ridge, just down from our house. The heart carved on it is dated just five days later, and I helped carve that heart. They were just down the hill from us, less than a quarter mile or so, moving into an old, empty single-wide that was tucked tight between the dirt road and the creek. There were Buckmans over on West Street, I think, and a few down in town. I now understand that any town probably has it's own version of the Buckmans. I didn't know any of them, really, my world being limited to my own family, the people in my school, and the congregation of my church, First Baptist, down in Randolph. But I remember my mother saying something to my father, while she was putting the plates on the table. We kids were washed up and sitting in front of our plates, being quiet. She told my father that some Buckmans had moved into the old Brassard trailer. They didn't say much to each other, at least around me, so I remember paying attention, wondering what my father would say back. He was quiet, even when he was angry, which seemed a good deal of the time. I could see his mouth go a little tighter, his lips thin out a bit. He shook his head, then turned to my sister, Sue, and told her to sit up straight. She did, and then, we had dinner.

I wondered if there were more Buckman kids who would be going to my school. We already had two Buckmans, both boys in the older grades, who came from time to time, usually in the fall, when their mom and dad were helping with the hay on the Campbell farm. They were rude, got strapped by Mr. White, laughed about it, and terrorized the girls and the younger kids. Crop-headed and bony, with raccoon eyes and worn out clothing, poor, like most of us, but harder, and meaner than we ever were. We were all glad when the hay was in, and they disappeared for another year. They had a sister, a couple years older than Susan, who had already quit school, and gone to work at the sock factory.

My school was just a little place, not the big school they have there now, with only enough kids to fill two classrooms, so Mrs. Billings, who lived in town, took the little kids, including me, and my brother James, who was a year younger. I was ten, and was just finishing the fourth grade. Mr. White, who was also the principal, took the older kids, which included both of my sisters, Ellen, who would have been eleven, and Susan, who was a year older. Mrs. Ferris was the third adult at the school, an older woman who smelled of cows. She cleaned the building, and watched over the lunchroom, making a peanut-butter sandwich for any of the kids who forgot to bring their own. She put her hand on your head if you felt sick. She was nice.

I didn't ask my mother about the Buckmans. We didn't butt in when our parents were talking, and all of us had learned to keep a low profile, at home, and at school, too, of course. I don't know that there was a rule that the kids were to be quiet at the table, but we were. We asked for the butter or the salt, and always thanked my mother for the food, even after my father had said the prayer. He always thanked the Lord, and "my good wife", as my father put it, for the food spread out on the table. Cooking was a lot of work back then, with bread to be made, twice a day, if you counted the biscuits in the morning, and everything that came in from the garden, or up from the cellar, needing time to prepare. My sisters helped, of course, with snapping green beans, or shelling peas, or peeling apples. Washing up, or stirring a big pot of soup. James and I worked outside with my father, hauling hay bales down from the loft, shoveling manure, and bringing in wood from the shed. We washed the cows twice a day, for milking. We'd talk, us kids, some nights, all in whispers, over the wall, about who had it worse, the heavy work outside, or the finger work inside, and had decided that it depended on the season. Winters were long, and being in by the stove was a better thing. Summers made it nice to be outside, away from the heat of the kitchen and the house.

We didn't question our life, then. We knew only ourselves, and more families like us, at First Baptist. We didn't see families on the TV, where the kids all had their own room, and the house was big and fancy, and there was a maid that did all the work. I saw that later, when we got a TV, when I was older, and it always seemed silly to me, that people could live that way. But when I was growing up, all I knew was what was around me. If I compared my luck to anyone, it was only to my brother and sisters, and they all had pretty much the same life as I had, although we each had good days and bad days. I never felt poor, even with all of us kids sharing the low-ceilinged room with the half-wall between the girls and the boys, or the soap-scummed bath water, passed from the girls down to the boys, already cloudy and losing much of its heat. I never felt mistreated, because my father treated all of us the same way, hard, of course, but not really mean. Parents were harder then. But I never felt lucky, either, until I had a chance to know the Buckman kids.

Roy Buckman was on the school bus Monday morning, looking a little like his cousins, only my age. He might have been eleven. He had the same lice-cut hair, showing his bony head, and the same darkened eyes, where not enough sleep had settled, and his clothes were dirtier than what my mother would have ever let me out in. His sisters were with him, both worn thin and wary, but really pretty, unwashed blond hair pulled back, the older girl's face scrubbed until you could only see the bleeding holes where the pimples had been. Roy told them both where to sit, his younger sister, who seemed only a little younger than me, and even his older sister, who was as old as Sue, and seemed maybe to be a bit simple. He had them sit next to each other, right in front of me and my brother, and across the aisle from where he took his seat. Roy looked around on the bus, like he was trying to see how things worked, and then sat down, and looked at his sisters some, then looked hard at me and my brother. I looked away, and then looked back, and saw him reading a book, even though he was only my age, a thick book with a wolf on the cover.

I was only reading little kid books at that point, although reading was something I already loved. I tried to forget the hard look, and leaned across the aisle and whispered, "What cha reading?"

He looked at me, and you could see that he was trying to decide whether he should talk to me or not. He finally thrust the book out to me, his thumb still marking his page, and said, "*Fang of the North*. It's about a sled dog up in Alaska that's half wolf. That's him on the cover." He pulled the book back, and then looked back at me. "Do you read?"

I could see Mr. Beller's face in the big mirror, looking up, and I tucked back into my seat, out of Mr. Beller's aisle. I whispered, "He doesn't like it when we lean into the aisle." I nodded towards the driver. I thought about the thin books I read, with a cute bunny on the cover, or a cat. I said, "I like to read, but I don't have any books like that."

Roy nodded. "You can borrow it when I'm done. Maybe next week. It's pretty good."

I looked back up at the big mirror, where I could see Mr. Beller looking towards the next stop, where the Campbell kids were waiting by the road. I stuck my hand out to Roy, across Mr. Beller's aisle. "I'm Toby Landers," I said.

15

Roy stuck his hand out. "I'm Roy, he said, leaving the Buckman off, at first. "Roy Buckman," he added. "They're my sisters." He nodded at the girls. "Tina is the big one, and Trish is the little one. I'm looking out for them," he added. His handshake was hard and quick, and we pulled our hands back before Mr. Beller had a chance to see us out in his aisle again. If kids acted up on the bus, Mr. Beller went in and had a word with Mr. White, and then you started you day holding onto the edge of Mr. White's desk, wishing you had stayed out of the aisle on the bus.

The Campbell kids got on, and found their seats. Mr. Beller checked the aisle again, then set the bus into gear, and pulled out onto the road, the big tires digging into the spring mud, and the old bus pulling a bit, with Mr. Beller working to stay out of the deep ruts in the road, with mud season only being about half way done. We rode along in silence, a few whispers in the back, but the bus was a quiet place, because Mr. Beller wanted it that way. I thought about Roy Buckman, and wondered if he was as different from his cousins as he seemed. I didn't think that they read at all, and they certainly didn't shake hands.

But back behind that little question was a bigger one, one that nagged at me for the rest of that school year, and the whole summer, a question, really, that has interested me my whole life. I didn't really have the words for it then, words like "destiny" and "free will", but now I know that I was wondering if a Buckman could ever be something other than a Buckman. I was a Landers, and at that time I had no doubt that I would grow up to be a lot like my father, and that my sisters would grow up to be like my mother, and that we would likely have a life that was a lot like the life my parents had. This was the first time I had thought about what we can become, who we might be able to decide to be something other that what we had been put in place to be. Roy Buckman read books, and shook hands, and offered to share his books with me, something I could never have imagined.

This thought scared me a little. It felt like a rebellious way of thinking. It wasn't a thought I would share, or a question I would ask, but thinking about it suddenly opened up the world. If Roy Buckman could swing away from his expected life, and become something different, maybe we all could, too. Not that I had ever thought about it, before. I was a Landers, and there wasn't anything wrong with that. But it was interesting to think that that maybe we could have a choice.

When we got to the school Mr. Beller pulled up next to the building, set the brake, and pulled the lever that opened the door and swung out the big, red stop sign on the side of the bus. We children stayed in our seats, waiting. Mr. Beller then stood, and turned around and faced us, and then quietly said "OK". We silently filed past him, Roy following his sisters, and then my brother and me. Mr. Beller seemed to look extra hard at me as I walked up the aisle, and I nodded, but I didn't say anything.

My sisters moved to Mr. White's classroom, and Roy looked at me. "That the big kid's room?" he asked.

I nodded, and said, "Mr. White. We have Mrs. Billings. She's pretty nice. Mr. White's the principal," I added.

"Is he mean?" Roy asked.

I nodded. "Sometimes," I said.

Roy brought his older sister, Tina, into Mr. White's classroom, then came back to ours, with his younger sister in front of him, and stood by Mrs. Billings, introducing his sister and himself, and asking where they should sit. She looked unhappy to have two more children in the class, bringing the number to thirty-one, and then looked out at the classroom, where the brown metal desks were set in straight lines, the girls to her left, and the boys to her right. She put Roy's younger sister, Trish, in the one empty desk towards the front, and then sighed, lacking an empty desk on the boy side. She finally took a metal folding chair and set it beside Tommy Blaisdell's desk, telling Tommy that he would share until another desk was brought up from storage in Randolph. She marked off about a third of the desk top with masking tape, and pointed at it, telling Roy that this was his part of the desk, and to stay on it. She then looked at Tommy and narrowed her eyes. "No problems," she said. Tommy nodded.

Roy scooted his chair a little way out from Tommy, towards the window, trying to be a good desk neighbor, I guess, then stood, along with the rest of the class, waiting for the prayer and the pledge. I guess where Roy went to school before, they had the same start to the day.

After the pledge, Mrs. Billings told us to sit, and we did. Mrs. Billings had the younger kids in the front of the class, and the older kids, like me and Roy, in the back, and she moved between them and us, teaching a lesson to them, and then a harder one for us older kids. We always started with math, with the little kids doing counting, and us having to do adding and subtracting, and multiplying, on paper. I settled into the work, and didn't think about Roy until it was time for lunch. We lined up from the front of the class to the back, putting the younger kids in front of the line. Roy was watching his sister, who was peering into her lunch bag. My brother, James, was up there, too, but I didn't worry about him like Roy did Trish.

We were quiet, walking down the hall to the lunchroom, with Mrs. Billings walking beside us. Most of the kids had a lunch box, or a paper bag, like me and James, ours filled today with a peanut butter sandwich, an apple and two Oreos. The school sold milk for a nickel, and there was a nickel in each bag as well. We brought the bags back at the end of the day, folded flat in our book bag. There were four long tables set up in the lunch room, where they also had a school play twice a year, and played dodge ball or basketball if the weather was too bad to go outside for recess. The room smelled of unwashed children, with a bit of cow, since many of the kids, my brother and me, included, came from dairy farms. There was chlorine bleach in the air as well, from where Mrs. Ferris and a couple of the older girls had wiped the tables just before.

We were already sitting, with Roy crowded next to his younger sister, Trish, when Mr. White brought in the older kids, including Tina, who Roy waved over to sit with him. She looked like she wanted to sit with the girls she was walking with, but she went to him first, and pretty much got his permission. Roy kept his eye on his older sister the whole time, talking some with his younger sister, and eating a sandwich he pulled from a paper bag.

One by one, kids started raising their hands, which brought Mrs. Ferris to them, to check if they had eaten their lunch, and could be released to go outside to play. Most kids got told to eat more, including James, who had to clean up his apple core. He chewed at it angrily, gnawing it distractedly as he watched his friends heading out to play. He held the core up to Mrs. Ferris, who nodded, and he speed-walked out the door, tossing the apple core and the empty milk carton in the trash can by the door, and putting the folded paper bag in his back pocket. Mr. White and Mrs. Billings stood at the back of the room, watching the kids and talking quietly.

Roy was finished with his sandwich, but stayed in his seat, watching his sisters eat, and waiting for them to be done. I was eager to go out and play kickball. I could hear the game already started. I hoped that the big boys hadn't taken the better ball, a big red one that stayed pumped up and could be kicked all the way across the playground, but I knew that they probably had, leaving us the smaller, blue one that was usually about half flat. James was probably already on a team. Both my sisters had finished as well, with Susan and Ellen probably standing by the wall with the other girls, watching the boys play. The younger girls would play clapping games, or jump rope, but the older girls just stood watching the boys, and whispering to each other. But I waited for Roy, who was waiting for his two sisters to be finished. When they finally did, and had been given permission by Mrs. Ferris, he put up his hand, got the nod from Mrs. Ferris, and followed them out the door.

I found Roy out on the playground, a stretch of worn grass out behind the school, where there was a kickball game already started, mostly bigger boys. Roy was watching, from the side, and still keeping an eye on his sisters, who were both jumping rope right by the building. I walked over and stood beside him. He looked at me, said nothing, then, kept watching his sisters.

I stood there for a bit, wishing he would have said "Hi". I said, "How do you like the school?"

He looked at me, hard, again, like he had on the bus, then, softened a bit. "It's OK," he said. "Smaller than Barre."

I thought about the Barre school, a three-story brick building right in the middle of town, with a whole pile of stone steps leading up to the giant wood doors. "Yeah," I said, "It's pretty small. Smaller than Barre, for sure." That sounded stupid, but I didn't know what else to say, so I said, "I just live up the hill from you. The grey house with the old barn next to it?" He nodded, but didn't say anything. "That's us," I said. Nothing. I just stood there, watching him watch his sisters. After a while, my brother called me to the kick ball game. I asked Roy if he wanted to play, but he shook his head, so I jogged over and got on my brother's team.

I was bugged about Roy not talking to me. When James asked why I was hanging out with a Buckman, I shrugged my shoulders. I didn't know. I didn't like his cousins, and I'd never heard anything nice about the Buckmans. But already I knew he was different than me and my brother, different than the other kids at school, or the kids I knew at church. I knew my parents wouldn't want me hanging out with him, and I wondered if James would tell on me when we got home. I let the ball roll right past me, not paying attention to the game, and everybody yelled at me. I shook my head and tried to think about the game. Roy was still standing by himself, watching his sisters jump rope over by the building.

Mrs. Billings rang us all back in, with the big, brass hand bell that was already about a hundred years old, even back then, and we settled in our seats, quiet, but still breathing hard, and a little sweaty from the game. We got out our readers, and went over the day's lesson, then pulled out paper to answer the questions at the end of the reading. The reader had a bunch of little pieces taken out of real books, and sometimes I liked the reading. There were always ten questions at the end, some of them with short answers, like "who did the dog belong to?" but a couple of them were longer, and you had to think some, and write a couple of sentences to answer them. I like reading better than arithmetic, even with the ten questions, but not as much as history, or science, which we only had a few days a week.

When we were done, we could raise our hand, and Mrs. Billings would come and check your work, and then let you free-read until the rest of the class was finished. I did that, and then went to the bookshelf to pick a book. I thought about the wolf dog on the cover of the book that Roy had been reading on the bus, and wished that there were some bigger kid books here, in our classroom. I finally settled for a book about a mouse that runs away from home, one I had already read a couple of times. I liked it well enough, but it felt younger than what I wished I was reading, now.

Roy had finished up, and when he saw me raise my hand, he raised his, too, and Mrs. Billings checked him out, and said "Very good," which she didn't usually say. Roy was reading the wolf dog book, holding the book up close to his face, I guess because the print was so small. I opened up the *Runaway Ralph* book, and tried to read some, but I couldn't get interested in it. I wished I had a better book. I thought I would go to the library in the school, and see if they would let me borrow a big kid book. Maybe tomorrow, I thought. I didn't want to call attention to myself.

Roy sat his sisters in the same spot on the bus on the way home. When we were almost to my house, he shoved his book out to me, and said, "You can borrow it for tonight. We have to move the metal tonight, so I won't have a chance to read until tomorrow, anyway."

I took the book, thick and heavy and with a snarling wolf dog on the cover. "Thanks," I said. "What metal?"

Roy looked out the window, until the bus was just pulling over in front of my house. "Scrap metal. My dad sells it, sometimes. We still have a big pile at the old place. The truck doesn't have plates, so we have to go after it gets dark. Bring the book to school tomorrow."

I smiled, and said thank you, again, but Roy just looked at his sisters, then back out the window again. The bus was stopped, and James was already up, and walking past me. My sisters were following him. "See you tomorrow," I said. But he didn't say anything back.

CHAPTER TWO

I had tucked the book in my bag, and went with my brother to the barn, where we would help my father with the chores until it was time for dinner. My father had the milking pump all apart, and was in a foul mood. He told me to lime the gutters. I went to the stack of lime bags beside the spider-webbed window, brushing the fat, grey barn spiders off the bags with a handful of soggy hay, and the lugged one of the bags upright, and took my knife and cut through the thick, soft paper of the bag, opening it up about half the way. I wiped the lime off my knife, and took the scoop, pushing it into the lime, and carefully carried a full scoop to the end of the south gutter, and began to sprinkle the white power into the concrete gutter. "Don't use too much," my father said. "Six scoops should do it." I tried to sprinkle it less as I went, trying to think three scoops per gutter, and where one third of the way might be. He hadn't worried about lime before, and I wondered if it was because he was upset at the milking pump, or worried about money.

James had been sent to bring wood up to the house, a chore that would take him an hour or more, since he was little, and could only carry a single split each trip. I knew my mother was inside the house, working on the laundry, which she had set the girls to bringing in, and then having Susan cut the best parts out of a basket of bad potatoes. Susan had gotten into trouble with my mother yesterday, for having not kept after the potatoes in the bin in the cellar, and letting a few go bad, and these, left in the bin, then threatening to spoil the rest. The cellar was one of Susan's jobs, with my mom hating to go down there, in the dark. I'd heard her going at Susan last night, down in the kitchen, angry about the potatoes, and the wasted food, her sharp words punctuated by the sharp crack of the hair brush on Susan's backside, Susan's gasp after each crack, like a quick echo. Old potatoes smelled especially rank, and my mother would have Susan out on the porch to do the work. Ellen would be at the kitchen table, helping to fold the laundry, and putting our clothing and sheets away. I had guessed a pot roast for dinner tonight, since there had been a roast thawing out in the big roaster last night, with onions, potatoes and carrots baked around it, probably. I liked mashed potatoes better. I hoped there would be a pumpkin pie for desert, but that wasn't a sure thing. And the apples were all gone at this point.

By the time I had the gutters limed, my father had the pump back together, and hooked up to the vacuum line. He flipped a switch, and listened to it run, putting his hand over an open valve, feeling the pulsing suck of the machine. He nodded without smiling, and sent me out to the south pasture to bring the cows in. I picked up a cane from beside the door, and headed out into the cloudy afternoon. Spring was a wet time, with the cows leaving deep hoof marks in the mud, cutting through the newly greening turf and pressing up the clay from beneath the black soil. I watched where I stepped, trying to stay out of the holes, which would likely suck the rubber boot right off my foot, leaving me tipping wildly, trying to keep my sock from the mud.

It was still light, with the sun just behind the hills to the west, but the sky was still filled with the yellow light of early evening. I saw the cows up ahead, lined up patiently by the gate, mud and clay up to their knees, and their backsides and tails splashed with the runny manure they had this time of year. It took them a while to get used to the fresh grass again, after a winter of hay and grain. I sighed, hoping that James would be finished with the wood, and back in the barn to help me wash the cows off for milking. Having a boy on each side of the cow was a big help, compared to squatting here, and then, there, trying to do the whole cow quick enough, and well enough, that my father didn't lose his temper. Summer would be easier, I knew, with less mud, and less manure.

I opened the gate, and stepped aside, letting the cows make their way down the path towards the barn, keeping the cane low so as to not spook them. I knew that a few would stop beside the pen where the calves were, and look at their babies, fenced away behind the heavy wire stock panels, and need a whack or two from the cane to make their way on down to the barn, leaving their crying babies behind. The sound of the mother cows lowing to the calves, and the calves bleating back, that sound still bothered James, but I was used to it, now, and it no longer bothered me as much as it once did. Cows had to make calves in order to make milk, and milk was what brought the milk check every month, paying the mortgage on the farm, and buying the groceries and materials from the stores down in town. My father had said, once, "You want to eat, don't you?" I had nodded. I did want to eat.

I left the gate open, for the cows to find after they were milked, and followed the last cow, number 23, as she picked her way on down the pock marked trail, watching my step as the holes in the wet ground were doubled and deepened, and fresh, streaming piles of manure were plopped down. I hoped James was there in the barn. As I followed number 23 into the barn, I found James there, with the buckets, brushes and rags, and joined him in cleaning up the first cow. We got through the seventeen cows we were milking at this point, and I took the cows back up the hill, while James and my father cleaned up the barn, and put the milk in to cool. I was tired, and ready for dinner, the sandwich and apple having worn off a few hours earlier. I was eager to settle into my bed, and use a little time to get at the book I had borrowed from Roy.

It was getting really dark by the time we were back at the house. I had been right about the pot roast, and the rest. The potatoes were cut into odd shapes, with the bad parts cut off. My mother made Susan explain about the potatoes to the rest of us, and why they had gone bad. They tasted fine, though, even if they looked a little funny, along with the normal looking carrots and onions. And there was pumpkin pie, after all. I ate until I was full. My mother had Susan take a trip down to the basement, with a flashlight, to be sure that everything was as it should be, and then she sent the girls upstairs for their bath, while James and I sat at the table and did our spelling list and a few math problems. My mother sat by the wood stove and pulled out a basket of mending, and worked at putting a new zipper into the back of one of my sister's dresses. My father sat in his chair, reading one of the journals that came every month, a tooth pick still in his mouth, and his hard, calloused hands pulling at the thin pages as he read. It was quiet, with the wind making a shushing sound in the trees outside, and the soft sound of truck tires out on the highway, over the rise and out of sight, but still something you could hear on a quiet night.

I felt sleepy, after the day's work, and all the pot roast and the pie, but I wanted to spend some time with the book that Roy had loaned me, so I went and got a big glass of water and drank it down. I was done with my homework, but hadn't taken the book out of my bag, worried that my mother or my father would ask where I got it, and then be angry that I had spent time with one of the Buckmans, so I just checked and rechecked my work until Susan's voice called down the stairs, "Done." James and I went upstairs, stripped and got into the tub, soaking for just a bit in the cooling water, smelling of the soap and shampoo that the girls had used. They had left two wash clothes on the side, and we scrubbed until most of the day's dirt was in the water, which then looked a bit like old dish water, then we each stood, and rinsed off with a plastic pitcher of fresh water drawn at the sink. When we were clean and dry, we wore our towels down the hallway to our room, and got dressed in our winter pajamas. It was still cold at night, and my father had mostly stopped firing the wood stove over night, except a single log, just enough for coals to be there in the morning.

My mother came in, after we were dressed, and watched us kneel beside our beds and say our prayers, and then kissed us both, and went to do the same with our sisters, on the other side of the wall. There was a single bulb on the ceiling, that she flipped off as she left the room, but we were allowed some time with the bedside lamps on, to read, if we wished. I flipped mine on, and James complained, but I told him to turn over, and face the other way. I lay on my elbows, the pillow tucked under my chest, and opened the book up. *Fang of the North.* Above the northern border of Canada, a lonely trapper made the rounds of his traps, riding his dog sled across the frozen snow, the dark arctic winter howling around his thick bear coat, and heavy fur hat. The howl of a wolf sounded in the darkness, closer than he would have liked, and the sled dogs shivered in their traces, hearing in the wild song something they had lost and left behind. Something they feared...

I read until I heard my parents climbing the stairs, then quickly shut off the light, and hid the book back in my bag. I called to my mother, and told her I needed to pee, and she told me I shouldn't have had that big glass of water, but to go ahead and go. They let me pee, and then I headed back to bed. I heard the bath drawn again, this time for my mother, and then my father. He often stayed in the bathroom while my mother bathed, sitting on the toilet, I supposed. I tried to imagine it, and then I tried not to. Sometimes, I could hear their voices, soft and indistinct, my father's voice sounding like someone else, and even a rare laugh, once in a great while, but tonight I heard nothing except the tub water running, and I fell asleep before the water was turned off.

CHAPTER THREE

The next morning, when Mr. Beller pulled the school bus over in front of the trailer where Roy Buckman had moved in, there were piles of scrap metal all over the place. The dirt road was only about ten feet from the side of the trailer, and the creek dropped off a few feet on the other side, so there was barely room for the trailer itself, much less piles and piles of old metal. I looked out the window, forgetting about Roy for a moment, and tried to make sense of what I was seeing. To the left, beside the old truck, was a stack of truck radiators, black and brass colored, with some green stain on the fins where they had leaked. Flat, rusty bars stood in another stack, including pieces of rebar, bed rails, car springs, tee posts, and some angle iron. Beside that was a stack of pipe, some short, some long, big fat, black pipes, that must have once carried sewage, thinner iron pipes, for gas, maybe, black or galvanized, and so corroded that they now only looked like the ground. Copper pipe was off by itself, mostly straight, but some twisty pieces as well, some green with age, others a dull brown. A stack of old car batteries was set by the trailer steps, maybe thirty or more, some of the cases cracked, with the acid leaked out and dried into a white, toxic power on the sides. There was a stack of used metal roofing, striped and cratered with rust, stacked out a foot or so into the road. I knew that Mr. Cummings, who drove the town plow, would hate that. The tiny yard around the trailer was filled, with only a narrow slot for the truck to park, and a thin, winding path for a person to pick their way up to the trailer steps.

By the time I had taken it all in, Roy had shepherded his sisters onto the bus, and was walking down the aisle, directing them into their same seats from before. He looked deathly pale and tired. They all did, with his sister's hair still unwashed, but flecked now with what might be old paint chips. Tina sat with her mouth hanging open, her yellow teeth un-brushed, looking like she might fall over at any minute. Her right cheek showed the only color on her face, a dull purple bruise roughly the shape of a hand. Trish saw me staring at her sister, and nudged Tina, whispering something in her ear. Tina covered her face with her hand, and looked down at the floor, while Trish looked angrily at me, like she might jump up off the seat and try to fight me. Trish herself looked only a little better than her sister, white faced, hollow eyed and dog tired. I wished she wasn't mad at me, and looked away.

Roy was turning to sit, just as one of the older boys in the back, I wasn't sure who, whispered "Junkyard." Roy, who was maybe even a little smaller than I was, stopped, and looked back at the older boys, and brought his hand up quickly, making a rude gesture with his hand, and whispering something foul. He stood long enough, his finger still up, and staring down the bigger boys in the back, that Mr. Beller said "Sit!", which Roy slowly did. Mr. Beller checked his mirror, his face angry, and planning, I was sure, to have a brief talk with Mr. White once we got to school. I hated that. Roy looked terrible, and now he was going to get strapped by Mr. White, and then beaten up by the older boys at recess.

As we pulled over for the Campbell kids, I held the book out to Roy, who hadn't said a word to me yet. I felt sorry for him, and I knew he wouldn't like that. I was scared for him, and I knew he wouldn't like that, either. I didn't want to talk about the piles of metal in his yard, but I finally said, "That's a lot of metal. Did you haul all that last night?"

Roy looked at me with the same look he had given the big boys in the back, but then softened, and said, "How'd you like the book?"

The door had opened, and the Campbell kids were climbing onto the bus. Roy pushed the book back to me, and said, "Keep it another night. We have to do more metal tonight, anyway, and I won't have a chance to read."

I was happy to have the book back for another night, but the idea of more metal got me stuck. "Where you going to put it?" I finally asked.

"I don't know," said Roy, too tired to be annoyed at me, looking first at his sisters, then out the window.

We were done talking, I guessed, so I opened up *Fang of the North*, and fell once again into the boreal forest and the wilderness of the arctic. I glanced over at Trish, when I was turning a page, and found her looking at me, no longer angry, but just looking. She saw me and turned away, but I thought that tired and dirty as she was, she was probably the prettiest girl I had ever seen. I wondered if she liked me. I rode the rest of the way to school, sometimes traveling with the dog sled, trying to picture the unseen wolves in the shadows, and sometimes thinking about how pretty Trish was, even when she looked so awful.

When we got to school, I still didn't know if Trish hated me or liked me. I had looked over at her twice more, after checking to see that Roy was looking out the window, and it looked like she was dozing, maybe, having managed to fall asleep right on the bus. Trish had freckles on her cheeks, tossed out like the stars in a winter sky, and a tiny little nose. She was leaned up against her sister, who had forgotten to hold her hand over her cheek, where I could see the lines of fingers in the darkening bruise, and looked like she could barely hold her eyes open, too. I thought about my mother, checking each of us, after we had finished our breakfast, eggs and sausage this morning. She made sure the boys' shirts were buttoned up right, and tucked smoothly in, that the girls' dresses were even and straight, our hair in place, and our teeth brushed. I thought of how annoyed I was at standing in line, every morning, having her fix my shirt, smooth my hair, and then making me bare my teeth, checking that I had done a good job brushing them, before passing me out the door and doing the same for James. I thought for once that maybe it would be worse to have no one there to do that, to be the Buckmans, and walk out the door every morning, without anyone caring if you looked nice, had been fed, or had had enough sleep.

Mr. Beller stood by his seat, instead of sitting, like he usually did, and I figured he was getting ready to go into the school and have a word with Mr. White, about Roy. He stood, watching the kids get off, but stuck his arm out in front of Roy, and said, "You sit, right when you come in. You stay out of the aisle. You don't make any noise. Save your fighting for the playground, if you want, but never on my bus. That's your warning. There won't be another." He dropped his arm, and Roy moved on past, without nodding or saying anything. I followed nervously. I'd never seen Mr. Beller give a warning before, and I wondered if he felt sorry for Roy, the way I did. I had a hard time imagining that Mr. Beller would ever feel sorry for anybody.

Roy sat next to me at lunch, pulling out the same kind of sandwich, baloney, maybe, or ham, on bread with mustard. He had an apple this time, too. He'd almost fallen asleep in class, twice. I asked him how late they had worked last night.

He grinned at me, like what I'd said was funny. "We worked all night. Did five loads, from Barre up to Brookfield. Probably have five more to do, tonight. Water tanks, a couple refrigerators, and a bunch of lumber. We might build a shed, or something, I guess. And there's a couple of little tractors. Lawn tractors. They don't run yet. And some bicycles." He tried to think. "There's probably some stuff I'm forgetting. I'm tired. Oh, yeah, there's a bunch of wire, and a stack of cable, too. If we had a trailer, we could do it faster."

I could see one of the big boys, Danny Bowman, big and scary, the boy from our bus, staring at Roy. "He's looking at you, kind of mean," I said.

Roy glanced over, and nodded. "Yeah. He's the guy on our bus that was mouthy. I'll have to let him know who I am." He took the last bite of his sandwich, and chewed it slowly. "What does White do if the kids fight at school?" he asked.

"He straps them, and then sends a note home to their parents." I thought about the time I had gotten into a scuffle, last year. "Maybe you can just stay away from him." I said.

Roy shook his head. "New school. There's always a fight. I just don't want to get thrown out, and leave my sisters here alone. I don't mind the strapping, or the note. My dad won't care, anyway, unless I lose." He looked at the boy, maybe a foot taller, and probably twice his weight. "And I won't lose, not to him, anyway. Will the other kids pile on?"

I thought about that. "No. I don't think so," I said. "They'll watch, though."

"Good," said Roy. He handed me his apple. "I'll have that later." He raised his hand, and Mrs. Ferris came over, and checked us out for recess. On his way out, Roy made it a point to stare at the older boy, and mouth something again, and then nod out to the playground. I couldn't understand it at all.

Roy headed off to the side of the playground, in the new shade of big maple just setting its leaves on. Roy looked at the ground, stepping over the roots, and kicking a loose rock off to the side. He looked over at the door from the lunch room from time to time, and then stooped down to tie his shoes up tighter. The older kids were coming over, Danny Bowman in the front, walking right towards us. There were maybe fifteen kids behind him, and when the other kids on the playground saw, they dropped what they were doing and came jogging over, too. Nobody shouted, not wanting to bring the adults in sooner than they would come, anyway, but they were excited to see a fight, a fight between Danny, who we all knew was the toughest kid in the school, and this new kid, a Buckman, who stood in the shade of the maple, shifting his skinny frame from one foot to the other.

Danny was moving fast, but something in the way Roy looked at him made him slow up, a few feet away. Danny said something about the little kid that lived in the junkyard. Roy just stood there, shifting his weight back and forth, up on the balls of his feet, his arms a little out from his sides, his hands

opening and closing, and his eyes sharp on Danny's hands, and Danny's face. Danny had just said, "And his sister's a retard," when Roy sprang, not yelling, or swinging wildly, not shoving, not punching for the stomach or the chest, like school yard fights usually did, but silent, swinging up to Danny's face, scraping Danny's top lip up, right through his front teeth, and folding Danny's nose over to the side, flat, with the sound of a carrot breaking. Danny made a gagging sound, and Roy hit him again, hard, with his other hand, short, fast jabs, this time over Danny's left eye, twisting his fist as it moved into Danny's forehead, splitting the thin skin there, and sending a torrent of fresh blood down into Danny's eyes. Danny's head rolled back, and Roy punched deep into his throat, then, hit Danny's mouth again, low this time, cutting the lower lip and breaking out two more teeth. Danny fell back, crying now, tripping over one of the roots, and fell, blinded and bloody and terrified, trying to say something that might have been "please", over and over. The kids all around were silent, now, staring like they couldn't turn away, but sickened I guess, like I was, by the swift blood and needless cruelty of it.

Roy was standing over Danny, both hands bleeding from where he had cut himself on Danny's broken teeth. He turned away from Danny, and looked back at the crowd of pale children behind him. "Again?" he asked, and the bigger boys in front pressed back against the crowd, their hands open and at their sides, a few shaking their heads in a silent "no". Roy watched Mr. White moving across the playground, slow but steady, and then said, low and quiet, "You leave us alone. Me, and my sisters." A few kids nodded, but all of them had heard it. "Don't mess with us, at all," he repeated. "Ever."

Mr. White usually strapped both of the boys who had been fighting, but today he just stood over Danny, and shook his head. "He's a Buckman, Bowman," he said. "Didn't you know that?" Mr. White tried to grab Roy by the shoulder, but Roy shifted just a bit sideways, out of reach, and looked at Mr. White. "Go on, then. Inside," Mr. White said, letting Roy walk ahead. I thought Mr. White sounded just a little bit scared.

The crowd of kids started to fade away, nervous and silent, not yet talking among themselves. Two of the older boys helped Danny up, and, with one on each side, hanging back so as to not get bled on, they walked him over towards the school. I looked at the ground, where the blood sat in pools on the dirt, with two big flies already landed in one puddle. I looked at the apple, bright red and perfect in my hand, and thought about this boy who had moved just down the road from me. A boy my age, who read big-kid books, and who

looked after his sisters, and who had spent the whole night moving loads of scrap metal, then fought, and almost killed, Danny Bowman.

"Is that Roy's apple?" asked a voice beside me. Trish stood there, picking at a new scab on the back of her hand. "Can I have it?" she said.

I looked at her again. She had on tights under her skirt, black and thin, worn out, with holes in both the knees, and a run up the side of one leg. Her white blouse was stained with food, and what looked like rust, and her hair was slicked back with oil and dirt, and tied with a piece of string. The toes of her shoes were scuffed way past the shine, and one had a broken strap that had been cut off, rather than repaired. All that, but when I looked at her, I couldn't talk, or even hardly breath. She was pretty.

"Apple?" she said, again. "Roy won't want it after he's whipped. Not me, though. I'm always hungry."

I handed her the apple, and she took a big bite, her scummy teeth sinking through the bright, red skin, into the moist flesh inside, a trickle of juice running down her chin. She grinned at me. "He's a good fighter, isn't he? Even with bigger kids. He's fast. And he hits really hard."

I nodded, staring at the apple juice running down her chin. She held the apple out to me. "You want a bite? I already had mine, and I ate the core of Tina's, too. I'll probably get the shits if I eat all of this one." She held the apple towards my mouth, a grin on her face. I looked at her freckles, and her eyes, laughing, green and brown and gold, and then I opened my mouth. She gently pressed the apple in, between my lips, and held it there while I took a deep bite. She pulled the apple back, watching me try to catch my breath. A bit of juice ran down my chin, and she slipped her finger out, and softly wiped the juice up, off my skin, then popped her finger into her mouth and sucked the juice off. "They're good apples, aren't they?" she asked.

I nodded, still having a hard time with speech. Finally, I said, "Where did he learn to fight like that?"

Trish sat, cross-legged, on the grass, and patted the worn grass with her hand, inviting me to sit down next to her. She still had her mouth full of apple, juice now dripping out the corners of her mouth and down her chin. I looked out at the other kids on the playground, no one playing, really, just talking in little groups, talking about the fight, I guessed. I sat, watching to not sit in the blood, and sitting close to her, but not quite touching. She held up her hand, chewing away, with her mouth a little open, and made a sign for me to wait a bit. When she had swallowed the apple, and wiped her lips with

the back of her hand, she grinned at me again. Then she said, "Our dad puts him up against our cousins, ever since he was little. Most of the cousins are bigger than us, 'cause dad's the youngest one in his family. The uncles all get together, up at the farm, for the weekend, sometimes. Without the wives, usually. Beer and nudie magazines, mostly, and some cards and shooting. They have the boys fight, for money. They call it "dog fights", and when Roy wins, dad gets to keep the money in the pot. Roy's got to where he wins pretty much all the time, even against the big kids, and sometimes even two on one. He's really tough."

She took another bite of the apple, then handed it towards me. I started to take it from her, but she pulled it back. "Nope," she said. "I feed you."

I felt my heart pounding in my chest. I was breathing hard, and still not getting enough air. I felt sick, kind of dizzy, and worried that I might throw up. I wondered if it was the fight, and seeing all the blood, some of which still pooled bright red and shiny on the ground beside us. But I opened my mouth up, and let her put the apple there, and slowly bit down, taking another bite.

She watched my mouth as I chewed, and I wanted her finger on my face again. I finally closed my eyes, trying to settle my nerves, and I heard her take another bite of the apple. When I opened them, she had leaned a little closer to me, and was grinning like I had done something funny. "You like me?" she said. I nodded. "Good," she said. "I like you, too."

Suddenly everything that felt sick inside me felt fine, better than fine, and I couldn't help but grin, and almost giggle. She liked me! Then she looked back at the school, and said, "I hope Roy thinks that's OK. He's kind of protective."

Mrs. Ferris rang the kids back in from recess. Trish ate the core of the apple, spitting out the seeds and the stem as we walked. When we were about half way there, I felt Trish's sticky fingers on my hand, wrestling my fingers in around hers, until we were holding hands. I thought about the teasing I would take if the boys found out I liked Trish, and I thought about Roy, and started to pull my hand back. But Trish held on tight. "If we're going to like each other, you can't be ashamed of me. That won't work." she said, soft, almost a whisper, but not quite.

"I'm not ashamed." I said, and squeezed her hand tight, swinging our hands as we walked. When we got to the knot of kids working their way in through the door, I could see about half of them staring at our hands, and then at me and Trish. I wasn't ashamed of her, or me, at all, then. I was still worried about Roy, who was 'kind of protective', but I wasn't even thinking

about that, really. My chest felt like it was all filled up with bird song and sunrise. Before the 'sitting in a tree' thing even had a chance to start up, with Susan and Ellen staring in shock, and Mrs. Ferris turned to go in the door, I leaned over and kissed Trish, our very first kiss, right on the mouth, right in front of God and everybody. She kissed me back, so it took a little while. The whole crowd of kids was silent, for the second time that recess. Then we turned and walked on into the building, still holding hands, right up until we got into the lunchroom, where Mrs. Ferris was, who didn't permit that kind of thing. Susan and Ellen had looked at me coming back into the lunchroom, though, Susan glaring, and Ellen looking like a stranger had taken over her own brother's body. I wondered if Susan would tell my folks about the fight, and about me and Trish.

CHAPTER FOUR

Mrs. Billings spoke with me once, then a few minutes later, rapped her ruler on my desk, telling me to quit daydreaming. We were doing science, which I usually liked, an electricity unit where we had a lantern battery, some wire, and switches, bulbs and a buzzer. I liked that sort of thing, but I couldn't stop thinking about Trish and her brother, Roy. It was like having five or six different feelings, one after another. I thought about Roy, leaping up into the air to split open Danny Bowman's face, and his calm focus beforehand, picking the place of the combat, with the roots and the shade working to his advantage, I thought, and even taking the time to tighten up the laces in his shoes, as Danny was moving swiftly, stupidly, towards his own disaster. I thought about Trish, who must have seen her brother fight this way over and over, enough times to be a little bored with it. I thought about the kind of dads who would fight their own kids, in a ring, for money. The idea of beer and nudie magazines caught my attention, too.

But mostly I thought about Trish, about the apple, and her finger on my cheek, and her eyes, her laugh, her freckles, and her cool, dry fingers holding tight onto my hand. I thought about her voice, asking if I liked her, and the way she had said, "Good," when she knew I did. I thought about our walk up to the school, bold as brass, holding hands, with her wanting to be sure I wasn't ashamed of her. And I thought about the kiss, my lips closed tight at first, and pressed up against hers, and then her lips softening, opening, and her mouth alive and moving on my own, I felt the blood rush up in my face, and I thought I still might pass out, falling straight from my desk onto the grey tile floor.

Trish had smiled at me, just before she sat down, but hadn't turned around to look at me since. Roy had come into our classroom a few minutes late. I suspected that Mr. White had wanted to keep strapping him until he cried, but that the principal must have given up after a while, his own class just down the hall, with only Mrs. Ferris to watch the kids. Roy walked into the class, dry-eyed and calm, and took his seat with none of the caution that kids usually did after a long chat with Mr. White. His knuckles were cut, for sure, on both hands, torn up along the back of the fingers. He'd wiped them off, maybe on his pants, but there was still some blood there. His shirt didn't look any worse than it had when he got on the bus, except for a deep blackening stain on his chest. Not his own blood, we all knew. He caught my eye as he walked in, cupping his hand out as if he were holding an apple. I had pointed at Trish, who had grinned at her brother, rubbed her belly, and mouthed "Thank you".

I wondered what would happen when Roy found out about the hand holding, and the kiss, and the public fact that his sister and I liked each other. I wondered what "kind of protective" might look like, directed towards me. I worried what my parents would do, too. I worried a lot back then. I stewed all the time on whether I was in trouble or not, stewed on the things I wish I had (a green, two-speed Schwinn bike being on the top of the list these days, closely followed by a lever action, Remington .22 rifle), what kind of grades I would get in school (although, so far, I had gotten good enough grades to please my parents, and not so good as to irritate my classmates), how tall I would grow, and if I would be as strong and as frankly male as my father was, when I got older. I even worried about hell, but only on Sunday afternoons.

Trish didn't seem worried about Roy, or the other kids, or the second night in a row of hauling scrap metal from Barre to the already full trailer lot in Brookfield. Maybe she didn't worry about anything. She didn't seem embarrassed about the trailer they had moved into, or the huge pile of metal that was growing up around it, how her dirty clothes were, or her unwashed hair or teeth. My sisters would have died if they had gone to school with a little stain on their shirt, or their hair not brushed. Trish seemed proud to have me as her boyfriend, even though I wasn't one of the boys that the girls would ever brag about. I got the ruler smacking down on my desk, again, with a sharp, "Toby! Pay attention!" from Mrs. Billings. Trish turned around just then, grinning at me, and made a kiss with her lips. She thought it was funny.

Somehow, I got through the rest of the class without getting into real trouble. Finally, we were dismissed, after standing up, pushing our chairs in, and making sure that the classroom was picked up. It was a Thursday, so we had a spelling test, and a math test the next day, with Mrs. Billings reminding us to study as we lined up by the door. James was right behind me, where he usually was, and he whispered, "Dad's going to kill you when he finds out." I shushed him, not wanting Trish to hear him, but she was up in the front of the line, leaning a little against the wall, thinking about another long night of hauling scrap metal, I guessed. I could see the back of her head, and noticed that her hair was tied back with a blue wire bread tie, instead of the string from yesterday. I wondered if she would smile at me on the bus.

Trish seemed to fall asleep on the way home, along with her sister and her brother. She was leaned up against the window, and I could hear her head make a soft thumping sound when we hit the bumps, but she didn't seem to wake up. Our stop was just before theirs, and as the bus pulled away, I wondered if Mr. Beller would be sure they were off the bus, or just let them sleep all the way back to the parking lot in Randolph, where they kept the bus.

As the bus pulled away, I turned and found Susan standing right in front of me. She pointed her finger right in my face. "You can't do that with her. You embarrassed me to death. And dad won't want you hanging out with Buckman kids. And she's so dirty." Susan added this last part, sounding not so much angry as puzzled, like she couldn't understand how I could like Trish.

I backed up a little, away from her finger, but I looked right at her. "They don't have water yet. The electricity isn't turned on at the trailer, and they have to haul their water in buckets, up from the creek. And they all worked all last night, hauling that metal up from their old place. It's not her fault that she's dirty. You're not being Christian," I added, knowing that Susan would worry about that. I didn't think too much about the sermons I heard at the Baptist church every Sunday, but I remembered something about judging, and not getting down on someone just because they were poor. Susan had been baptized back in September, with the minister making her wait until he thought she was old enough to be making her own decision. Susan had been asking for it since she was five or six, I guess.

"Her brother sure knows how to fight," James said, not wanting Susan and I to be at each other. I thought about telling about the "dog fights" that Roy had grown up with, but I didn't. I didn't want my family having any more reasons to not like the Buckmans.

"If I tell mom, she'll make you stop," Susan said.

"If you tell mom, I'll tell her about you and Steve Morris." Steve Morris was an eighth grade boy that Susan was sweet on, a boy she had held hands with a few times at recess, when he wasn't with one of the other girls. Mom wouldn't like it, both because she thought Susan was too young to have a boyfriend, and because she didn't like the Morris family, for some reason. They might have been Catholics.

Susan dropped her finger down at that point, started to say something, then just turned around and stomped on up to the house, followed by Ellen, while James and I headed over to the barn. I wondered how long it would be before my folks would find out about me and the Buckman kids, and what would happen when they did. I already knew I wasn't going to stop liking Trish. I'd never before decided that I would do something my parents didn't like, even if I got caught. That felt a little scary, and good, somehow.

There was a chicken for dinner, with carrots and a new loaf of bread, steaming in a dishtowel there on the cutting board. Green beans from the freezer, still good from last summer, and of course, a pitcher of milk, raw, but cool, from the fridge. Dessert was canned peaches, from the store, a half peach for each of us, and two for my dad. I wondered if Trish and Roy had dinner, and I wondered where the apples had come from. Store apples were high, this time of year, and were free in the summer and the fall, with apple trees pretty much everywhere you looked on the mountain farms.

After the dishes were done, my mother sent the girls up for a bath, and James and I got out our spelling and math, still sitting at the table, while my parents took their coffee over to the couch. I wondered how old my parents had been when they first liked someone, and if it had been each other, the first time. My mother looked pretty, her apron off, and her print dress with the little blue flowers all smooth and nice. She sat next to my dad, his shirt sweat-stained, but he had brushed his hair before coming to the table, and he looked nice. She leaned towards him a little, touching at the sides, and smiled as she read, pleased to have the day over, I guessed, and some time with my dad coming up. I thought about the bath, with her soaking in the fresh drawn water, and my dad there in the same room, seeing her there in the water. Suddenly it was me and Trish, there in the bathroom, with our kids put to bed, the day's work done, and Trish was laying in the clear, hot water, grinning up at me. This picture just about killed me, so I bit my tongue hard enough to clear my thoughts, and tried to think about spelling words, and measurement.

I tried to study, up until we heard Susan call "Done," from the top of the stairs, but the thought of Trish and me, all grown up, and sharing a life, with kids and everything, kept rising up in my brain, uninvited. It was really nice, even if it was confusing. I got through the bath, and into bed, and finally managed to escape into the far North, where *Fang* had found his new owner freezing to death out in a blizzard, and dragged him through the snow, by the collar of his coat, all the way back to his wolf's den under a fallen tree. It was exciting, but my dreams that night were of Trish.

CHAPTER FIVE

"You just better not get lice," Susan said, under her breath, as she stepped off the porch, heading out the where the bus would pick us up. "My hair is just about grown out from the last time, and I'm not cutting it off again."

I guessed that this meant Susan had decided to not tell my parents about me and the Buckmans. "I'm not going to get lice," I said. There was a little bit of a kerosene smell in Trish's hair, so I though she and her sister might have had a run with it before moving down here. Lice needs some hair to work with, and James and I got buzzed by our mother every week or so, like most of the boys at school. But the girls all pretty much had long hair, unless somebody's mother just got fed up with the kerosene and all the laundry, and buzzed their daughters. That happened to Susan and Ellen two years ago, and Susan still wasn't over it. She had a bumpy head, and looked a little like one of the boys when she got buzzed. She hated it. Ellen had actually looked OK with her hair off, and had wanted my mom to keep on buzzing her, just like she did me and James, but my mother wasn't having any of that.

As the bus rolled up towards the trailer where the Buckmans were living, I could see the new piles of scrap metal, piled higher and higher around the trailer. The two lawn tractors, both painted a rusty yellow and white, were propped up on the tail ends. A pile of bicycles was now on top of the metal roofing, rusty and broken, it looked like. The two refrigerators were there, one old enough to have the little, round, finned top on it. The cable and wire had been piled on top of the pipe. The piles were high enough now that the trailer was mostly hidden from the road. Trish was standing in front of her brother and sister, when Mr. Beller pulled the bus over and swung open the door. She bounced up the steps, still wearing the same tights and skirt from the day before, but she had on a cleaner white shirt, with some ruffles along the neck. Her hair had been washed and brushed out, and I could see how blond she was, almost white. She grinned at me, and waved, then sat down on the aisle, making her sister, Tina, climb over her to sit by the window. Trish turned and grinned back at me, again, and made a little kissing thing with her lips.

I was too happy to be embarrassed, since I had woke up thinking I must have imagined the whole thing yesterday, and that Trish couldn't really like me that way. Roy scanned the bus again, looking at the boys in the back, who looked away, and then took his seat across from me. When he looked at me, I could tell that he already knew about his sister and me. When the bus pulled over for the Campbell kids, Roy said, "She got up early and washed out in the creek, when it was still dark, for you, I guess. I heard she made you her boyfriend." I didn't say anything. I guess she had. As the doors closed, Roy said, "I like you well enough, but you better watch your step."

That seemed more than fair. I nodded, then, Mr. Beller put the bus in gear. The driver looked up at the mirror, catching my eye, and shaking his head. I wondered what he meant by that, and if I were in trouble, again.

Nobody on the bus commented on the extra scrap piled around the trailer, even though Mr. Beller had to park out in the middle of the road when he stopped. Danny Bowman was on the bus, in the back with his friends, and he didn't say anything. His friends didn't, either. Danny had a bandage over his eye, which was black and puffy, and the cuts on his lips were still a little open. His lips were so swollen it looked like maybe he would have had a hard time talking, even if he had something to say. I wondered what his folks had thought when he got home.

When we got off the bus, Trish was waiting, and took hold of my hand. She peeled her lips back, showing me her teeth. They were white, with a little chip on one of the front ones, and a line of blood showed along her gums. "I cleaned up for you," she said, "so you wouldn't be embarrassed to be going with me. If I smell like lemon, it's 'cause the only soap we had was dish soap. Stings some, but it gets you really clean. So. How do I look?" She stepped back from me and twirled around. Her hair was loose, and shiny gold, lying over her thin shoulders. I smiled really big, and told her she looked great. Which she did. She leaned up to me, and said, "Sniff!" I sniffed and smelled the lemon dish soap, and something else. Something that smelled like the ladies in church. "It's powder!" she said. "My mom left it behind, and I took it. Sort of smells like roses. You sprinkle it on, after you take a bath." She looked right into my eyes, her face only a foot away or so. She still had her mouth way open, so I could see her scrubbed teeth.

I felt so lucky, right then, and happier than I'd ever felt. "You look beautiful," I said.

She leaned in and gave me a quick kiss. "Roy said we can't kiss all the time at school. He says to wait until recess." My thinking was already too scrambled to know what to say, so I just nodded. The doors opened, and the children started to press inside. Trish was still holding my hand when we got inside, but we both turned loose when we saw Mrs. Billings eyeballing us. Trish grinned. "Recess," she said.

I forgot the words to the pledge, and only thought about Trish during the prayer. I prayed that God would keep her safe, and let her keep liking me. I knew that Susan would have hated that, thinking that the last thing I should be sharing with God was my sordid new love life. It sounded kind of selfish, to me, but it was what was in my heart, as my mom says, so I thought it was OK. As Mrs. Billings was getting the spelling list for our test, I thought about what Trish had said about her mother. How she left the powder behind. I wondered where her mom had gone, and how long ago she had left. I hated to think of Trish without a mother, and only her dad and her brother there to look out for her. I tried to picture a day without my mom at home, cooking supper and looking after us, and I couldn't do it.

When Mrs. Billings called out the first word, it caught me by surprise, and I didn't really hear it. Then she repeated it, the way she does, and I still didn't catch it. My head was still all filled up with Trish, and I couldn't even think about my spelling list. I shook my head, trying to get my focus back, and managed to get through the rest of the list, hearing each word, but doing worse than I usually did. We swapped papers to grade them, and Roy swapped papers with me. His handwriting was neat, and at the top of the page was a drawing of a house, out in the country, with a dog out in front. You could tell that the dog was a shepherd, and there were trees, and a road, and even a barn off to the side. It looked like the drawing out of a magazine, not something a kid could do during a spelling test. I looked back at him, and he looked embarrassed about the drawing. "You missed "ceiling", he said.

Roy didn't miss any of the twenty words, and I guessed that he hadn't slept, or had time to study, for at least the last couple of days. He only got the spelling list on Wednesday. I put "minus 0", then added a "100%" at the top, and an "A+", next to it, even though Mrs. Billings just wanted the number wrong at the top of the page. I put my name as the grader, and handed the paper back to Roy. He flipped it face down on his desk without looking at it. He marked mine a "minus 3", and put his name below. "I fixed your "sleigh", or you would have missed four," he said. "Did you study last night?"

"Some", I said. "I had a hard time thinking last night."

"I'll bet," he said. I wasn't sure what that meant, but I didn't like the way that sounded.

I shrugged, and looked over my paper. It looked about like my papers usually did. I looked at "sleigh", and could see the "i" now tucked in between the "e" and the "g". You could hardly tell. He made the dot on the "i" a little slash, just like I did. It felt bad to be cheating on a test. I'd never done that before, but I couldn't think of anything I could do about it at this point. And I only got a "B" anyway, which is what I usually got. Mrs. Billings made her way down the aisle, picking up papers as she went. She paused by Roy's seat, looking at his spelling test. She looked surprised, her eyes flipping back and forth, checking my grading, I guessed. "Very nice," she said.

Roy looked away, and didn't say anything. Mrs. Billings stood there a moment longer, then sighed, and went on collecting the papers from the other kids. I wondered what she thought about having a Buckman be the smartest kid in her class.

We got through the math test, with Roy not sketching a picture this time, although he finished way earlier than the rest of us did. We swapped papers again, and I wasn't surprised when Roy got everything right, again. When we lined up for lunch, Trish had turned around and grinned right at me, her head tipped a little sideways, like she was asking me a question. I didn't know what the question was, but I felt my mind tip off to the side, and all my thinking slide off onto the floor, again. Happy, but stupid. I wondered when I would get back to feeling sort of smart. As Roy and I sat down, Trish was there, and said, "Mind if I eat with you guys?"

She was looking at Roy, not me, and Roy sat there for a second, looking annoyed, checked to see that Tina was sitting with a group of girls, and then said, "Sure". Roy turned to me, and said, "Don't give her my apple again. She's a pig, and will eat everything, if you let her."

Trish grinned, and made several, loud snorting noises, rooting her nose at her brother, sounding a lot like a pig, I guess, and getting the kids around us to look, before they turned away. "Three apples was too many. I was on the bucket all night last night".

The three of us sat off to the side of the lunchroom. I was taking my sandwich out of the waxed paper, and trying to understand what bucket Trish was talking about. Trish held her sandwich in her hand, lifting the white bread up and looking at the meat inside. She sniffed it, then, happily took a bite. "Good thing I like baloney," she said. "Three slices?"

Roy was eating his own sandwich. "Might as well eat it up," he said. "It won't last without a fridge. There's pickles, too, but no more apples. And there's a couple of Oreos in your bag."

Trish rooted around in her paper bag, and came up with two Oreos. She held one out to me. I started to reach for it, but she pulled it back. "Eat your lunch first," she said, grinning wildly at me, and then eating the Oreo in her other hand. I opened my bag, and took out a peanut butter sandwich, and a little plastic bag of raisins. There were also two chocolate chip cookies, from a batch Susan had made the day before, and I offered one to Trish. She snatched it up, and ate it in two bites. "Thank you," she mumbled, her mouth full of cookie. "That's really good. Homemade. We never make cookies."

Roy said, "We don't have an oven. Where's my cookie? I was your friend, first, before this little piglet came along." Trish snorted again, and tried to root at her brother, who poked a finger in her ribs and drove her back, with her giggling and spitting cookie crumbs over the table.

I could see Mrs. Ferris watching us, disapproval in her face. I didn't know if she was disapproving of the noise, or of me sitting with the Buckman kids. "Shush," I whispered to Trish. "You're going to get us in trouble." She nodded, still giggling under her hand, and tried to be quieter. I handed the other cookie to Roy, who took it and put in on the paper bag he was using as a plate. I worked on my sandwich, which was kind of dry, and offered the raisins to Trish and Roy. Trish ate the raisins, then, finished off her sandwich.

We sat that way for a bit, Trish picking crumbs up off the table and eating them, while I finished my sandwich. "I'm done," I said, just like I was at home.

Trish grinned, and picked up the Oreo, cleaned off some cookie crumbs that had landed on it, and then held it in front of my face. I had just opened my mouth when Roy pushed the Oreo back towards his sister. "Maybe you two can keep that stuff to the playground, and not here in the lunchroom," he said.

Trish said, "You're no fun," but she took the Oreo back. I raised my hand, and Mrs. Ferris came over to our table. She nodded, but looked at me first, like she wanted me to know she didn't like what she was seeing. Mrs. Ferris went to our church, and would be seeing my folks on Sunday. I wondered if she would tell them about the Buckmans and me. I worried about that, up until we were out the door, onto the playground, and Trish's hand found mine, her cool fingers moving on my own. She fed me the Oreo, while we three sat together in the shade of the maple trees, breaking it into pieces, and slipping each piece

41

into my mouth, her fingers brushing my lips. I stopped worrying about Mrs. Ferris and my folks.

Roy looked out on the crowd of kids, watching Tina as she stood with a group of girls. "Tina always does good with the other girls, unless someone is mean to her. Trish is the one I usually have to worry about. Scrapping and fighting."

Trish poked her brother, hard, in his ribs. "Don't go talking about me that way, not with Toby here." She poked him again. "You try getting along with the fancy-girl crowd. I'll be fine, now. I just needed a boyfriend." She put her finger on my nose, pointing out the "boyfriend" thing, I guess. "And now I got one," she said, happily.

Roy looked at me, an odd look, and shook his head. "Yeah," he said, "I guess you do."

CHAPTER SIX

That Friday afternoon, watching the bus doors swing shut, and seeing the bus give a big puff of diesel smoke and move down the road, with Trish, and Roy and Tina inside, I felt awful. I usually liked Fridays, having two days without school, with chores on Saturday morning, and church on Sunday, but free time in the afternoons, both days, time to wander in the back woods along the ridge, or head up to the old stage coach stop, and sit in the cold foundation stones that were still there. This Friday, I was only aware of the big emptiness in this new heart I had grown in the last two days. It felt like Trish had moved in, and made a room for herself, and decorated it with flowers and cushions, right there in my chest. Bringing in sunshine and happiness in a way I really hadn't felt there before. And now that room was still there, but it was empty for the next two days, and that felt awful.

I thought about Trish, and Roy, while I did my chores. I had to be careful to not think a whole lot about the hand holding, or the kissing, because if I did, I'd forget what I was supposed to be doing in the barn, and maybe get stepped on. But I could think about other things, like how their mom had moved out about a year before, having been knocked around by their dad one too many times, Trish had said. She'd moved right in with another guy, and they were still living in Barre, but the kids never saw her, really, except at the store or on the sidewalk. I'd asked Trish if she missed her, and she had said, "Sometimes. Like if I'm sick, or something. But there's less fighting with her gone, and what are you going to do, anyway?" I thought about that, and how my sisters and I would pretty much just fall apart if our mom was gone. My dad, too, I guessed.

Roy had let me keep the *Fang* book, telling me to finish it up over the weekend. I was looking forward to that. He said he had another book for me, one that he'd bring in on Monday, about the French and Indian wars. I was still in the habit of worrying, and I worried some about Mrs. Ferris telling my parents about me and the Buckman kids, but even that didn't scare me too much, since I had already decided that Trish and I would be together forever, whether my folks liked it or not. I heard an echo of Trish's "What are you going to do about it, anyway?" I thought I'd try to be like her, that way, and now worry too much about stuff I couldn't do anything about.

Dinner was pork chops, with creamed fresh spinach on the side, ladled out by my mom, who caught my eye with a warning to clean my plate. I liked pork chops just fine, but spinach had never been a favorite of mine, although the fresh stuff in the early spring was a little better than the stuff from the can in the winter, which was brownish green, like old army pants. I got through dinner, though, thinking about Roy trying to cook for his sisters, with no fridge, and only the bits of food that had been moved into the trailer, and I had no problem eating all my spinach. I knew that the Buckman kids would have loved what was on my plate. I pictured Trish sitting at our table, reaching over and taking another pork chop, chewing with her mouth open, and making all the noises she made when she ate something, and laughing and telling some story about her family.

In my imagination, I could see my parents happy to have her at the table, laughing right along with her, loving her almost as much as I did. Trish laughed and grinned all the time, and I realized that there wasn't much of that laughing thing in our house. Except the faint, hidden laughter I had heard once or twice from behind the bathroom door, while my mom took her bath, and my dad sat with her, after we were all supposed to be in bed. It was like Trish brought that into my life, and opened the door to the secret happiness that I now thought my parents had, kept hidden until they were together, at the end of the day, after the kids were all put to bed.

As I thought about that, I could feel a little bit of Trish move back into my heart, and I didn't feel as lonesome as I had before. I read, seeing Fang into a snowstorm, and then a fight with trappers in a log cabin tavern, and then fighting for his life with a pack of wolves who hated him for leaving the wild. It was a great book, and I got about half the way through it that night, until my eyes started to close, and I finally turned off the light. There was a little light in the dark hallway, coming from beneath the bathroom door, where I could hear the water running for my mother's bath, and the soft voices of my parents. I listened hard, and could hear the water splash a little, and then, a little laughter, and my father's voice, low and soft and happy. Then I fell asleep, thinking not about the bath, but about Trish, sitting at our dinner table, laughing with us, and stealing a pork chop off my plate with her fingers.

44

We wake up Saturdays at the same time we would for a school day, early, with it still a little dark, this time of year. My dad says cows don't care about the weekend, so the rest of us don't get to really, either. After breakfast, mom put the girls out to the garden to clean up for planting, and after we did the milking, dad took us boys up along the back pasture fence line, with him cutting back the brush from the fence, and James and me pulling the cut brush off, and tossing it onto the woods side of the fence. It's good work for gloves, since lots of what grows along the fence is brambles of one sort or another, raspberries, blackberries, and nettles. There's thorn apple trees that are dangerous as well. We both had decent gloves, James and I, kept on the porch, right next to Dad's.

We worked our way steady around the back pasture, coming back to the barn right around lunchtime. It was cool enough that we didn't sweat too much, and we took a break from time to time, as dad worked on the fence, patching wire and setting staples, wedging a post with rocks, getting it all back into shape for the summer. I usually like fence line work, since it's outside, doesn't involve cows, directly, and looks pretty great by the time you're done. Working with my dad, outside, felt good, even though none of us said hardly anything. My dad pretty much only said things like, "Get that, there", or "Leave it be". My brother and I didn't talk while we worked, mostly because Dad wanted us paying attention to the job at hand, but also because there wasn't a whole lot to say. We talked in the bath, some times, and in bed, if I weren't reading, usually about school, or one of us getting into trouble at home. But we were pretty quiet together, most of the time. My sisters didn't talk much to each other, either, even though they talked to the other girls at lunch and recess, pretty much non-stop.

The creek was still pretty much up, high enough you could hear it from the house, and fishing it would have been a waste of time, but James did mention maybe going fishing at the Floating Bridge, and catching some crawdads, and maybe seeing if the water was still too cold to swim. I knew the water would be cold, but we swam it, anyway, sometimes. Saturdays, in the summer, my folks let James and me walk up the hill, then down to the bridge, maybe a couple of miles, pretty much every Saturday, and some week days, too, if the chores were done. We swam and we fished, coming home wet and tired and a little muddy from the road, sometimes with a sunburn, and sometimes with a sack of fish or crawdads. The bridge was a favorite spot for kids on the hill to gather. My sisters went, too, if it was warm, and if my mom let them.

Grownups would fish along the bridge, and some of them would swim, too, on the really hot days.

Dad said we could do the low pasture next week, and we left our boots and gloves on the porch, splashing a little bit of water from the hose on our hands and arms, drying off on our shirts, before we headed in for lunch. There were bananas, still a little green, the way I liked them, sandwiches made from lunch meat, and a new jar of applesauce brought up from the cellar. A pitcher of milk, of course, and what smelled like a spice cake, still in the oven. Mom sent Ellen back to wash again, and I checked my hands, just to be sure.

When lunch was over, I asked about James and me going to the bridge, and my mother looked over at my dad, who looked at James and me, and then said we could go, as long as we planned on bringing back dinner. Susan looked at Ellen, and then asked my mom if the girls could go, too, and my mother nodded. I knew the girls weren't wanting to fish much, but were hoping to see some friends from school. James and I waited until the girls had the dishes done, and then the four of us headed up the dirt road, James and I with the poles and an empty feed sack, the girls up ahead of us. My parents stood by the front door, and watched us walk away. I wondered, for the first time, if they might be glad for a little time with us gone on a weekend, and then thought about all the school days when the two of them were home with each other. The thought of my parents feeling that way about each other was something I had never considered, before. I wondered if Susan and Ellen thought about them, that way.

There were a few folks already at the bridge, but no kids. Mr. Norcross was there, in his regular place, his battered aluminum cooler underneath him. It was filled with beer, we thought. He fished pretty much every day, when he wasn't doing odd jobs for the people that would hire him. He had a cigar going, and I sniffed as we walked by. I liked that smell, sort of like leaves burning in the fall, but with some manure smell thrown in, maybe. I could see Susan and Ellen slowing up, disappointed that there weren't any kids here yet. Ellen walked across the bridge, and filled her hands with some stones from the gravel road, bringing them back, so she would have something to drop in the water while she and Susan waited for kids to come along.

In the summer, people swam off the north side of the bride, and fished off the south side. But it was cold enough that there weren't any swimmers here, or likely to come, I thought, so James and I cast off the north side, fresh worms twisting on our hooks. We leaned onto the rail, and looked out at the water, black and shimmery. I thought about the milk truck and it's driver, sunk down there in the deep water, below us. My dad had told us the story, as a warning about trying to do the easy thing, about the penalty for short cuts. The bridge was marked at six tons, with a clear sign at both ends, and if you were driving something that weighed more than that, you had to go around the water, either taking the Crossover road, a few miles to the south, or Stone road, a couple miles to the north. But Miles Burnham, who used to drive the milk truck for Cabot, he was in a hurry that day, maybe having slept late, my dad said, or not willing to wait for his fun, and he took the milk truck, already more than half full, right across the bridge. Or he tried to, anyway, with the bridge flipping out from underneath him, like a raft with too many kids on one side, and he and the truck spilled off the side, breaking out the rails, and then sinking down into the cold, black water. The bridge was a floater, set on big barrels, because the water here was too deep for pilings to ever be set, so the truck and it's driver were never recovered. Miles Burnham could take the rest of eternity to wish he had done the right thing, instead of taking short cuts. You could still see where maybe thirty feet of rails had been replaced, a little newer than the rest. We only heard the story once, dad not being the sort of man to repeat himself, but it stuck with us. I was careful not to let out too much line while we fished, not wanting fish that might have been there on the bottom with Mr. Burnham.

Susan and Ellen were down the bridge a ways, with Ellen dropping a stone in from time to time, watching the circles spread out across the water, and Susan looking up and down the road, hoping for some kids she knew. I wondered if she had made arrangements at school on Friday to meet someone here. Sure enough, Steve Morris and his little brother came walking up from below the old fork shop, carrying poles, but probably not really planning on fishing much. I could see Susan perk up, standing straighter, and brushing her hair back with her hand. She was kind of a sloucher at home, with my parents always telling her to sit up straight, and here she was, standing like a girl out of a magazine. I looked at Susan, thinking for the first time that she probably wished she was prettier than she was, even though I thought she looked just fine, not as nice as our mom, but growing into it.

I had my line hooked around my finger, and the tug brought my attention back to fishing. A little tug at first, just tasting it, and then the set, a big enough tug that the line hurt my finger, and the tip of my pole bent down almost to the water. I locked the line, and looked down into the deep, as if I could see what was happening down there. I moved off from my brother just a bit, to give myself some room to work, and began carefully reeling the line in, trying to keep the hook from tearing out as the fish jerked back and forth, trying to pull loose. It fought hard, and felt heavy, and I figured I must have hooked a bass, not the trout we usually pulled from the water. Some men from Barre had poured a barrel of live bass into the lake years before, wanting to spice up the local fishing, and the bass had slowly taken hold in the lake. They were fat and strong, ugly, really, compared to a trout, but a good-sized bass could feed two or three people, and they fought all the way to the shore. There were pickerel here, too, a thin, toothy fish that could take the end of your finger off, and snappers, as well, giant mossy turtles that stayed along the bottom, coming to the surface to take a breath every hour or so, and threaten the privates of any little boys silly enough to skinny dip in the lake. I'd hooked a turtle before, and all you could do was to cut your line, and say goodbye to your tackle, but turtles pulled hard and slow, not this frantic set of tugs that I was feeling. I felt pretty sure I had a bass, my first one, and a fine start to the dinner my dad had told us to bring back.

I leaned out over the rail, trying to keep the fish from getting in under the bridge, where my line could get tangled on the wood, and kept reeling in a foot here, and then another foot, taking my time, and trying to not lose him. I almost lost my pole, with one hard tug, but I held on, and managed to bring him up to the surface. James had reeled his line in, and set his pole on the walkway of the bridge, and was leaning over watching the water. Even as the fish had tired, it was still heavy and strong, and took line back out from time to time. My arms were starting to hurt, and the sweat had dripped down into my eyes, salty and stinging, where I couldn't wipe it away, when the giant speckled bass had broken the surface, one side up, showing his stripes and color. I could see the hook, just barely still in the torn lower lip, and I started a slow walk to the end of the bridge, back to our side, where I could bring him into the shallows, and have James help lift him out. I wished we had brought a net.

James was in the water, ready in case the line broke or the hook tore out, and we got the fish up to the gravel, then I lifted him up, onto the shore. One last twitch tore the hook out, but he was over the gravel at that point, and James was on him, trapping him, and then lifting and tossing him up, higher on the shore, and away from the water. I dropped my pole, and gathered him up, getting him onto the grass, and far enough away from the water that I could relax a little. I was exhausted, and let James thread the stringer into his gill, and out his gaping mouth, clipping him shut, and making him mine. "I'll bet he weighs five pounds, or more," James said, holding the stringer out to me. He weighed a lot, for sure, the biggest fish I had ever caught, and still my favorite one to think about. I sat down on the gravel, and set the fish, still twitching a bit, on the grass beside me. I wished that Trish had been there to see me catch him, and that I could give my fish to Roy, and have him take it home and cook it up for his sisters and him to have for lunch.

My sisters, and Steve and his brother, had run down the bridge, watching me as I pulled in the bass. I saw Steve's hand on Susan's, and felt happy for her, and happy for myself, and glad for this thing to have entered my life, and changed me, and given me a sense that I had a future that was good and exciting. I clipped the stringer onto the bridge, after checking that there was no way my fish could escape, and James and I put a fresh worm on, and set out lines back in the black water, my breathing still a little fast, and my arms still sore. James caught a couple of eight-inch trout, the sort of thing we usually caught, but my mind elsewhere, back on Trish, and the Buckman kids, and after two worms were eaten right off my hook, I reeled my line in, and called it a day, and just stood by the rail, watching my fish slowly twist in the water below.

THE BUCKMAN KIDS

CHAPTER SEVEN

My dad had smiled when I pulled my fish out of the burlap sack, brushing the wet grass I had packed him in off out on the porch. "That's a nice fish," he said, and I felt myself puff up a little at his praise, a rare thing, indeed, back then. I carried it over to my mom, and showed it to her. She was at the sink, filling a pot with water, and she stopped, and turned off the faucet, looking carefully at the fish. She leaned over and kissed the top of my head, and called me a real fisherman. She admired the two trout that James had caught, but we could both tell she was only trying to be fair. James was a little jealous, but he understood that my fish was something special.

My mom cleaned the fish at the sink, then, had me take the guts and heads out for the chickens. She had my dad help her with the bass, it being big enough to fillet, and he showed her what he knew about cutting the meat off a fish that big. She dressed the fillets with some of the corn bread batter, then, put the corn bread in to bake, and fried the fillets and the trout in the big cast iron skillet. Ellen had caught some crayfish, and had tossed them in the bag as well. My mom put them in a bowl of water, with some salt, until they puked up all the sand, then she rinsed them off and boiled them on the stove.

The kitchen smelled pretty great by the time we sat down to say grace. The table had a big platter of fried fish, boiled crawdads, the steaming pan of corn bread, and some fiddleheads my mom had picked out by the road, steamed and dressed with butter. My father's prayer stepped up from the usual, with an added, "Lord, look at the bounty my good wife and children have provided for our table. Bless them, Lord, and this good food, in your name, amen." Having my fish shown off to God was something, as James pointed out later that night, in the bath.

Fried fish and corn bread are my two favorite things for dinner, especially if the fish came from me. I was all filled up, with pride and a good dinner, and I lay heavy on the mattress, James shifting around and still wanting to talk about the fish. We had prayed beside the bed, with my mom watching, of course, but I had another prayer, quiet, just between me and God, before I finally went to sleep. I thanked Him for the good things he had brought into my life, the fish, of course, and my family, but mainly my new friendship with Roy, and what I knew to be my love for his sister, Trish. I prayed that Trish and her family would be fed and safe tonight, and then, with a little of my old worried self, that she would still like me on Monday. As I fell asleep, there in the dark, lying beside my restless brother, I could hear my sisters whispering about Steve Morris, and maybe about me and Trish. I slid into sleep, looking forward to my dreams.

Sundays start off early, even earlier that the rest of the week, because my dad is a deacon at the church, and we have to get the cows done, and then all of us cleaned up and out the door in time to get there by eight-thirty. The deacons are supposed to be the first ones there, unlocking the doors and welcoming people. The deacon's wives set up the coffee and the Sunday School rooms, and most of them teach a class themselves. My mom does the nursery, missing babies, she says, and my dad does a class for the high school boys. The deacons do their own Bible study on Wednesdays, with the pastor, so they can keep up with the Word themselves.

Our pastor, Reverend Sikes, is old, with white hair and spotted hands, but he's still strong, and can shake the church when he gets going about sin and redemption. My parents both like him, although sometimes my mom will shake her head a little bit on the way home, praising the sermon in a way that it seems like there might be something in there she didn't really agree with. Reverend Sikes is big on the Gospels, and not so big on the Old Testament, so my dad likes that. Dad reads the Bible, but almost only the New Testament, and usually just the Gospels. His Bible has the words Christ actually said all printed in red, and Dad has underlined a lot of the red words.

Sundays are pretty much full of Church, with us hurrying in the dark-early morning to get ready, then getting there while the building is still mostly empty. Sunday School starts at nine, and runs until ten-thirty, then we have a half hour to eat cookies and drink punch, with most of the kids running around outside, trying to play and not get dirty. The real church happens at eleven, and runs until twelve-thirty or so, or sometimes almost until one, or even later, if Reverend Sikes is holding out for folks to walk down the aisle to be saved. My parents usually talked about the sermon on the way home, or quizzed us kids about Sunday School lessons. We had no chores in the afternoon, Sunday being a day of rest for the family. Our lunch and dinner were light, and we ate mostly what had already been made, so my mother

and my sisters wouldn't spend all afternoon in the kitchen. In the winter, we stayed in, reading or maybe listening to the radio, but when it was warmer, we could fish in the creek, or down at the pond, as long as we didn't swim. Sundays were supposed to be quiet and thoughtful, and my parents saw fishing as being that way. I knew some parents at church didn't let their kids fish on Sundays, and mostly made them stay inside.

This Sunday, after the sermon, while my dad was setting the pews back in order, and the Reverend Sikes was out front shaking hands and saying a few words as the congregation left, I saw Mrs. Ferris go up to my mom, who was putting away the coffee cups that she and one of the other wives had washed. Mrs. Ferris leaned in close to my mom, helping her with the cups, and brushing the crumbs off the tables into her hand. I could tell she was talking about me, because she and my mom turned to look at me once, then, turned away, still talking. I could feel a sudden anger at Mrs. Ferris, who I had always liked, now butting into my life and trying to make things hard for me. I felt a streak of fear run up my spine as well, cold and sharp and filled with panic, the feeling I always had when I thought I was about to get in trouble. I wrestled it back down with thinking about how Roy had faced up to a fight with a kid twice his size, and then a strapping by Mr. White right after, never even seeming worried. I thought about Trish, and her eyes and her freckles, and my own commitment that we would be together, come heck or high water. That made me feel a little better, but not completely.

They finished up with the cups, and Mrs. Ferris headed off to find her husband, who was already outside, I guessed. My mother looked at me, again, like she was trying to figure something out, but I knew she'd tell my father whatever it was that Mrs. Ferris had told her. They were a team, and she never kept a secret from him about us kids. She loved us, I knew, but she was on his side, first, and we all knew that. I understood that, and figured it would be the same way when Trish and I were raising our kids.

My mother didn't say anything on the way home, other than the usual conversation between my mom and my dad about the sermon. My parents both took the sermons to heart, and stewed some on how they could do better. Reverend Sikes was a good pastor that way, in that he liked to push his congregation, even if he had to say things some people really didn't want to hear. He said that going to church just wasn't good enough, you had to be the church, and that meant living with some sacrifice. My mom felt that way, and my dad did, too. I was still worried about what Mrs. Ferris had said to

my mom, and how that was going to work out for me. I hadn't connected it to the sermon at all, but later I understood that Reverend Sikes had helped my mom see things in a certain way, and that Mrs. Ferris must have, too.

Today's sermon was from one of my dad's favorite parts of the Bible, and had Jesus say that the way people treated the poor was really the way they were treating Jesus, himself. The first part is where Jesus thanks someone for giving him food when he was hungry, and a place to sleep when he was homeless. The person he is talking to says they never did those things, and Jesus says something like "What you do for the least of them, you do for me." And then he turns around and yells at someone else, who didn't do those things, didn't feed him when he was hungry and all the rest of it, and tells them they're in big trouble for not caring about the poor. It's a pretty strong message, especially when you include that last part, and my mom was glad the Reverend Sikes had put that part in.

"I think we don't do enough," my mom said, as we got out of the car. My dad thought about that for a while, thinking, I'm sure, about how much work he already did, and how thin the money was sometimes, but then he said, "I think you're right. We probably don't."

At lunch, my mom looked at me, and then put her hand on my father's arm. "Toby", she said. "Mrs. Ferris told me that you had been the only child at the school to be welcoming to the Buckman children. She said you ate lunch with them, and that you spent time with them at recess, even when the other children were being mean. I wanted you to know that your father and I are very proud of you."

This was so different that what I had expected that I couldn't say anything back. Susan dropped her jaw, and just stared at me, like I had just robbed a bank, and the judge had thanked me and given me a free car. I finally said, "Thank you. I really like them. They're really good kids."

My mom smiled at that, and looked at me like I must be the best kid in the world. Even my father smiled, just a little bit. I couldn't believe how it was working out. Then my mom turned to Susan, and said, "I understand that the older Buckman girl is in your class, Susan. It wouldn't hurt for you to be nice to her. Sit with her at lunch, like your brother does with the younger two."

Susan looked like she couldn't believe how this was working out. Mom saw the resistance in Susan's eyes. "Do you have a problem with that, Susan?" Susan shook her head, but my mom narrowed her eyes. "I'll check with Mrs. Ferris next Sunday."

Susan managed a "Yes, Ma'am," suspecting that she was about to get in trouble, again, but you could tell she wasn't very happy. I was pretty happy, though. And tomorrow, I'd be back at school, spending time with Trish and Roy, with my parent's blessing.

THE BUCKMAN KIDS

CHAPTER EIGHT

Roy shepherded his sisters onto the bus, Monday morning, with Trish wearing a checked yellow shirt, a longer brown skirt, and knee socks. Her hair was washed, and her eyes were sparkling. She winked at me, something that was hard for her to do. When she winked, the right half of her whole face screwed up tight, she bared her teeth, and she tipped her head, way over sideways. Sounds odd, but she looked really cute doing it. I waved, my face just about splitting with my own smile. Roy sat down across from me. He and his sister, Tina, had a bath, too, it looked like. He saw me looking. "Dad found a propane tank with some gas still in it," he said. "We boiled buckets on the stove, and filled up the tub with hot water. Took some time, but it felt great. I miss the tub up in Barre. Hot water right out of the wall. How's the book?"

I checked to see that Mr. Beller had his eyes on the road, and handed the book over to him. "All done," I said. "I finished Sunday night. It's a great book, but it was sad at the end."

"Don't tell me about it. I haven't read it, yet." He took the book, looking to see that it was all there, then dug into his bag and pulled out another fat paperback. The cover had what looked like a guy in a canoe was going up into a jungle, with vines hanging down all around him. It was called *Heart of Darkness*. "You can read that for a while. Some white guy living over in Africa goes crazy and starts killing everyone," he said. "It was really good." I looked at the book, and found a piece of paper folded in the front. "Don't open that here, " Roy said. "It's a note from Trish. She wouldn't let me read it, but I guess it's a love note."

I tucked the note back into the book, and looked up the aisle, where I could see the back of Trish's head, her hair clean and bright gold. Her hand was on her knee, and I could see her fingers picking at a scab. I could feel my heart starting up again, so I looked back at Roy. "I caught a bass down at the Floating Bridge. We cut it up and shared it for lunch." I showed him how big it was with my hands.

"That's a big fish," he said. "I didn't know they had bass in there. I shot a turkey hen on Saturday, and then got the tom when he came looking for her. Turkey sandwiches, today, and tomorrow, if it keeps."

I could see Mr. Beller look up in the mirror, so Roy and I rode along quiet for a while. As we pulled into the school, I asked, "You have a gun?" Roy nodded, tying his bag closed. "What kind?" I asked. I still really wanted that Remington .22, but knew that my dad thought I was too young to have a real gun.

"It's a Savage. It's got a 22. on the top, and a .410 on the bottom. I had to hit the hen and the tom with the .22, cause I'm out of .410 shells. It's a good meat getter, for little stuff, anyway. I've had it a couple of years. You can get a lot of groceries with a brick of .22s," he added. "I'll show it to you some time. Let you shoot it. There's partridge up along the creek." I like the idea that Roy was my friend, and that we could get together and shoot some time. I wondered if my dad would let me shoot partridge.

That week, starting on Monday, Susan had made a friendship with Tina, and Susan and Ellen and Tina all had lunch together, and even talked together out by the wall, watching the older boys play kickball. Trish and I and Roy had our regular recess out by the maples, talking, with Trish and me holding hands, and kissing some. Roy seemed OK with it, although he had asked that we hold off the kissing stuff until the very end. "Once you kiss him, Trish, he gets all stupid and cow-like."

She had grinned at me, and then said, "Yeah. He does. I don't think he's used to having a girlfriend, yet." She turned to me and pulled me over, kissing me again. "My little moo-cow," she said, kissing me again, turning my brain into jelly, and making my breath disappear. "Say 'moo', little moo-cow," she said. I moo-ed. I was happy.

"Yeah," said Roy, sounding pretty disgusted. "So, how about leaving him in people shape long enough for him and me to talk some?"

"OK", said Trish, her finger making circles on the back of my hand. Sometimes she played with my ears, running her finger inside the bumps, or tugging on them. Sometime she flipped my nose back and forth, or pushed the tip of it up. She liked my face, she said. All of it drove me crazy.

Roy and I talked about books, mostly. He had boxes of books that he had found somewhere, in abandoned places while his dad was scavenging metal and stuff. They were a mix, including some yellowing paperbacks that had mostly naked women on the cover, but he said that the good ones were where the story was important, and you could see people learning and changing as the story went along. We talked about the *Heart of Darkness* book. Roy liked it a lot. He thought the title wasn't just about the jungle, but was about the darkness inside everybody. I used the word sin, but Roy shook his head. "It isn't sin," he insisted. "God has nothing to do with it. Look at Fang. He did what he had to do, because of who he was, and the places he ended up. He killed when he had to. The darkness inside him was what kept him alive. Sometimes darkness is what you need. Sweetness and light doesn't go that far." Roy stopped. His voice was becoming a little loud. He shook his head. "I don't know. I like the books where it isn't easy, and the main guy has to figure it out, and do what he has to do, even if it looks like a bad thing. It's more real. It isn't easy, most of the time. Maybe it's easy for you," he finally said.

We just sat there, with Trish still holding my hand, but not doing anything to stir me up. I wanted to argue that my life wasn't easy at all, that I had to get up every morning and do the cows, and then do them again, before dinner, and that my dad was hardly ever pleased with what I did, and that Susan tattled on me, and tried to get me in trouble. By the time I got to the point of complaining to myself about having to eat spinach, all in my head, still, thank goodness, I knew I sounded pretty silly. So what I said was, "Yeah. It's pretty easy for me, I guess. Stuff is pretty much the same, every day, and none of it is really hard." I would never have thought that, a month ago. We looked out at the kids, running and yelling. "But I like my life a lot better, now, since you guys moved down the hill," I said. Roy nodded, and his sister went back to playing with my ears.

The Buckman kids became something in my family. James thought that Roy Buckman was a superhero of some sort, I was smitten with Trish, of course, and closer to Roy than I had even been with another kid. Susan and Ellen became real friends with Tina, Ellen, especially. My mother was not one to take her focus off a potential problem, and she asked Susan about Tina that first Monday night, right after dinner. The girls were washing up the dishes, and James and I were still at the table, working on our lessons.

"Did you sit with the Buckman girl at lunch today?" my mother said.

Susan had to know the question was coming, and she seemed relieved to have the right answer. "I did, me and Ellen, both. She's really nice, and smart, too. Her face droops a little on one side, so she looks kind of slow, because of that, but she's really not. She just looks kind of funny."

My mother didn't like the "looks kind of funny" part, I could tell, but she was pleased that Susan had done the right thing. She wiped at the counter at some flour that had hardened into a dried paste. "What happened to her face?" my mother asked.

"She got hit, I guess, when she was little, and it broke a nerve or something," Susan said. "She can scrunch it up where it looks kind of normal, but most of the time her cheek sort of droops down. It's weird looking."

Ellen, who was usually quiet when Susan and my mom were talking, spoke up. "She's really pretty. As pretty as her sister. And she draws like a grown up. I like her."

"I wasn't saying she isn't pretty. I was just telling mom about her face." Susan didn't like having Ellen butt in, you could tell.

"Dry them all the way, before you put them up," said my mother. You could see her thinking about the Buckman kids, worrying about them, maybe. "They need clothes?" she asked. We usually saved the things we grew out of and gave them to our cousins down in Pittsfield, where my mother's sister lived.

"They dress pretty poor, and I guess there's no water in the trailer yet. Power's still off." Susan was scrubbing out the sink. I found myself getting a little defensive of the Buckman kids, for some reason. My mom was worried about them, and everything Susan said was true, but I knew the Trish and Roy would hate to have us talking about them this way. I wanted to butt in and say that Roy was doing the best he could, but nobody had asked me, and I didn't really know what to say, anyway.

"Maybe we can get something together," my mother said. You could hear her worrying about doing the right thing, and worried about still having enough clean clothes for us to get through the week without having to do the laundry twice. She used her fingernail on the dried flour, and it came off. She polished at where it had been with her dishtowel. "Ask the Buckman kids to come up next Sunday. After lunch. Susan, you and Ellen can make some brownies, and we can churn up some ice cream, once they're here. I'll sort through the clothing and see what we can spare." She still sounded worried, but happy to have a plan in place.

I was the one who was worried, now. What if Trish started fooling around with my ears, right in front of my mother? Or if Roy went off about God or something? There seemed to be a lot of things that could go wrong, with the Buckman kids right in the same room as my parents. I liked things the way there were, and I didn't want to put any of it at risk. Then I got after myself. I was acting ashamed of Trish, and I'd promised her I wouldn't do that. "I think that would be great," I said. "I'll talk to Roy about it at school."

Ellen looked happy, Susan looked relieved to not be in trouble, and my mother was happy to made a decision. But James looked up at me with his eyebrows raised. "Are you nuts?" he whispered.

THE BUCKMAN KIDS

CHAPTER NINE

Trish was first on the bus, again, a pattern she would keep up through the rest of that school year. She was freshly scrubbed, back in the river, again, it turned out, as the propane in the tank had run out. She beamed at me as she climbed up the three metal steps, her eyes so full of life that I could feel it pour into me, filling empty places I hadn't known were there until I met her. She pooched her lips up, blowing a kiss to me, then turned and sat, with Tina having to climb over her to take the seat by the window. Roy would look at me before he sat down, see my grinning moo-cow face, and shake his head, smiling, sometimes. Today he hardly glanced my way, sitting heavily in his seat and staring out the window. I said "hi" at the Campbell stop, but he might as well have not heard me.

When we got to school, in the press of kids waiting for the doors to open, with Trish's hand in mine, and her quick kiss still alive on my lips, he looked at me. "Do you know William Morgan?"

I did. Mr. Morgan had an ever expanding horse farm in East Brookfield, a big house, a fancy horse barn that was heated with oil in the winter, and bought a new, black Lincoln every year. His horses were taller than what we were used to, the kind they used in horse racing, and cost more than I could imagine. He was from Boston, and had a bank there, his own bank, they said, that paid for his horses, an addition to his land every year or so, and the hired help that worked in his home and his barn. His kids were grown, and his wife was in Boston most of the time. He was Catholic, and went to church two or three times a week, up in Montpelier. He bought a little more land every year, usually a failing farm, often tearing down the farmhouse that came with the land. There were few complaints about him, other than speculation about his odd marriage to a wife in Boston, his Catholicism and his habit of tearing down perfectly good houses. I explained all of this to Roy, and it didn't make his feel any better. "Why?" I finally asked.

The press of kids was starting to move into the building, past Mrs. Billings, who stood at the door. Trish was squeezing my hand in some pattern that might have been a code of some sort, three shorts, a long and then three more shorts. She grinned up at me, and I almost forgot about Roy. Roy shook his head. "My dad got a job with him, clearing off some land, old fences, brush and stuff. We're all going to be working at it after school, and on the weekends. This summer, too."

I thought about that. It sounded like a lot of work, but Mr. Morgan paid well. "It's probably good money," I said, hoping to make Roy feel better.

"That's not the problem," Roy said. He didn't say any more, and we headed into class, Trish risking another quick kiss in the crowded hallway before entering the classroom and moving to take her seat.

I had to wait until lunch to hear what the problem was. "My dad doesn't do well with bosses," Roy said. "Never has. He does OK when he's working for himself, like with the scrap metal, or buying and selling cars, or livestock, or something. But when he works for someone else, he ends up getting mad, and then there's a problem." Trish was quiet, but I could tell she was worried about it, too.

"What kind of problem?" I asked.

Roy shook his head, again. "Big problems, usually."

I had brought some cinnamon rolls from home, three extra, one for each of the Buckman kids, at the suggestion of my mom. I wanted to make Roy feel better, so I pulled them out of my bag. "My mom made an extra batch this morning. She sent these in for you, and Trish, and Tina." The rolls were big, starting out the size and shape of a hockey puck, but rising and browning into something bigger than your fist. They were sticky with brown sugar and butter, and were one of the favorite things my mom made.

I put one into Roy's hand, then gave another to Trish, and set the third one on the table. "Two for me!" said Trish.

Roy pointed at Trish. "Take that over to Tina," he said. "If you take a bite out of it, I'm giving her yours, too."

Trish sighed, grinned at me again, then, delivered the roll to her sister. "Roy is so mean," she said. "I don't know why you like him." She bit into her roll, and moaned. She closed her eyes, and rolled her head back and forth, then panted a little bit, and taking another bite. "This is soooo good," she said, her mouth full, and her words a little hard to understand. "I love your mother. Can I have yours, too?" I nodded, my big moo-cow grin on my stupid face.

Roy shook his head again. I thought about Mr. Morgan. I knew that he had bought up the Carson farm, on the ridge road, which butted up to his land up in the woods. I could remember some pasture out by the road, a tiny farmhouse, and a barn, with the back half of the roof caved in a few years before. When the roof went, and nothing was done to repair it, my father had been really upset. The Carson family had sold the cows and moved into Barre a few years before, where Mr. Carson got a job as a stonecutter. They had let the house and the barn just set, with some shingles flipped up on the house roof, and water getting in, he knew. He had stopped on the road, back in the fall, and laid it out for my brother and me. "Thirty minutes to fix the shingles, and maybe another hour to replace the glass in the side window that had broken. Now the rain's come in every time it falls, the plaster is soaked and probably fallen down, and the boards in the roof are rotting away, and probably the floor as well. It would take weeks to make things right now, all because no one had fixed the shingles when they first flipped up. Don't you ever do things that way!" he finished up, scaring me and my brother, with us promising not to.

"Is he going to tear the house and barn down?" I asked.

Roy nodded. "He wants it all gone, and the cellar hole filled in and sodded over. All the fencing took up, too. Not an inch of barbed wire left, he said. We have to cut a road back through the woods, to his place, so he can run his stock over, and back, when he wants to. It sounds great." Roy didn't finish, but it was pretty clear he thought that it wasn't great at all. I finished my sandwich, and ate the carrot sticks my mom had packed. Trish had eaten her lunch, some cold potatoes and a piece of dark meat, rabbit maybe, that looked like it had been cooked outside. It smelled good, and she sucked the grease off her fingers with a happy smile.

"What do you think will happen," I asked.

Roy just shook his head, and didn't say anything.

We sat there, working on our lunch, Trish having already finished her cinnamon roll, and reaching out and petting mine from time to time. I told her she could have it, but she looked shocked. "Me? Eat your cinnamon roll? After I already had my own, and a big, old slab of rabbit or kitty cat or whatever this is…?" Here, she held up a piece of the meat, eyeballing it carefully, and then looking at her brother suspiciously. "Where's Fluffy?" she asked, in a scared, little kid voice.

I thought she was the funniest thing ever, but Roy was used to his sister, and only smiled a little. "Fluffy went bye, bye," he said. Trish shrugged and popped the last of the meat into her mouth, chewing happily away.

I told Roy and Trish about my mom's invitation this coming Sunday, up for ice cream and brownies. I didn't mention the clothes, because I thought that Roy might not like the idea of my mom wanting to give them clothes. I thought my mom would probably think of a way to bring it up so that the Buckman kids felt OK about it. She did that with our cousins, in Pittsfield, always thanking their mom for helping her make room in the closets.

Roy just sat there, not looking pleased at all with the invitation, and Trish looked angry, of all things. "Why does she want that?" she asked. I didn't know what to say, so I started in with how Mrs. Ferris went to our church, and had told my mom that we were friends.

"Is that why your sisters are eating with Tina?" I felt trapped, and the more uncomfortable I looked, the more upset Trish got. "So this is like a church thing," she said. Roy didn't look too pleased, either. I couldn't believe how everything had gotten messed up so fast.

I was suddenly miserable. "You don't have to come, if you don't want to." Trish pushed my cinnamon roll back towards me. "I thought you would like it," I said.

"Was this your idea?" Trish asked.

I could tell she wanted me to say yes, but I shook my head. "Nope. My mom said we should do it, last Sunday, after she talked with Mrs. Ferris." I've never been able to lie very well, and both my parents pretty much trained what little lying ability I might have once had right out of me. Trish was looking at me, like she had noticed something she hadn't seen before.

"Is it about her feeling sorry for us?" Trish asked. I thought back over the sermon that had started the whole thing. I couldn't say yes, but only because my throat was closing up, so I just nodded. Trish colored up, and then started picking away at a scab on her elbow. Roy chewed at the rabbit, and looked at his sister, waiting. Trish popped off the scab, and held it up by her face. I thought she was going to eat it, but then she flipped it off, over the table, where it stuck in the back of Missy Holdman's hair. Trish smiled a little at that, but the smile faded away. She put her finger on my arm and looked right into my soul. "Do you feel sorry for us?" she asked.

I was startled by the question, not yet knowing much about Trish's history with other people. I found my voice, dry, but usable. "No. I think you and your brother are smarter than anyone I ever met, funnier, tougher, and stronger. I think you are so pretty I can't even look at you for long without forgetting my own name. I don't feel sorry for you at all." I was telling the truth again.

Feeling sorry for Trish and Roy, once I had a chance to know them a little, seemed impossible. Trish looked harder into me, and I understood that she was, in her own way, just as scary as her brother, maybe more so. She pressed her finger into my arm, hard enough that there was a little bruise there, the next day. I looked right back at her, and didn't blink.

"Well, OK then," Trish finally said, knowing that I was telling the truth. "I don't feel sorry for you, either." She pulled the cinnamon roll back. "How about your sisters?" she asked.

I took a deep breath. "Mom told Susan to eat lunch with Tina, and Susan did it so she wouldn't get in trouble. But once she met Tina, all she could say was how great she was. And Ellen seems pretty much in love with her. I don't think anyone that really knew you could ever feel sorry for you. Not like that."

Trish grinned at her brother. "I like this boy. He's honest, and well spoken, for a rube. And he has cute ears, a nice, floppy nose, and he feeds me. I think I'll keep him." She kissed two of her own fingers, then reached over and pressed them against my lips. Even though Trish's words sounded like she was kidding, the kiss and the touch felt serious, like carefully putting something back into place that had almost slipped away. I took in a breath, breathing in the air around her fingers, tasting the smoked rabbit that I knew Roy had shot with his rifle, some cinnamon from the roll, and a bit of the tang that I was learning was the taste of Trish.

"We can come," said Roy. "What time?" he asked.

CHAPTER TEN

Ellen wanted to make the brownies, herself, which was the first time I remembered her trying to take something over from Susan. There was some quiet argument, with easy going Ellen surprisingly insistent, and Susan trying to hold on to her role as the older sister who decided things. Both of them acted like they wanted to impress the Buckman kids, which I didn't understand, at the time. I had spent Saturday afternoon moving the ice cube trays to the chest freezer, where each batch froze hard in an hour or so. I kept dumping them into a plastic bucket I had in the freezer, and making more and more ice. We had a big churn, and it took a lot of ice. We made ice cream pretty regular, having a separator in the milk house, and about as much cream as we wanted, provided you're willing to take the separator apart and wash the disks, which was a job and a half. My dad put up cans of cream twice a week, usually Mondays and Wednesdays, but this week he did another can on Saturday. We had plenty of eggs as well, the days getting long enough for the chickens to be pumping them out.

Sunday, after church, I was so nervous I had to be reminded by my mother to eat my dinner. Mrs. Ferris had chatted with my mom again, after church, and she looked pleased that we were having the Buckman kids over. The sermon that morning was on rebirth, tying the coming Vermont spring to a spiritual renewal, and the Kingdom of God returning to Earth. There was nothing in it that was really about having the Buckman kids over for ice cream and brownies, but this last bit got my parents talking in the car, on the way home. There was a discussion of heaven, with my dad taking the position that heaven would be made here on earth, and my mother thinking that heaven was up above, gold streets and all. There were bible verses to support either position, and my dad had thought that Reverend Sikes had favored the redeemed Earth as heaven, with my mother committed to the Rapture and flying away. I had heard them discuss this before, and it all made sense to me, with my father's love of the soil, and the woods, and my mother's longing to escape the endless cleaning and work that seemed to her a part of living on earth. I finished my meatloaf and potatoes, usually a favorite of mine, without hardly tasting them, and went to check the ice bucket in the chest freezer again.

The girls had the dishes done, and had found a quick compromise on the brownies, after their whispered argument came to my mother's attention, my mother's voice, the voice that Ellen called the hairbrush voice, saying simply, "Susan? Ellen?" That was sufficient to end the discussion. My father went out to walk the fence line, something he did from time to time, usually when he was wanting to think about something, but always taking his fencing tools and a bit of wire along, even though we had just done the spring fence work. My mother checked the kitchen, then, retired to her chair, working through her Bible, the soft, black cover worn to mostly brown, her lips silently moving as she read the familiar verses. James was reading as well, slowly working his way through one of the *Little House* books, worn at the corners, passed down from Susan to Ellen, to me, and now, to James. I watched the clock in the kitchen, trying to finish up *Heart of Darkness*, the title of which I was careful to keep somewhat hidden from my mother, who I knew would not approve of the amount of killing the book contained. We had decided on the Buckman kids coming up at two o'clock, that being enough time for lunch to be put away, the dishes done, and the brownies to have a good start.

After school, on Friday, while we waited to get on the bus, I had asked Trish if she thought her dad would let her and her brother and sister come up to our place, and she had said, "It'll be fine. He'll be asleep, probably. Mr. Carson won't let him work on a Sunday, and it not a home farm day, either." She looked uncomfortable, then, and she scanned my face as she spoke, looking for some sign that I would be judging a man who slept in the daytime. Trish was fiercely defensive of her family, although that sure seemed like an uphill battle to me. I worked to keep my eyes neutral, but she could tell I thought it odd for him to be sleeping in the daytime. She reached out and took my nose in her fingers, one of her favorite things to do. She looked into my eyes, and said, "My dad's different than yours, but he's still my dad. I don't want other folks to be judging him." She gave me a quick kiss, erasing any thoughts I had of her father as cleanly as Mrs. Billings had the board erased at the end of the day. Trish looked like she was working on whether to tell me something, then she said, "He didn't have anyone like Roy to look out for him when he was growing up. Tina and I are a lot better off than he was." She smiled just a little, and then tapped my nose again. "So hush. It's your folks I'm worried about." That confused me. Why would she worry about my folks? She saw me thinking again, read my mind, and simply said, "First impressions, silly. If your parents are going to be my in-laws, I want them to start off by liking me."

She said this just as we were climbing up the metal steps, and she gave my hand a quick squeeze before sliding into her seat, with Tina climbing over her, again. I rolled the word "in-laws" around in my head, and felt my chest do that thing where it puffed up all full of happiness. The future looked pretty sweet.

My dad was just back from his walk along the fence lines, and Susan and Ellen had poured the brownie batter into two big pans, and then slid them into the hot oven, when there was a soft knock at the door. Both Susan and Ellen ran upstairs, without even bothering to see who was at the door. My dad was upstairs, changing back into a Sunday shirt, and my mom was still in her Bible. James was oblivious on the couch, so I was the one to go to the door. Usually the whole family was there if someone came to the door, since visitors were such a rarity. My mother looked up from her Bible and gave me a quick smile, and nodded, as if giving me permission to go to the door. I went, and found Trish on the front porch, with Tina standing beside her, and Roy, holding a bag of something in his hand. They were cleaned up to the point I struggled a bit to fit Trish's smile, her freckles and her beautiful eyes to the scrubbed and well-dressed girl who shyly reached out and touched my chest. "Hi," she said. "Roy brought your folks a bag of fish. He caught them this morning." She looked nervously past me into the house. "Anyone else here?" she asked.

I stepped back, just as Roy stepped up, trying to hand me the grocery bag of fresh-caught trout. "Come in. Sorry," I said. "Everyone's here." I reached to take the bag of fish from Roy, who looked way more uncomfortable than he had been waiting for Danny Bowman on the playground that first day.

My mother had appeared, smiling and reaching past me for the bag of fish. "Oh! This is so perfect. We were just wishing that we had some fish for dinner! You must have guessed. My! What a heavy bag! You must have caught the whole stream. You're Roy, Toby's friend. And your sisters. Trish, and Tina? Come in. I'm so pleased to meet you." Roy blushed up as red as a plumb, grinning a little, but saying nothing at all.

Trish did the tiniest curtsy, and said, "Mrs. Landers, I have wanted to meet you since I first met your sons and daughters. They have been such good friends to me and my brother and sister. This is Tina, and Roy. Roy's the one who caught the fish, but I cleaned them for you."

I felt like I was watching a movie, with Trish and my mother playing the kind of people you might see down at the Playhouse theatre. Polite, well spoken, pretty much perfect. My mother never spoke to any of us that way, and Trish seemed more like *Anne of Green Gables* than the girl I had first met on the playground. My mother ushered us all back into the house, and took the fish to put into the fridge, peeking into the damp bag, and going on about what beauties they were, and even how well they were cleaned. "No one ever brings me cleaned fish," she said. I wondered if this was the way you were supposed to be with company. We didn't have folks over much, with my dad's parents being too old to travel much, and my mom's folks already dead. Aunts and uncles came and went without much fuss, usually dropping kids off, or borrowing a ladder or some such thing. I vaguely remembered Reverend Sikes and his wife coming to dinner once, and my parents being this polite, but that was a long time ago, and I couldn't be sure.

We ended up in the kitchen, which was beginning to smell like brownies, when Ellen and Susan came down, clean, and back in their Sunday dresses. Their hair was brushed, and Susan had even put on a pair of shoes. We all stood there, no one saying such of anything, all of us feeling uncomfortable, when my mother said, "Well, Susan, why don't you get the ice cream started. The brownies will be out in forty-five minutes, and it would be nice to let them set for just a bit, and then have them with the ice cream. The recipe card is out on the counter. I'm going to go see about your father."

Roy and I sat at the table. I noticed his hands were pink from scrubbing, and then he noticed me looking. "What 'cha looking at?"

"Nothing." I tried not to grin too much. "You want some milk or something, while we wait? We can take turns with cranking the churn, when the girls get it filled and the ice in. I made a whole bucket of ice."

Roy was looking around the kitchen. "This is nice," he said. Susan told me to get the ice out of the chest freezer, and bring a couple of towels for the churn. She had filled the churn with cream, sugar, eggs and vanilla, almost all the way to the top, and she and Ellen set it down into the wooden bucket, then, set the crank in place on the top. Trish and Tina volunteered to carry it out to the porch, with both of them swinging the heavy churn as they walked. I brought up the bucket of ice, and Susan came out with the bag of rock salt, still half full from last summer. We set a towel, folded up, under the churn, then filled the wooden bucket up with ice, then poured the salt over it, nice and heavy. Susan folded the other towel and set it on top of the churn, as a seat for the kid who would sit there, while the other kids took turns cranking the handle.

We had done all that about a thousand times, but it was new to the Buckmans, and we explained the process as best we could. James took the first seat, and I started to crank, until Trish put her hand on mine, and asked if she could turn the handle. "This is easy!" she said, trying to find a way to squat down buy the bucket in her dress and still look like someone my mother would approve of. I got her a footstool from the front room, and she settled in.

"It's not so easy once it starts to set," I said. "You know it's done when you can just barely turn it without tossing the sitter off."

Roy had taken a seat in one of the two rockers set on the porch. "OK if I sit here?" he asked. "You have a nice view from up here. Looking out over the valley. All the way down to town," he said.

I felt kind of bad, for some reason. "We don't sit out here, much. Dad usually has me and James working, and mom keeps the girls pretty busy inside." I felt dishonest, and worried that I was making my parents out to sound bad. But I knew that Roy and his sisters couldn't even see out of their windows in the trailer, the few good windows covered with sheet plastic, and the broken windows just plywooded over.

Roy smiled, like he knew just what I was thinking. "It's OK," he said. "It's just a nice view, that's all." Ellen and Tina had disappeared, upstairs, maybe. I looked over and found Susan standing by the porch rail, staring at Roy. I looked at him, myself, to see if there was something wrong, but he looked OK to me. Trish was still cranking away at the ice cream, with James sitting contentedly on top, his toes on the porch on either side, to keep his balance. When the ice cream started to set, that crank handle would slow down, and the churn would rock. James had been tossed off a few times, before.

My mom and dad came out on the porch. Roy stood up, and offered his hand to my dad, introducing himself and his sisters, even though Tina was off with Ellen somewhere. My dad shook his hand, and then complimented Trish on what a good worker she was, saying that she'd get the first bowl of ice cream, and mine too, if she kept on churning. Trish smiled, and said, "I'm used to hard work. And Toby gives me some of his lunch, most days, anyway. I wouldn't want to take his ice cream away from him." She smiled over at me.

"Maybe you three can come up and help with the hay this summer. It's supposed to be a heavy year, and we could use the help." My dad had made it a point to never hire help, with what he called "four big, hungry kids already here on the farm". I was getting used to surprises, though, since the Buckman kids moved in.

Trish smiled, and Roy said that he and his sisters would be glad to help us out, and that they had worked hay before. Trish slid up the sleeve of her dress, and showed off her muscle, bigger than mine, really. "I can keep up with Tina and Roy," she said. My dad agreed that she looked like she was strong enough, and that he would be sure to have them up for putting up the first cutting.

My parents went back into the house, still smiling. "Your folks are really nice," said Trish.

I felt a little like I had when Roy had talked about the view off the porch, but I said, "Yeah, they are, most of the time. They sure like you three." Ellen and Tina came back, and we took turns on the churn until the handle was too stiff to crank any more, even for Trish. The brownies were out and cooling, but still pretty hot when Susan cut them into big squares and set them on lunch plates, with a big scoop of ice cream on each one. My parents sent all the kids back out to the porch, and had their ice cream there at the kitchen table, with a fresh pot of coffee my mother had made.

After we had eaten most of the brownies, and almost all of the ice cream, the four girls cleaned up the dishes, and then all of us went out to the barn to swing on the rope. There was a fat, splintery rope that had been hanging there forever, from back when they used to put the hay up loose. Dad retied it over the center of the loft, and let us swing from one end of the barn almost to the other. There was about two feet of loose hay on the floor, and a small stack of bales left over from the winter, that we tried to hit, dropping some fifteen feet or so onto the floor of the loft. Susan usually hung back from the rope swing, both being afraid to fall, and not wanting to do anything unseemly in her dress, but today she swung with the rest of us, shrieking and laughing as much as Trish did. Roy climbed the rope to the top, and then Trish did, too. Ellen tried and only made it about half way, and I knew enough to not even try, having never been able to get all the way up before. I just sat on the bales and watched, the four Landers kids playing and laughing with the three Buckman kids, like we had know each other since we were born. Way better than us and our cousins ever did. Roy sat beside me, having chapped up his hands a bit sliding on the rope.

"This is good, isn't it?" I said.

74

"Yeah. It is good," Roy said. "I hope we can stay here on the hill for a while, at least." He looked worried.

I hadn't thought there was anything to worry about. "Why wouldn't you stay?" I asked.

Roy shook his head, and didn't say anything for a bit. "We'll have to see how this job goes for my dad," he finally said. "That's usually why we have to move."

I didn't understand it, but I knew to not ask anything more. I felt really happy to have the Buckman kids here, packed full of ice cream and brownies, swinging in our barn, and planning of bucking hay with us in the summer. And I was glad my parents liked Trish, since, as she said, they were going to be her in-laws some day.

THE BUCKMAN KIDS

CHAPTER ELEVEN

Looking back, it was almost two weeks where everything seemed easy and good. I relaxed into loving Trish, seeing her climb onto the bus every day, then the two of us standing together in front of the school, holding her some, getting a quick kiss, and then looking up to see the back of her head in class, her hair brushed out clean and straight, or braided in a single pony tail half way down her back. Lunch brought us together, Roy and Trish and I talking about everything, the coming summer, which we expected to be filled with haying, swim holes and fishing, what it was like to live in Barre, even our favorite pie. Trish and Roy never talked about what happened at home, but I could tell they were both worried about their father's job.

Trish had already carved half of the heart on the beech tree, a big, old beech that stood, as beech like to do, pretty much by itself. My dad said that they put out something in their roots that keeps the other trees away. Smooth-barked and grey, looking much like an elephant's leg, the beech has the perfect surface to invite carving by those intent on marking their passing on this earth, and celebrating the joy they might be lucky enough to find here. Trish wandered back up through the woods that Sunday, the Sunday of the ice cream, wanting to maybe see me, not to talk, but just to see me, again. She had come up the ridge, not wanting to be seen herself, and had found the beech on her way up. She'd seen me, finally, moving the cows into the barn, and had blown me a kiss, she said. She thought I might reach up and touch my cheek, feeling something soft and sweet land there, but I had only followed along after the cows, staring at their butts, she said. In spite of this glimpse into the real me, she stopped at the beech on her way back down the hill, and used her boy scout knife to carve in half of the heart. She had carefully cut the left half of a heart, maybe ten inches tall, deep and smooth, with a neat "T.B." on that side. She told me the next day that I could finish the other half, and that she would check to see that it was a neat as hers. Then she asked me what it was I really liked about cow butts.

The only cloud on our horizon seemed to be Mr. Buckman starting to work tearing down the barn at the old farm that Mr. Morgan had bought. Roy and Trish were worried about it, I could tell. I tried to reassure them. I had heard nothing but good things about Mr. Morgan, in spite of his being a Catholic. I told them my father and my brother and I worked for him some, every summer, ourselves. My father had sold him hay, since I could remember, eight hundred bales or so. Mr. Morgan always wanted the second cutting, or maybe the third, mostly pure timothy, with a little clover being OK, all put up dry and sweet. Mr. Morgan paid well, almost twice a bale more than my father got for the excess hay he sold other dairy farmers. My father looked out for the best cuttings, all from the high field, where none of the saw-grass grew, and when the hay was perfect, put up with no rain, and quickly dried.

We took wagons of the fresh-baled hay over behind the tractor to Mr. Morgan's barn. Mr. Morgan would greet use, offer us each a cold bottle of grape soda, and then push his hand deep into several of the bales, pulling out a bit of hay from here and there, eyeing it carefully, and sniffing it, watching out for mold or weeds. He saw me watching him, once, and put the hay in his mouth, chewing on it carefully, watching me as he chewed, my eyes getting big, until I realized he was teasing me. He was always careful about the hay, but always pleased. My father had been making hay since he was younger than me, and knew just what Mr. Morgan wanted. The four of us, with Mr. Morgan in his wool pants, and rolling up his white sleeves, would load each wagon of hay into Mr. Morgan's barn, setting an electric elevator, with traces of yellow paint and a rattly chain, at one end on the wagon, with the other end up in the barn loft. I admired that elevator something fierce, having bucked bales by hand up into our barn until my arms were useless and on fire. Mr. Morgan just plugged it in, clack, clack, clack, and with my father loading from the wagon, the bales would magically rise up and into the barn loft, where Mr. Morgan, James and I would catch them as they came off the steel rails, and stack them just so. Mr. Morgan was as picky about the stacking as he was about the hay, being sure we gave the bales some air, and making neat, sturdy stacks that lay like giant, green bricks, piled high and even and strong.

My brother and I loved this work in Mr. Morgan's barn. It was hot and sweaty, and sticky, of course. We were working with hay, and there's no way to avoid the sweat and the prickles. But the same work with my father was silent, my dad offering a rare word or two, only to correct. Mr. Morgan talked constantly, loud enough to be heard over the clanking elevator, telling us about his life in Boston, his experiences in the war, and most of all, his prize horses. He mostly talked about his stud, Peacemaker. Peacemaker was out of Man of War, a horse Mr. Morgan told us was known around the world. Peacemaker was six years old, too old to race, now, but he just getting started as a stud, and mounted the brood mares that Mr. Morgan brought up from the south, siring horses with great potential, as Mr. Morgan put it, with the best yearlings trailered over to a training barn near Woodstock.

Mr. Morgan clearly loved this horse, a giant, muscled monster that turned into a puppy for his owner. He came when whistled for, and nickered and nuzzled Mr. Morgan's hand for dates, sweet, sticky brown things that looked like giant raisins. Mr. Morgan always kept some in his coat pocket, the pits carefully cut out, and had given James and I some once. They were wonderful, and not something that I had ever seen before, down in the grocery store in Randolph. Mr. Morgan brought them back from a store in Boston. I still buy dates, and think of Mr. Morgan when I eat them, Mr. Morgan, back when he was happy, in his clean, fresh barn, looking at the horses he loved, and chatting with James and I.

Hearing about what a great guy Mr. Morgan was didn't help Trish or Roy feel any better, so I stopped talking about it. We talked some about the summer, which was coming up pretty soon, and wondered when the water at the pond would get warm enough you could do more than grit your teeth and jump in, lose all your breath, then scramble back out again, shivering on the bank. Summer swims were glorious, with the sun hot on your skin, and the top few inches of the pond warmed up like bathwater. There was a little piece of cleared grass, right next to the pond, that served as a beach of sorts for the folks from Brookfield that went swimming. It was right by the bridge, and while the parents floated and soaked in the water, the kids would climb up on the bridge, and hurl themselves off into the water below, over and over. I could do a back flip, sometimes, and James just tossed himself in, hoping to make as big a splash as possible.

Ellen was a diver, standing thin and uncertain, balancing for a bit on the top rail of the bridge, then arching up into the air, and then turning to enter the water with almost no splash at all, just slipping into the deep, cold water, with only a quiet ring at the surface to mark her passing. Susan accused her of showing off, not something we were allowed to do, but Ellen dived the same way when it was just us there at the pond, and I knew she didn't care about showing off for us. I think she just liked the idea of doing something perfectly. Watching her arc up into the air, and then slip silently into the water, that's one of the pictures I still have in my head, as clear as if it had only happened yesterday.

While the three of us, Trish, Roy and I, sat in the shade at recess, Trish talked about our kids. This embarrassed me, at first, but she kept at it, naming them different things each day. I remember "Inky, Blinky and Stinky" being one possibility, with accompanying descriptions of each child. "Rumble, Bumble and Tumble" came up as well. "Charlotte" was offered more seriously, Trish sometimes wanting to talk about names she really liked, with Roy then suggesting "Wilbur" and "Pendelton", for the remaining two. It was always three kids, sometimes all boys, sometimes all girls, sometimes a mix. The house was big and clean and smelled good, and the aunts, Susan, Ellen and Tina, and uncles, Roy and James, would come by, maybe on Sundays, and all the cousins would play outside while the parents all sat on the porch and drank lemonade and made ice cream. Trish had their rooms all planned out, the breakfasts she was going to make for them, and even how our kids would be expected to behave. Trish said she wasn't going to take any sass, but that she didn't want her kids too afraid of her, either. "And you'll only hit them if I tell you to," she added. "Sort of like your folks," she added.

I thought about that, and decided that she was probably missing a few details about my folks, but I didn't say anything. I could tell she had been planning this family thing for a long time, and that she thought about it a lot, even if she made up joke names of the kids, sometimes. I sometimes had pictured myself all grown, maybe driving a tractor, and a shiny new truck, or shaving every morning, but I hadn't thought much about the family details. I decided that Trish needed the picture of her future family to help her live with the reality of the trailer she went home to each day.

Trish had come to school one morning, on the day that things started to go south, her smile for me on the bus a little off. When we got to school, I could see that her upper lip was swollen, with a little split on one side. She had been slapped, hard, and I could see a finger-lined bruise starting up on her cheek, the same as I had seen that first day on her sister, Tina. She saw the worry in my face, and grinned. "We gotta kiss on the other side for a bit, I guess," she said, trying to be funny. She was watching me carefully, but I couldn't help feeling a white hot rage rise up in me, my breath suddenly short, and my vision blurring a bit at the sides. I hadn't ever been angry like that before, and afterwards, it kind of scared me. "Easy there, Killer," Trish said. "I just got a little mouthy this morning, and my dad was kind of surly, anyway."

"Your dad?" I started, but Trish put her finger up to my lips.

"Hush. Roy keeps it from getting out of hand," she said. Roy looked embarrassed, and turned away. I only wanted to kill her father. "Dad knows the three of us could take him if we had to," she added, tapping my nose. "Besides, he has to sleep sometimes, and he doesn't want to wake up on fire." She grinned at her brother. "Roy told him that, once, when he was going after Tina. He hasn't forgotten it, I'll bet".

Roy looked back at his sister, and said, "He knows I mean it." Roy was as serious as a funeral. I looked at his eyes, so old to be there in a schoolboy's face. I knew that what Roy said was true. I thought again about the way Trish had said Roy was "kind of protective", and I suddenly knew that it was a full time job for Roy to keep his sisters safe, not just on the bus and at school, but at home, as well. We headed into class, and took our seats, with Trish blowing me a little twisted kiss before she sat down. Roy turned to me, just before Mrs. Billings came in, and said, "Don't worry. I got it covered." I forgot the pledge that day, and had to mumble, thinking instead about Trish and Roy and Tina, the Buckman kids.

I was still stewing on it, trying to find a way to make sense of this kind of life, a life that was happening just down the hill from our house, and happening to kids I had quickly come to love. When I got home, my father was quiet in the barn, and my mother seemed upset when we washed up and got inside. Susan and Ellen were washed up and clean, and a roast chicken sat on the metal platter, still sizzling from the oven, with a pot of white gravy, some steamed green beans canned last fall, with a bowl of mashed potatoes topped with streams of melted butter. It was one of my favorite meals, and yet, I drifted through the prayer with no thoughts for the food on the table.

Before my father started to cut up the chicken, he stopped, carving knife in his hand. "You ought to know," he said, picking his words carefully. "Mr. Morgan's stud was killed last night. Peacemaker. Someone shot him in the head, from close up. Mr. Morgan found him this morning, in his stall." My father seemed to be trying to think about how much else he should say. "Mr. Morgan's going to move back to Boston. He's sending the brood mares and the rest down to the farm in Woodstock, and then selling the place here, I guess. He gave you boys the elevator he had. Brought it over today. It's out in the barn." I looked at my dad, and knew that there was even worse news coming. "Mr. Morgan had an argument with Mr. Buckman, the day before, about the work on the old Carson place. The work was poorly done, and Mr.

Morgan fired him. He thinks Buckman is the one who shot the horse."

My father's face was white with anger. He didn't say any more, but sat, looking at the chicken in front of him, as if he had forgotten how to carve one up. I knew that he had lost a good customer, and a friend, in Mr. Morgan moving back to Boston, but I thought he was angry at more than that. I knew my dad had a clear idea of how the world should work, and someone shooting another fellow's horse out of spite was a sin, in a big way. My mother handed the bowl of green beans to my brother. "We don't know that," she said. "But it looks that way, certainly." She glanced at my brother's plate, where some five green beans lay in a tiny pile. "More, James," she said. James took more. Susan had started the mashed potatoes, and had taken to top part for herself, taking the big melting pat of butter with it. She passed the bowl on to Ellen, who looked quickly at her sister, but said nothing, and put a scoop of dry potatoes on her plate. "There's no reason to bring it up with the Buckman kids," my mother said. "We don't really know it was their father who shot the horse, and it's not their, fault, anyway, even if he did." My mother eyed Susan's plate. "Susan, please trade plates with your sister." Susan did. "Greed is a sin, Susan," my mother added. Ellen took the most of the butter from the potatoes on what was now her plate, and returned it to the bowl, earning a brief smile from my mother. Susan wasn't smiling. She had no butter at all, and was now in real trouble with my mother. Again.

"What's going to happen?" I asked, wondering some about the police being called, but mostly wondering if my parents would still let the Buckman kids come up to our place. My dad was carving up the chicken, having remembered to start at the breast, laying perfect thin slices off with the sharp, dark carving knife. "I don't know," my mother said. "Mr. Morgan spoke with the sheriff, and gave him the value of the horse. It cost as much as his farm did, I think. But no one saw anything. And Mr. Morgan said the sheriff didn't seem very willing to confront Mr. Buckman about it." My father laid the first slices of chicken on her plate, and she thanked him. We each held our plate towards him, and he laid slices of chicken on it. When we all had a full plate, we sat in silence for a bit. "We'll just have to give it time. We can pray about it, tonight," she added.

CHAPTER TWELVE

We prayed about it, that night, praying for Trish, and for Roy and Tina, calling the Lord's love and blessing down on them. We prayed for Mr. Morgan, even though he was a Catholic, praying that the Lord would ease his grieving heart. We didn't pray for Peacemaker, because he was a horse. We didn't pray about Mr. Buckman, either, our church not believing that calling the Lord's wrath down on evil doers was our proper role, but I know my father would have prayed down the plagues of Egypt on Mr. Buckman, if he'd believed that way. But I prayed again, that night, myself, alone, after my mother had left the room. I prayed for Trish to be kept safe, and selfishly, for Trish to be kept mine, and for the Buckman kids to find a path to safety. "Make them safe," I prayed.

This last bit was the tricky part. My mother had cautioned us that the best prayers were prayers of thanks, and prayers that others be blessed with the Lord's love. When you prayed for things to be different, especially different in a certain way, you were stepping up into a role that wasn't really meant for us, she said. Best to be content in God's wisdom, and not try to take the wheel ourselves, she said. But in my mind, I saw Trish's sweet face, split and bruised, and Mr. Morgan ripped from pretty much everything I knew he loved, his giant horse now waiting to be hauled by a backhoe out to a fresh hole in the ground. I saw Roy, sent in to fight his cousins, for the entertainment of his own father and his uncles, and Roy sleeping light every night, worried about his sister's safety, in their own home, and when I saw all those things, I wanted change. I prayed for change, and I knew, even at the time, that the core of hate that had bloomed along my spine for Mr. Buckman, when I had first seen the heavy hand print on Trish's face, that hatred had not gone away. Like food tainted by a poisoned dish, I knew my prayer was colored by hate, but then, at that time, I was young, and I didn't much care. "Give them a path the safety, Lord", I prayed, knowing as I prayed, that I would be pleased, inside, where only God could see, to have that path paved with the broken bones of their father.

The next morning was much like any other that Spring. We rose early, with the hard darkness of winter only just starting to give way to the finest hint of a pale glow in the East. It was still cold in the mornings, and the heat of the cows felt good on my hands. Breakfast was hot and good, our usual eggs and sausage and toast. My mother had left the butter off the toast on Susan's plate, and she watched Susan eat it dry, without complaint. My mother always thought a reminder would be helpful for each lesson taught. I had heard the lesson about greed last night, my mother's lecture punctuated as usual with the hairbrush, and wondered this morning at Susan's ability to catch twice the grief that the rest of us did.

When the bus stopped at the Buckman trailer, I held my breath, suddenly afraid that Mr. Buckman had disappeared into the night, taking his children with him, but then Trish hopped on the bus, pretty and magic and smiling as she always was, making the tiny kiss that she did, before taking the aisle seat, and having her sister Tina climb over, again. She had told me she sat there so she could feel me looking at the back of her head. Roy looked stretched thin, though, and I could guess that he had heard about Mr. Morgan's horse, probably from his father. I nodded "Hi", and Roy nodded back, but he sat without saying a word. I wondered how his father had talked about it, about shooting the horse, if he had bragged and laughed, or if he had been ashamed and afraid. I never knew, but I guessed that it was the first, and nothing I have ever heard about Mr. Buckman has ever made me doubt that guess.

We didn't talk about it, us kids, that morning, and the day went on as well as it usually did. We often lived like we were passengers on a train, never guessing that a switch has been thrown, that, miles down the track, this act will plunge their train into an abyss. That's a blessing, I guess. Who would want to know what troubles lay ahead? We had math, we had spelling, we had history, and then, we had lunch. It was after lunch, when the three of us were sitting, as we did, under the greening maple, watching the other children at play, that Trish said, "You heard about the horse?"

I nodded. "My dad told us last night." I stopped myself from saying how upset he was, and about poor Mr. Morgan moving back to Boston.

Trish chewed on the muffin I had brought for her, made with blueberries from a can, it still being a month or two before the fresh ones could be found, but still mighty good. My mother had taken to packing my lunch bag extra full since she had met the Buckman kids, but never saying a thing. I guessed that Susan's bag might have had some extras in it as well. We sat, without talking, Trish's hand on my knee, moving my leg back and forth as she chewed. Roy sat like stone, his eyes open, but closed off, somehow. He had a muffin as well, untasted, in his hand, and with the other, he smoothed the dirt and pick up tiny rocks, which he tossed out into the field in front of us. We sat where the blood had pooled from Danny Bowman's surprised wounds, but the rain had long since washed the blood away. I somehow had the idea that the ground was ours, marked by a sacrifice of sorts, like in the Old Testament. At any rate, we were never challenged there, even as the days grew hot, and the shade beneath the maple became something the older kids might have wanted for themselves.

Trish had finished her muffin, and nudged her brother, and he silently handed hers the one in his hand. "You mom sure makes good muffins," Trish said. "Maybe she can teach me, and I'll make muffins like this when you and I are married. I'll send Huey, Lewy and Dewy off to school with warm muffins in their bags." Her certainty about our future seemed a little risky, that day, for some reason. I nodded, but was quiet. I was lying on my back, looking up at the leaves overhead, moving just a bit in the breeze. Trish balanced a piece of muffin on the tip of my nose, and then carefully bent over and took it with her lips, breathing her warm breath into my skin and tipping my thoughts like a card table tossed by an drunken player. She hovered over me, staring into me, her green and gold-flecked eyes reaching deep into mine. She moved to my lips, and kissed me there, softly, her lips still sore, drawing in her breath to keep the muffin crumb from falling into my limp mouth. "You OK?" she asked.

I started up at her, trying to focus, which was hard, since she was only an inch of so away. "Yeah", I said, taking another kiss, careful to stay on the better side of her lip. "I'm just worried, that's all. What do you think is going to happen?"

Trish pulled back, trying to get me into focus, as well, I guess. "Nothing, maybe. Nothing yet, anyway. We thought the police might show up yesterday, but they didn't. Not this morning, either. They usually come really early, when they hope everyone is asleep and easy to take." I wondered at the word "usually", but didn't ask. Trish sat up, and looked out at the playground, finding her sister Tina standing up against the wall, with Susan on one side, and Ellen on the other, Ellen leaning into Tina, and saying something to her. Trish looked back at me. "You still like me, though, don't you? I mean, the marriage and the kids and everything is still on, right"? She tried to sound like she was kidding, but I could tell she was worried.

I sat up, too, and leaned up against her. "Married when I turn eighteen," I said. "I love you. I don't care about anything else." I tried to kiss her, but she pushed me back down again. I could tell there wasn't anything I could say that she would really trust, and I think she knew that, too. She pulled a blueberry out of the muffin in her hand, Roy's muffin, and tired to balance it on my nose again. Even though it was a soft one, from a can, it kept rolling off. She would pick it back up again, and press it a little harder onto my nose, trying to get it to stay. The blueberry and her finger looked huge and out of focus, and I looked cross-eyed as I stared at it. A little bit of the juice ran into my eye.

"Close your eyes," Trish said. "You look awful with them crossed." I did, and she put the mushed blueberry on my lips. I felt her above me, and then I felt her breath on me, again, and her mouth over my eye, and her tongue, I guessed, just a little rough, like a cat, licking the run of juice off my nose and eye, and then her lips carefully taking the blueberry of my lips. "You make a nice plate," she said. My breathing had gotten all confused, and my heart was pounding again, and I had to open my eyes. "You better keep loving me," she said. "Even if my daddy is a crazy man."

"I will," I said. And I did, of course.

The last weeks of Spring moved on towards Summer, with my mother asking the Buckman kids up almost every Sunday afternoon, for ice cream, and brownies, or a layer cake, or chocolate chip cookies, hot from the oven. Trish pestered my mother into letting her help with the baking, just saying she wanted to learn, not mentioning Eeny, Meeny, and Miny, or her future role as my wife. My mother seemed pleased to have a way of responding to the horror of Mr. Buckman's act with kindness, and even my father continued to talk about the coming hay season, and the role he expected the Buckman kids to play in it. He was even talking about haying some of the land of a neighbor, who had taken on a full-time job up in Barre. He took me, and James and Roy, out to the barn, and had us watch while he tuned up the tractor, the haybine and the baler.

"Do your repairs before you're out in the field," he said. "You have to make hay while the sun shines, and in Vermont, it doesn't shine that long." He was replacing a bearing on the haybine, and had the roller dropped out on a jack, and his tools spread out on the barn floor beside him. "Crossing your fingers won't help. Wishing won't make it happen. If this bearing had spun out while the hay was half cut, we would have lost the day. If it rained, we'd lose the hay. You want to have everything in place, ready to go, when you need it. I heard this bearing last summer, towards the end, and I should have fixed it then, probably, but I'm sure not going to wait until the hay is ready. That bailer ran fine. It's a John Deere, and a good one. The 14T is the best bailer Deere ever made. I know I can trust it, but I'm going to go over it, anyway. Better a little work beforehand, than being surprised."

I had heard the lecture a hundred times, but I could see that Roy was really listening. I realized that Roy's father and mine were worlds apart, and that the things I had grown up with, and had taken for granted, were new to Roy, and appreciated. My father could see this, too, and he invited Roy to spin the old bearing, and feel the catch where the bearing had started to go. Roy took the thing in his hand, spun it, and asked questions. I felt a little jealous, watching them together, my father's voice soft, his explanation slow and detailed. But then, I had never seemed to listen the way Roy did, and I never asked questions that my father might have been pleased to answer. I think I always assumed that if I were to have a problem with the haybine, my father would be there to fix it for me, lecturing me all the while about how I could have done it better, but still, doing it for me.

So my father took Roy in as a third son of sorts, one who really wanted to hear about how to do things right, and my mother took Trish and Tina in as two more daughters, all be it only on Sunday afternoons, at that point. It seemed that Mr. Buckman had found no apparent consequence for his murderous act, except the increased dislike the people on the hill had for him, people who had, to be fair, disliked him from the start, anyway. I thought that my relationship with the Buckman kids could go on, uninterrupted. Mr. Morgan's life had changed, certainly, and Peacemaker's had ended, and yet, it seemed, on the surface, that my world would maybe be untouched. I sometimes thought of my prayer that night, my prayer for action, a prayer tainted with hatred, and I was careful from then on, to this day, really, to only pray with thanks and for blessings. I thought then that perhaps no harm had been done. And maybe that was the case. It's hard to know what thing causes the next, and we all tend to look for ways to blame ourselves when bad happens.

School wound to a close, the sun rose a little earlier every morning, as the first cutting of hay began to wave in the breeze, and the air grew hot. It seemed that we might all have a summer of hard work, swimming and fishing, with Trish, Roy and Tina up to the farm several times a week. Sometimes they were called away on work of some sort by their father, but usually they came. The money my father paid them was regularly taken by their father, until Roy began stashing a portion of their wages with me. I kept the money in a canning jar, tucked in the back of the wood shed, behind that last cord of wood that we never seemed to use. Trish continued to easily stir my brains into mush, much to my delight, and hers. The summer sun brought out her freckles, and bleached out her already blond hair to something the color of sunlight. Her beauty grew and amazed me every day. We were happy.

It seemed that Susan had an interest in Roy, although Roy, as he said, had no time for that nonsense. I found her staring at him, and when I paid attention, I could see that she stood differently when he was around, her shoulders back, and her chest out a little. She kept at her hair, and had even stopped chewing her nails, so they could grow and look less like a little kid's. Ellen and Tina continued to seek each other out, and when we all weren't working, they would disappear off into the woods, looking for mushrooms, or flowers, or berries, or whatever. The three Buckman kids had slipped into our lives as if they had always been there, as if they belonged. Everyone in my family felt that way, even though it wasn't talked about. We all were a little excited on the days we could expect the Buckman kids to make their way up the trail on the ridge, and stand there on our porch, with Trish's soft knock letting us know they had arrived.

CHAPTER THIRTEEN

The hay was coming on fast that summer, with a decent amount of snow the winter before, and an early, hot spring. My father took the boys, which included Roy that morning, down into Randolph to Central Supplies, the feed store beside the railroad tracks. He needed to buy the bailing twine for the season, some grease, cotter pins, and some things for my mother, including a packet or two of flower seeds. We had left Trish and Tina in the garden, with my mother, Susan and Ellen, all putting in the first seeds and plants into the soft soil, which my father had plowed and harrowed the week before. Our garden was fenced against the deer and woodchucks, up on high ground, behind the house, and the soil there dried out pretty early. The Landers had kept a garden on that plot since the house was built, back in nineteen five, before my father was born, and the soil was rich and black, and good. When you walked across the garden, in the late summer, it felt like you were walking on a feather mattress, with each step sinking into the soil, and then springing up behind you. Trish and Tina had never put in a garden before, and they were all excited about it. Trish had asked about flowers, and my mother, who had ignored the same question from my sisters, had asked my dad to get some seeds. Geraniums, she thought, and maybe some marigolds, which helped to keep the bugs away. She liked the Buckman kids.

Central Supplies was built by the tracks, with a siding set behind the store to take in goods right off a boxcar. It had been painted a variety of shades of blue over the years, with the main beams dark brown, like they had been oiled. Inside, a worn oak floor sloped this way and that, creaking under foot. There was a row of shovels, hoes, scythes, rakes and the like all along one wall. There were boots in the corner, with a bench to sit on when you tried them on, heavy, lace up leather boots, for logging and tractor work, tall rubber barn boots, all black, and even a few fancy riding boots. Our black rubber barn boots had come from there. There were saddles, and some horse tack, and a wall of hand tools and hardware, with even a few welders and generators. There was a small shelf of milking machine parts and supplies, and where my father was, stacks of bailing twine, bound two to a bag. The feed was in big paper bags and gunny sacks out back, along with some dusty bales of hay and straw. In the spring, there were wooden trays of bulbs, packets of seeds, and some fruit trees and berry bushes, their roots packed in burlap, and watered from time to time with a slowly leaking red hose, which lay on the gravel beside them. Fly strips hung by the dusty windows, buzzing with stuck flies, and fly swatters, advertising the feed store, sold for ten cents up by the counter. I'm sure there was more. My father had let us wander free in the feed store since we were old enough to toddle around, with the only rule "don't touch", which we followed perfectly, after a few accidentally errors.

The Jacobs brothers ran the store, Elder and Younger. I can't imagine that these were their names. What would their parents have done if another son had been born? "Even Younger? But that's what they were called, here in the store, by the adults, any way. We kids called them Mr. Jacobs, or "Sir", of course. My father knew them and liked them. They went to our church, and were deacons, along with my dad. They were known to donate feed or supplies if a church family was short, donations that were off the books, and with no expectation of repayment. They were both married, living right next to each other in identical houses, and each had a slew of kids. I saw them all at church, but not at school, since the Jacobs both lived off in Braintree.

My father was talking about bailing twine with Elder, there now being, that year, a new twine, died blue, that came with some sort of added something that helped the twine not to rot, and kept it from catching in the bailer's knotter. It cost a dollar and a quarter more, for the bag of two spools, than the old yellow twine did, which we had always used before. Elder seemed to think it was money well spent, if you had a picky bailer, which gave my father a chance to start bragging on his John Deere 14T. We ended up with ten bags of the yellow twine, saving some twelve dollars and fifty cents, as my father pointed out.

When the decision on twine had been made, and Roy had been introduced to both Elder and Younger as the new hired help on the Landers farm, my father took Roy to look at the chore gloves hanging on a rack by the boots. We used the canvas-backed, leather-palmed barn gloves, made with a striped blue and white canvas, and thick, grey leather palms and fingers, going through a pair by the end of the season, if not before. Worn gloves were fine for firewood, but the twine would blister and cut your skin if the leather wore through. The gloves we bought had a high, stiff gauntlet, made of double-stitched canvas, which helped to keep the prickles from wearing out your wrists, even though it made the gloves hot and sweaty in the summer.

Children worked in those days, and you could tell that by the tiny gloves and the little boots for sale at the feed store. Children's gloves came in small, medium, and large, and the boots for kids came numbered, more like shoes, but in even numbers only. They went down to a size four, if I remember right, and I knew that four-year-old boys were expected to be out helping in the barn, just as my brother and I had been. My father had Roy pick out gloves for himself and his sisters, with Roy getting a children's large size for himself and for his sisters. My father showed Roy how to check the stitching and the leather in the gloves, once he had decided on the right size, and how to pick the best pair from the others. He pulled a few pairs out, and showed Roy the difference between them, with one pair sewed just right on both gloves, the stitches tight and neat and centered, and the other gloves being sewed too close to the edge of the canvas, where it would tear out with time.

Elder came over, and agreed with my father. "You don't want to buy a Friday glove, or a Monday glove, either, for that matter. The man sewing is thinking about the weekend coming up, and the weekend he just had, and not thinking about the sewing he's paid to do." My father nodded, but added that some folks just didn't care enough to do the job right, regardless of the day. He liked to think that the good gloves, the gloves he picked, had been made by a man who cared about his work. Elder nodded to that, as well. My father had Roy feel the leather in the palms and fingertips, where the gloves wore out first, and Roy could feel the thicker leather in one pair. I think he had tried to show me that, too, a few years before, but I couldn't remember. I leaned in and listened this time, feeling the gloves and looking at the stitching, interested to think that by being careful, you could get a better pair of gloves, for the same money. Roy Buckman gave me a second chance to listen to my father.

When the best gloves had been picked, my father had Roy try on barn boots, looking for a loose fit, as we always did, trying to get a few more months for growing feet. The barn boots smelled of new rubber, not a smell you might like if you came upon it without context, but for me, the smell always meant new boots, without the worn linings and stubborn foot smell that came with months in the barn. I loved that smell. Roy was uncomfortable with my father buying him boots, and said something about the gloves being a lot of money. "Well, you need gloves to help with the haying, and boots too, if you're going to work in the barn. Their mother won't have manure in the house." They stood there for a bit, neither saying anything. Roy suggested that my father take to cost of the gloves and boots out of his wages, and my father countered with taking half the cost out, since the job required the tools. "They don't make a fireman buy his own fire truck," my father said. Roy checked to be sure that my father would let him keep the boots on our porch, and my father agreed, looking puzzled at the request. I thought at the time that Roy was not wanting his own father to know about the boots, for some reason. That turned out to be true, but it was more complicated.

My father left Roy holding his new boots, and the three pairs of gloves, and went off to get the cotter pins and the grease, deciding on a small packet of zerks as well, master links for the roller chains in the haybine and the bailer, and a little round file for his chain saw. He studied a potato planter for a while, squatting down beside it, and turning the wheel, watching the mechanism move inside. You could see that he wanted one. He borrowed one from his brother every year, and he hated to borrow things more than once. But he sighed and eased back up, taking a last look at the planter before he headed up to the counter. While Younger tallied up the bill, Roy watched, seeming unhappy with the total. My father handed him back the gloves and the boots, and said, "We saved more than that just by not getting the fancy twine. Thank goodness for John Deere." We loaded our things and ourselves back into the car, and headed back up the road, towards Bear Hill, with Roy looking at the stitching on the three pairs of gloves in his lap. "Your dad sure knows a lot of stuff," he said.

We found the ladies still in the garden, summer dresses pulled up as they kneeled in the fresh soil. They were putting in onion sets and some broccoli, which my mother had started from seed back in the spring. My mother and the four girls kept working, their summer dresses like early blooms on the fertile land. Trish had her back to me, and she was kneeling, her dress up safe from the dirt, and her bare feet, the color of the earth, moving behind her as she edged her way down the string-marked row. She glanced over her shoulder, and smiled at me, clearly happy to be where she was. My mother sent Susan in to make a pitcher of lemonade, and she and the girls kept working to the end of the row, while my father and the boys made trips out to the barn, carefully stacking the twine in the corner of the back room. He set the tubes of grease on a shelf, and the tiny boxes of cotter pins and zerks into his hardware box, a long wooden tray with a broomstick handle, filled with tiny boxes of bolts and screws, washers, nuts, and all the bits and pieces that you find you must have when something breaks. It's eight miles from our house to Randolph, and the feed store is only open seven to five, during the week, and for four hours Saturday morning, so it's best to have your own stock of hardware.

Roy carried the new gloves and boots up to the porch, setting his boots beside the rest of ours. He stood there, eyeing them, like he was studying something, until Susan came out and handed him the first glass of lemonade. She filled it all the way up, and smiled at him, brushing the hair out of her face, and watching while he took a sip. "It's good," he said. "Thank you." Susan blushed and turned away, handing my father a glass only afterwards. The rest she set on the porch table, were we could all get our own. My mother took Ellen, Tina and Trish to the hose, and washed off their knees and feet and hands, the cold water making them squeal and jump a bit, once the Buckman kids saw that it was OK to do that. Trish lifted her sweaty hair off the back of her neck, letting the cool air in. "I'm going to have to tie this up," she said. She smiled at me, and took a lemonade off the table. Then she looked at the boots, and saw the new pair that my father had bought for Roy.

Roy was watching her. "New boots?" she said. "For you?" Roy nodded, looking down, and then said that he would be working in the barn some, and that Mr. Landers had bought gloves for all three of them, for haying. He handed a pair to Trish, who tried to smile as she held the gloves. But her eyes were still on the boots, and I could see what looked like the start of tears. Roy saw it, too, and tried to explain about his working in the barn, but Trish just smiled, and wiped her face, saying again how sweaty she was, and took a sip of her lemonade. "This is so good!" she said, "Thank you."

I wondered if I had got it wrong, that Trish wasn't really that upset by the boots, that maybe she did just have some sweat in her eye, but I figured it out, later. After the lunch, while the ladies again worked in the garden, my father and us boys cleared out the barn loft, sweeping up the old hay into a pile beside the drop, hanging the loops of twine we found on the nails on the back wall. After the day was done, and I had permission to walk with the Buckman kids along the ridge, as far as the big beech tree, I wanted to ask Trish about the boots, but she must have guessed, and she gave me a quick kiss, touched the heart on the tree, and then turned and followed her brother and sister on down the trail. "See you tomorrow," she said.

I walked back up to the house, still thinking about the boots. When I got up to the house, I understood. There, in a row, side-by-side, were seven pairs of barn boots, one pair brand new. There was a big pair for my father, and smaller pair for my mother, and then the kid's boots, all side by side. This is what Trish had seen. Evidence of family, the kind of family she had kept safe in her mind since she was little. I felt my heart ache for her, a physical pain, really, and my own eyes water up as I stared at the boots, and thought about the tear streaked, freckled face, trying to smile and thanking my mother for the lemonade.

I found my father still in the barn, putting the new grease into the zerks on the haybine. I stood over him for a bit, then squatted down beside him, and asked him how he knew when there was enough new grease. He seemed surprised by the question, but pleased, and showed me where to watch the old grease ooze out, along the sides of the bearing surface. He carefully wiped the excess grease off, and cleaned off the zerk each time, before moving onto the next one. "Twenty-eight zerks on the haybine," he said. "You need to count as you go, so you don't forget one. Forty-two on the baler". I watched him work for a bit, and then asked if I could try. He smiled and handed me the grease gun, showing me how wipe the zerk off, to push the nozzle straight on until you could feel it snap in place, and then the slow, pumping of the handle, while being careful to not let the gun drop down and break the zerk off. "There. You see?" he said, pointing with his finger to the old grease moving out from beneath the bearing. "That's good."

"Can I do the next one?" I asked, and he nodded, the smile still on his face. We worked that way for a while, and when we had counted up, together, to twenty-eight, we wiped the grease gun clean and put it back on the shelf beside the grease cartridges. As we walked back up to the house, I said, "Can we get boots for Trish, and Tina too?" We didn't ask for much, we weren't supposed to, and I'm sure my father was surprised by the question. He pointed out that Trish and Tina wouldn't be in the barn, other than to put the hay in. But he looked at me, and then said, "Why?"

I pointed to the boots, all lined up in a row. "Trish saw that, with Roy's new boots sitting there with ours, like family. It made her cry, even though she didn't want anyone to see. She wished she had boots there, too, I think," I said.

We sat on the steps, looking out over the valley, the sounds of dinner being made behind us, and the deep greening valley stretched out in front. My father took in a deep breath. "Looks nice, doesn't it?" I nodded. "You sweet on her?" I felt my heart skip a beat, but I nodded again. "She's a nice girl. They're good kids," he added, after a while. "Not much of a start, but you can tell they're going to turn out just fine." I couldn't say anything, but I looked out at the valley, and breathed in just like my dad had done. "I'll ask your mother to take the Buckman girls down to town tomorrow, and pick up some boots for them. I wouldn't have thought of that. I'm glad you noticed," he said, getting up, his hand on my shoulder, taking me into dinner.

THE BUCKMAN KIDS

CHAPTER FOURTEEN

The first cutting of hay was ready a little early, and my father was hoping that the weather would stay clear for three days. There was a slight breeze that morning, which pleased him. We had been to the barn for the morning milking, now with the sun now showing a sliver of gold in the East by the time we came out of the barn. It was still cold early on, but not the kind of cold that made everything hurt, and our heaviest coats had been washed twice, dried in the sun, inside and out, and then put away in the attic until November came. The wind was coming up out of the South, just what you might hope for, the warmer, dry air moving through the stalks, taking the heavy morning dew away and leaving the tall grass clean and dry, and ready for cutting. The low pasture had a head start, as always, with the saw grass and heavy brome soaking up the water, but it was the hardest to cut as well, uneven, and never fully dry without a hot, windy afternoon sun. My father hitched the haybine to the red International tractor, know in good times as "Old Red", and in bad times as "that old Red Devil". It was an International 718, a sixty-five-horse power gas tractor with a wide front, a decent three-point hitch, and a brand new set of rear tires.

My father's relationship with the International was complicated. He had gotten it used and neglected, and had spent the first year or two slowly getting it into shape. I remember a new clutch going in, which required splitting the tractor in two, with each half hanging from chains looped over the barn beams, an old railroad jack on cut ties providing a bit of safety, should the chains or beams give way. My mother had come into the barn, silent and tense, to stand in the doorway and watch as my father worked, afraid that he would be crushed, as her brother had been, only a few years before. Machinery was all cast iron, then, built to last, and simply made to be repairable by a farmer with more courage than money, but it was unbelievably heavy as well, and the scale of things made you stop and take notice. I remember wrenches from that job that were longer than my arm, and that I could barely lift with both hands when my father called for them.

The fact that the tractor ran on gas, and not diesel, made repairs a bit easier, but meant that the gears needed to be right, and the fuel costs were higher. One of my uncles had a newer John Deere, a diesel, that had cost an arm and a leg, and that my uncle was still making payments on, years later after buying it. When my father and he talked tractors, it was clear that my father wanted a Deere, but wanted to pay cash up front for what he bought. He already carried a mortgage on the farm that worried him in the night, and adding tractor payments would have been worse than continuing to fight with the International from time to time. The tractor savings had been taken by the new rear tires, and were slow to build back up. On the plus side, the tractor started up easy, gas lighting easier than diesel, especially in the cold, and it had enough power to run the haybine in second gear, uphill, if there were clouds coming, a thundering process that kept me watching from the sidelines, rather than sitting on the fender beside my father.

My father had backed Old Red up to the hitch on the Haybine, and looked over his shoulder at me as I stood by the hitch, cranked up high enough to meet the drawbar, holding a heavy forged pin in my hand. My father hit the money on the first shot, and I dropped the pin in, it clanking all the way through, and I slid the clevis through to keep it in place. My father raised the drawbar a few inches, and I cranked the jack in, folding the handle over. I could just barely lift the PTO shaft with both hands, squatting under the weight, but I got it up and onto the tractor shaft, and pinned it in place. The next step was hooking up the hydraulic lines, a tricky job that held the possibility of spilled oil, and pinched fingers. I looked up at my father, and he nodded at me. I pulled the plugs from the tractor, wiped the ends off, and took the first line in both hands, sliding the collar back, and shoved it in towards home. It wouldn't go, and a bit of fluid hissed out. The pressure was up, with the tractor running, and that made the job harder. My father shut the tractor down, and then dropped the drawbar, taking the load off the hydraulics, and letting me hook the lines in without a problem. I had hoped to be able to push the lines on under pressure, the way my father did.

We were going to do the high field first, since it was already dry, and to give the haybine an easier test run. I climbed up, stepping onto the drawbar, then the casting for the rear axel, then on up to the level spot next to my father's seat. I took hold of his jacket with one hand, and the fender with the other, and checked my footing. Riding the tractor with my dad was pretty great, but it went against my mother's wishes, something we rarely did, and so both of us were careful. James didn't ride with my dad, my mother having made that point early on. Ellen did, sometimes, on the other side, but this morning she and Susan were helping my mother with the garden.

The haybine followed us silently, swinging a bit from one side to the other when the path was uneven, it's weight sufficient to pull the tractor from side to side just a bit as well. My father pulled into the corner of the high field, and eased the throttle down, with the gas engine sitting at idle, while he and I swung down and walked around, checking that everything looked right. My dad tugged at the lines, peered at the clevis, and took another look at the engine of the tractor, which he had carefully gone over just an hour before, checking fluids and wire and even the front end links. "Check twice, and save yourself from trouble," he said. I nodded. We climbed back on, and my father eased the throttle back up, with the tractor roaring some now, and then he reached down and moved the PTO lever, suddenly setting the haybine into a loud, clattering action.

This was a big Heston, a seven foot, I think, and it met the hay with a seven foot long sickle bar that chattered loudly, low to the ground when dropped, the riveted sharp teeth rattling back and forth between cast iron fingers, eager for something to cut. Behind this, a set of giant rollers now spun, one rubber and one steel, the new bearing in the rubber one, rollers that pressed against each other like the rollers in my mother's ringer, only the size of logs. As they spun, they crushed the stems of the grass that was thrown up between them, and then spit it out the back, cut and now flattened and ready to dry. This material was gathered by wings into the gentle rows that would pour out behind us as we mowed through the field. The haybine combined the old sickle bar cutter with a hay conditioner, making for one less pass through the fields for the farmer with his eye on the weather and a short spell between storms. When the rollers were right, it made good hay, but Heston's had a hard time with reliability, and the roller chains, shafts, and, yes, the bearings, often needed attention. We did three cuttings, most years, and my father went over the haybine between each cutting, trying to prevent a breakdown during the haying.

My father listened carefully, hearing, I suspect, the new bearing silently running in its new grease. This is the thing that rumbled behind us, so loud that we could only point and nod. Were I to fall off the tractor, this would be the thing that would treat my body as just another piece of grass, something I tried without luck to not picture as we rolled along. Usually, once a season, or maybe twice, we would hit a nest of partridge, only finding the fine spray of blood and feathers when we returned to the field to rake the hay over in the sun. I held on tight with both hands, and checked my footing from time to time. My father eased the haybine blade to the ground, slid the transmission into gear, and eased the tractor and the roaring haybine into the field, taking our first pass along the fence line, the outer wheel of the Heston just missing the fence posts and rock walls by an inch or two. I knew that my father tried to not be a proud man, and he would never had voiced his feelings about this, other than to talk about getting the most hay out of the field that he could, but he loved to leave only the thinnest line of uncut hay, gliding along at a fast pace, so close to the edge he sometimes left black rubber tire marks on the fence posts. His eyes were up ahead, glancing only occasionally at the process just behind us, but I knew that he was listening to that incredible roar, hearing in it all the details of things working well, or not, just like a conductor in front of an orchestra.

As we bounced across the field, my fingers still white-knuckle tight on the jacket and the fender, I could see someone standing on the far side, beside the gate, waiting as if for permission to enter. As we came a little closer, I could see Trish, in her blue summer dress, and then, closer, I could see her smile, her hair tied up in a high ponytail, and her tall black-rubber boots proudly on her feet. She had worn the boots around whenever she came up, even for hikes up to the ridge, or working in the garden. Barn boots are hot in the summer, but she didn't seem to care. She set them in a line with the rest of the boots before she went home, and always turned and looked at them, twice, maybe three times, before heading down the hill. As we pulled up, Trish shyly waved to us, and my dad pushed in the clutch, leaving the haybine rumbling behind us, and tapped the fender on the other side from me. Trish scrambled up, taking her place, her smile like sunlight, her eyes full of joy. She took a hold of the other side of my father's jacket, and the other fender, and my father eased out the clutch, and the tractor moved on into the new grass, roaring and clattering, shifting beneath us like a row boat on rough seas, our bodies swaying back and forth, with an even row of green pouring out behind us.

Around and round we moved, the pattern for mowing the field something my father had learned deep in his bones, finishing with just exactly one cut down the middle, leaving the field cut low and even, with regular rows of what would with luck become hay, mounded up and smelling the way that only new cut hay can. My father raised the haybine, and took the PTO out of gear, and the haybine was silent, with only the idling tractor motor sounding in the warming morning air. My father took a deep breath, and looked around, at the work he had done, and at the green mountains and valleys around us, and he saw that it was good. We made our way out of the field, still slow in first gear, the tractor barely above idle, and parked it beside the barn. When he shut down the engine, the silence filled the air, our ears still ringing from the roar of the machinery. We didn't say anything. My father walked around the tractor and the haybine again, checking things as he went, laying his hand here and there to feel for heat, or tugging at this or that to check for looseness. Trish held my hand, and we watched. "Well," my father finally said, "haybine seems to be OK. That'll be nice hay, if the rain holds off." He looked into the cloudless blue sky, distrusting the appearance of good weather. He set his gloves on the tractor seat, where they could dry, and the three of us headed in towards the house. The garden was empty, which meant that my mother and sisters were inside, working on lunch, probably. I was hungry, even though I had done little that morning except to hang on and manage to not be run through the rollers of the haybine.

"I brought up some fiddleheads," Trish said. "Still really tight. Roy'll be up with Tina this afternoon. They had to go off with my dad to Barre. My dad's selling the batteries." She looked back at the field, all striped with neat even rows. The garden was planted, with the string still all that showed in some places, but lines of new green leaves showed where the peas were, and the beans as well. "This place sure looks nice," she said, almost to herself. Trish carefully set her boots in the line with the others, and then wiped her bare feet on the mat.

My mother gave my father a look as we came in. "Did you put that girl on the tractor?" she asked.

Trish looked panicked, but my dad smiled and said, "She might be a farmer, some day. She sees the beauty of the place, tended to. And she hangs on good, don't you, Trish?" Trish nodded, checking to see if my mom was really angry at her.

"Well, just make sure you do," my mother said. She smiled at my father. "Haybine behaving itself?" she asked. My father nodded, washing his hands at the kitchen sink. "Field looks nice, from here. Go wash up," he said, to Trish and me, "and we'll have some lunch. Trish brought us up fiddleheads, and they look just about perfect."

After lunch, my father walked down to the lower field, with James and

I and Trish at his heels. The grass was dry, and all but the lowest part of the field was dry as well. One corner was always wet, where a small spring make the heavy soil boggy, letting the swamp grass grow unchecked into an eight-foot tall wilderness. My father cut this area with a scythe once or twice during the summer, just to keep the brush out, but we never got any hay from it. We walked back up to the barn, and he checked the tractor and the haybine over, worrying for a bit over one of the teeth in the bar, and finally deciding to remove it and rivet in a new one. He checked the hydraulics, running his hand along the hoses, looking for leaks, then fired the tractor up, and let it warm for just a bit. James sadly headed back to the house, and Trish and I jumped on and found our places, and then we headed down to the lower field.

We had done the outside ring, and made three passes inside that, when we could see Roy jogging down from the ridge trail. He waved, and my father stopped the tractor, disengaging the PTO and brought the engine down to an idle. Roy smiled when he jogged up, but he looked tense. "Trish needs to come home," he said, and then took a couple of breaths. "Dad bought a trailer, and needs us to clear a place to put it. It's blocking the road now, and he already got into it with someone trying to get by."

Trish reached around my father's back, and gave my hand a squeeze. She hopped down without saying anything, and the two of them jogged back up the ridge. My father and I watched them go. When they had disappeared into the woods at the ridge, my father eased the throttle back up, set the PTO in, and with a roar and a clatter, we went back to cutting the field of hay. When we were done, we got the haybine cleaned off, greased up again, and backed into the shed, and the tractor parked beside it. It was when my father and I were walking up the steps to the front porch that I realized that Trish had run off in her new boots. I looked at the space where hers should have been, empty, and felt my heart lurch. I think my father noticed, too, but neither of us said anything. After we were cleaned up, and we were all sitting at the table, my father was asking the Lord's blessing on our dinner, and he added something new. "Lord, keep our young neighbors down the road safe in your loving arms. Amen." Amen, I prayed.

CHAPTER FIFTEEN

In the morning, we headed down to the barn for the milking, with just enough light up in the sky that we could leave the flashlights in the kitchen. It was still cool, and my father paused on the porch, taking in the air, and smelling the hay we had laid on the ground yesterday. He sniffed again, trying to scent rain, but there was only the morning chill, and the few brightest stars still visible in the paling sky. I stood beside him, with James yawning and still sleepy, trying to lean up against me. I pushed him back, but not meanly. It was time to be up, and trying to get a few last winks in while standing on the porch didn't make any sense. As we stopped to put our boots on, I remembered Roy and Trish running down the ridge, to clear a spot for the trailer their father had inexplicably gotten. I remember my pain at seeing Trish's boots gone from their spot with the others, and reached for my own.

I was still sleepy, and had to look twice to understand that Trish's boots were now there on the porch, set next to mine, and then I saw that there was a bunch of white daisies cut long, and standing out of my boot. My father caught me staring, and said, "She must have come back up, late." He looked at the boots she had returned, already the shine worn off from her constant use. He smiled and laid a hand on my shoulder. "Flowers, too. Set 'em in a water glass, and then we can go milk." I did, and when I came back out, I found my brother leaned up against my father, who was staring down the road. He sighed, and shook my brother awake, and the three of us made our way down to the barn, the stars above us fading, and the yellow daylight slowly taking the sky.

We were raking the high pasture, just before lunch, the light clatter of the rake spinning the hay up into a fluffy row, when we saw the Buckman kids on the ridge. The girls waved and headed towards the garden, where mom and the rest of the kids were weeding the rows, and Roy walked through the field, taking a line to meet the tractor. My father stopped just long enough to let Roy climb up to the other fender, and then let out the clutch, and we continued on, flipping and fluffing the rows laid down yesterday, where the days sunshine and breeze could get in and dry them out.

Roy looked tired, hollow-eyed, but no more, really, than he often did. The tractor was only at mid throttle, the rake taking no power really, and our speed in second gear sufficient to toss the hay, but leave a smooth row behind. The upper field was smooth and straight, and my father had let me do several rows before taking the wheel back, complimenting me on the job I had done. I wanted to tell Roy, but the tractor and the rake were noisy, and it seemed young to brag about driving the tractor, when I just now felt old enough to have done it. I decided to mention it later, maybe after lunch. Roy had left a fishing pole by the stone wall, and had his metal tackle box set on top.

There's not much in farming that's better than raking hay, when the sky is clear, and you have faith that the hay will get in, fresh and dry, well before the rains return. Mowing is first gear work, usually, and so loud that it hurts, with the haybine pounding just behind you. There's the constant worry of rocks turned up, especially on the first cutting, when you could find rocks the size of bread pans pushed up by the frost, where only grass had been the fall before. We had found a few rocks, yesterday, with me jumping off the tractor and running them to the side of the field, laying them on the other side of the stone wall, and running back, my father watching me from the seat of the tractor. We had walked the fields, of course, when the snow was first off, and cleared what we could see, but the first cutting always found more, somehow. Baling was work, pure and simple, with my dad on the tractor, and the kids on the wagon, moving in a line to take the fresh bales off the chute and stack them tightly on the wagon, from the back to the front, up four bales high, the sweat soaking our caps, and running down our backs, the hay pricking red bumps up our arms, our gloves wet and dripping in the first hour.

But raking was sweet, second gear work, usually, fast enough to make a breeze, and without the noise, pressure and worry that came with the haybine, or the constant press of work that came with the baler. My father could have left me in the garden with the others, working down the rows, leaving only our chosen plants and clean soil as we worked, but he said he needed me to run stones, and I think he liked the company as well. I had greased the rake this morning, under his eye, counting out the zerks as we went. I was super careful, cleaning the zerks before, not wasting grease, and cleaning the old grease up after, and had done with job without correction, and with a quiet "Good job" when I was done.

I looked over at Roy, his eyes out on the field, his hands red and worn, from clearing out a space for the trailer last night, I guessed. He caught me looking, and smiled, happy to be in the field, and back up at our place, with a good lunch ahead, and then fishing at the bridge. I smiled, too. It looked like a great day.

When we had raked the lower field as well, Roy jogged back up to the upper and brought down his pole and tackle box, setting them on the porch. My mom was hosing the other kids off, the well water icy after the first warm bit from the hose, and the kids were laughing and shrieking, but my mom seemed OK with the noise. All she said was "Hold still now," from time to time, without any anger. My father and I took the hose when she was done, and washed up in the yard as well. When we got inside, Trish was setting the table, where I had put the flowers in the glass early that morning. She smiled at me, and made a quick kiss in my direction, her eyes tired, but happy. Burger patties, green beans and a loaf of fresh bread came to the table, and a salad Susan had made, a head of lettuce, with tomatoes and carrots cut up on top, with a bottle of Thousand Island to go with it. There was a pitcher of milk, and a pitcher of water, and three more chairs pulled up around the old kitchen table. My mother had set the leaves in and just left them, stretching the table out to a full eight feet, with the Buckman kids being regular visitors for lunch this summer.

"Nice flowers," my mother said, setting the hot pan of burgers down on a cutting board.

Trish blushed, and said, "I brought them up when I brought my boots back. I picked them last night, in the dark. You could see the white daisies in the starlight, all along the ridge. Like stars. Good thing I know the trail. It was dark in the woods."

The food was blessed and passed, with James taking a few more beans, and Susan being careful with the butter. Little was said, the food being hot and good, and the morning's work behind us. I asked permission to go fishing at the bridge, and the girls asked to go along, and my mother requested enough fish for dinner. Trish and Tina looked unhappy, and Trish said that she and her sister had to go back and clean the trailer, but that if they got it done, they would head up the bridge.

"Dad'll be up in a bit," Roy said. "I'll head back with the girls and give 'em a hand. There's been leaks in that thing, and the walls are black with stuff growing on 'em. There was a cat in there for a while, it looks like, too. Might still be there." Roy looked over to me. "I'll leave the pole here, and maybe we can come back up, when it's done."

I was confused, and I could see my dad was, too. "This your house trailer you and the girls need to clean?" my father asked.

"No. It's the new one," Roy said. "The one dad brought back from Barre. It's not new, just new to him, I guess. He traded the batteries for it. It's pretty bad on the inside."

"Not so nice on the outside, either," said Trish, scraping bits of burger and bread crumbs off her plate. My mother reached over and put another burger on in front of Trish, and told her to cut another slice of bread.

Trish looked embarrassed, but pleased. "I shouldn't eat so much, I guess, " she said. "This is just so good!"

"Eat all you want, Trish," my mother said. "There's plenty, and none of this will be as good the second time around. Strawberry pie for desert, if you can stay that long."

Trish looked in agony at Roy, who nodded. "He won't be up yet. We can stay a bit, but not too long."

I had thought that the trailer was a farm trailer, something to haul scrap metal in. My uncle had one that he hauled fire wood, and delivered hay with. It held about as much as the bed of his truck did. This sounded like another house trailer, and I tried to picture how they had fit something that big into the tiny lot, along with the trailer already there, and the piles of scrap metal. But I didn't say anything. I asked my mom if I could cut another piece of bread, not wanting Trish to be eating by herself. My mom must have understood, because she smiled and gave permission.

My father wasn't saying anything either, but I knew he was thinking about the "Dad will be up in a bit" part of what Roy had said. I knew that the idea of a grown man lying in bed at lunchtime could only mean sickness, or worse. But my parents had so far refrained from asking the Buckman kids about their life just down the road, feeling that it would be best to just take them as they came, and see to it that they were fed and put to use when they came to visit.

My mother put the pie on the table, just as soon as Trish finished up her seconds, and the Buckmans did have time for pie before they headed out. My mom wouldn't let Trish and Tina help with the kitchen cleanup, saying that they had better get down the hill and start on their own chores. The kids all went out to the porch, and we watched the Buckmans head off down the ridge trail, hoping that they would come back in time for some fishing, or maybe a quick swim, the water being just warm enough now to not kill you if you jumped in.

"How could they fit another trailer in on that lot?" my brother asked. I shook my head, looking at the woods where Trish and the rest had disappeared. I knew she would touch our heart as she walked by the old beech, the bark there already a bit smoother and shiny from her touch. "What's he want another trailer for, anyway," my brother added. "You'd think one would be enough." I didn't say anything, and just stood there, looking at the woods.

The girls had gone back into the kitchen, and were cleaning up the pans and plates. My mother was on the couch, reading the Bible, and my father sat beside her, his face a little clouded with worry, still working over the Buckman kids, I thought. He saw me in the door, and said, "Mr. Morgan called, all the way from Boston. He said to put up the eight hundred bales of horse hay for him, and that he'd have it trucked down to the farm in Woodstock. He asked after you and James."

I hadn't thought much about Mr. Morgan, and now I felt guilty for forgetting him. "Why'd he have to leave, anyway?" I asked. "Is he afraid of Mr. Buckman?" I regretted the question as soon as it was out. I sounded whiny, and nosey, and Mr. Morgan's plans were none of my business, anyway.

I expected my father to remind me of that, but instead, he just looked at me. "Mr. Morgan told me that he was afraid to stay, but I don't think he was afraid of Mr. Buckman." He waited a bit, thinking, as he did, about saying more. "Mr. Morgan was in the war, on the coast of France, mostly. He told me he was a sniper, in the Army, and that he spent the daylight hours shooting German boys from a hundred yards or more, with a long barreled .308 Springfield. One after another, he said." My mother looked up from her Bible, clearly not happy about what my father was saying. He noticed this, and patted her leg, but he went on. "Mr. Morgan told me he had promised himself that he wasn't going to kill another man, after that, not ever again. 'Not one more', he said. He thought that if he stayed here, he'd end up breaking that promise. So, no, he's not afraid of Mr. Buckman."

I nodded. My mother gave my father a look, then, went back into her Bible, and my father patted her leg, again. I thought about the gentle Mr. Morgan being a sniper, shooting German boys, one after the other. I pictured the heavy, long-barreled rifles I had seen in the comic books, with what looked like a telescope set on top, bolt action, and with an oversized stock you set your face up next to. I thought of the way I knew some of the local farmers saw Mr. Morgan, as a spoiled, soft, rich man, a flatlander up from Boston, and wondered what they would think if they knew something about his history. And then, because I was only eleven years old, I wondered if he still had that rifle, and if I could maybe see it sometime.

The girls finished up in the kitchen, and my mother rose up off the couch to check their work, setting the ribbon in her Bible, and laying it on the table. With my mother's approval, and my father's words about Mr. Morgan still in my head, we gathered the poles and headed up the road, heavy with pie and ready for the pond. I was setting what I now knew about Mr. Morgan along side my thoughts about Roy Buckman, and working on the idea that so much of a person could be hidden inside, and thinking about the power we might all have to really decide who we would be in the world, regardless of who we had been born to be, and what we had been through.

The fishing that day was better than no fishing at all, I guess. James caught some nice ones, and I got a couple of trout who were willing to swallow the whole hook, but my thoughts were elsewhere. I sifted through my new images of Mr. Morgan, trying to make sense of what I now knew, and I wondered about the trailer the Buckman kids were now cleaning out, and tried to imagine how all of this was going to work out. Twice James called to me, pointing out that my line was jerking in the water, but I pulled too late, losing a worm, and not gaining a fish. The girls hung out with some kids from school, Susan spending some time with Steve, and Ellen borrowing a pole and doing some fishing, herself, catching enough to make up for my distracted waste of good worms. We stayed late, hoping for the Buckman kids to arrive, but it was close to dinner, and we knew to get home before we were in trouble.

My mom had made a pan of cornbread to go with the fish, and the first of the spinach was out of the garden, small and dark, steamed with butter, and so much better than the canned spinach we had over the winter. My father had reminded me that I knew better than to tell any of my friends about Mr. Morgan, and I nodded, and said, "I won't." I was good at keeping secrets, not being much inclined to talk much, anyway, and we had been raised to keep track of our own business, and not meddle in someone else's. But I thought about Mr. Morgan, and Mr. Buckman, and Trish and the kids, probably still up cleaning the trailer as my brother and I sat in the bath, him talking about his fish, and me trying to look like I was listening.

I had a western to read, that night, one of a set that Roy had brought up for me. I remember the cover, where a thin cowboy in a big hat managed to stay on a rearing horse, with one hand on the reins, and the other holding what looked like a lever action Winchester. There were mountains and a line of barbed wire out behind, and what might have been buffalos in the distance. It was a pretty good book, with robbers, a bad sheriff, and a Texas Ranger who needed to fix everything up without getting shot. But I had a hard time paying attention as I read, and I kept having to go back over the page, trying to find where I had drifted off. Finally, I gave up, turned off the light, and just lay in the darkness, hearing the soft whispers of my sisters across the low wall, and the irregular snorts and snores from my brother, who lay beside me. I could hear my parents in the bathroom, my mother, I knew, in the tub, my father sitting beside her, going over the day, I guessed. I couldn't ever hear the words, just the sound of their voices, and some soft laughter from time to time. I tried to think about Trish and me, all grown up, and having our own place, but all I could see was her on her hands and knees, scrubbing out the trailer, while her father, somewhere in the shadows, yelled at her. Then I thought of Mr. Morgan, shooting German boys in the head, one after another, and I knew that when I fell asleep, I would have nightmares.

Tomorrow, we would rake the hay again, and maybe be able to bale the top part of the high pasture, if the breeze that night kept the dew off. We were still almost two weeks early, and would get three cuttings this year, if things went well. I thought about sending the hay off to the farm in Woodstock, and if that meant that Mr. Morgan might come back up for a visit at some point. I thought about the hidden lives that people seemed to have, and how complex people were if you got to know more than just a little about them. When I finally slept, I dreamed of Mr. Morgan, but he wasn't shooting German boys. He was feeding dates to Peacemaker, or a horse that looked a lot like Peacemaker. I heard the chatter of children just outside the barn, playing, and thought I could hear Trish's voice, laughing with her sister and brother.

THE BUCKMAN KIDS

CHAPTER SIXTEEN

Things were changing. A few days, before, the girls had gotten into a water fight with the hose, when they were supposed to be cleaning off the dirt from the garden to come inside for lunch. Trish and Tina, and Ellen and Susan were all for horsing around, and my mother came to the door, hearing the yelling and laughter. I was walking up from the barn, with my dad and Roy, and I knew the girls would be in trouble, for getting their dresses and their hair wet, and for making a racket. I remember wondering if my mom was going to spank all four of them, or just Susan and Ellen, but then her pinched look went away, and she just stood there in the doorway. She smiled as she watched them play. We were almost up to the porch when she finally called a halt to it, saying, "Stop wasting water and come inside. I need your help with lunch." I could see Susan and Ellen look at her, not knowing she had been watching them, and unsure if they were in trouble, or not. But my mother just smiled at my dad, and sent him and us boys out to the hose to wash up before lunch.

I'd talked to Ellen about it, after supper that night. "Do you think mom and dad are different, happier, maybe, this summer?" She was washing dishes, and James and I were bringing in the plates and stuff off the table. My mother and father were on the couch, my mom with her Bible out, and my dad just sitting beside her, watching her read.

Ellen pointed for me to put the stack of plates in the sink. "I think we all are different, pretty much. Happier, maybe. It's just different, now," she said, putting another squirt of dish soap into the hot water. "I never met anyone like Tina." She worked at the dishes for a while, and then she went on. "Trish says the two of you are getting married, and that you're going to have three kids. Poopy, Croupy and Loopy." She looked over at me. I nodded. "And Roy is like an old man, so serious and kind of bossy."

I didn't know what I could add. Roy was bossy, I guess, to his sisters, telling them where to sit, and what they could do. And he seemed a lot older than he was, which was just twelve. And Trish and I were going to get married, even if the kids ended up named something else. I knew it then, and had for a while. I watched Ellen finish up the dishes. James wiped the table down, and settled in with one of my old comic books. Susan came up from the cellar, with a little basket of potatoes, all in good shape, it looked like, and two jars of green beans from the summer before. "There's still a lot of green beans down there. Maybe ten jars, or so. And the fresh ones are going to be ready in a couple of weeks. Looks like we're going to be eating a lot of green beans for a while." She set the jars up on the shelf, and put the potatoes in the bowl on the counter. Susan looked around the kitchen. "You ready for a bath?" she asked Ellen, who nodded, and the two girls headed upstairs.

I tried to read for a while, that night, but all I could think about was how this summer seemed so different from all the summers before. We were still doing the same things, milking twice a day, of course, and moving the cows in and out, with the girls working in the garden with my mother, me and James with my dad most of the mornings, doing the cows, checking the fences, cutting firewood, and getting the hay in. Evenings were the same, pretty much, with dinner served, the same meats and vegetables, salads, bread and desert. The same quiet table, when the Buckman kids weren't here for dinner, the girls cleaning up, then taking the first bath, with my brother and I following.

My body was much the same. While Susan was bursting forth into womanhood, looking less like a kid and more like my mother, Ellen and James and I still looked like little kids. When I looked in the bathroom mirror, less fogged now in the summer, I saw the same thin arms, the same thin chest, and the same boy parts, looking like a slightly bigger version of my younger brother. No hair, no muscles, no shoulders, yet, and my voice remained without the authoritative growl that my father, Mr. White and even old Rev. Sikes all had. But I felt more like a man, inside, with Trish and my future firmly in place. Three kids. That felt like some responsibility. The way I thought about things, wondering about my parents, and worrying about life in the Buckman trailer, just down the hill, those things felt older, more serious, like the kind of thoughts and worries a man might have.

I thought about the kind of man I would grow into. Like my father, I still assumed, tall and muscled, honest, quiet. But I thought I could be different, too. I had always thought I would live on the farm, build a place up by the high field. As the oldest son, my father had moved into his father's house, and taken over the herd. We still raised Guernseys, milking twice a day in the same barn, with a milking machine now, and new stanchions. The hay was baled, rather than put up loose, and the house had oil heat, in addition to the wood parlor stove which was still fired in the kitchen from December through March. But I wondered how much my father's life had changed from that of his own father, and how much my life would, as well. Trish was something new, for sure, and I knew she had changed me.

It was mid-afternoon when the Buckman kids made their way up the ridge. I was riding shotgun on the tractor, doing the second raking on the lower field. The upper field was ready to bale, or would be by the time the lower field was raked again. The sky was clear blue, and the sun was hot enough that I had my shirt off, working on the first sunburn of the summer. James and the girls were in the garden, with my mom, weeding, of course, thinning some rows, and setting out a second planting of something small and green. I had begun to wonder if the Buckmans were going to come up at all, when Trish gave a big wave from the ridge, jumping up and down so I would notice her. I waved back, excited enough to almost fall off the tractor. Trish and Tina headed to the garden, and Roy made his way to the field, waiting by the stone wall for us to reach him. He jogged over, and climbed up into his spot, without my father even having to slow down. I hoped my mother wasn't watching.

"Sorry we're late," he said. "Dad's all focused on the trailer getting ready by this Saturday. I hoped you hadn't started to bale yet."

I wondered how much sleep the Buckman kids had managed to get that night. Our routine, a good dinner, a hot bath, and a comfortable bed, and nine hours to sleep, seemed like something I had been silly to take for granted. Roy rode easy, his hand lightly on my dad's coat, swaying a bit when the tractor moved, but not gripping tight, like I did. It was easy for me to see Roy like a character in a book, one of the adventure ones, always brave, but I knew that was unfair, and that Roy had fears and worries and sadness, just like everyone else. He didn't show them much, though. He made things look easier than I knew they were.

There were few stones to pick on the second raking, this being the fourth time we had been over the fields, with the first walk, then the mowing, and the first raking, the day before. My dad could have had us in the garden, where we could have been of some use, but I was glad to be with him, on the tractor, turning the hay in the hot sun. I knew James would be jealous of Roy and me, Roy especially, maybe. There was a slight breeze, and it cooled our faces off when we went against it, and simply held the hot air around us when we went the other way. The garden would be hot, the only coolness from the jar of lemonade Susan had made and set in the shade of the milk house. James had his shirt off, as well, and he would be more burned than me, his back being up to the sun most of the day. I thought of that first jump into the pond, off the floating bridge, tonight, after we had gotten as much from the upper field into the barn as we could, and how the water would feel on my hot skin.

My mother had set three lunches aside for the Buckman kids, pork chops from my uncle, who kept pigs, fresh bread, of course, spinach and a salad. There was strawberry pie, again, the strawberries being a great success this year. My mom had the ice cream churn filled and cooling in the fridge, and I had made extra ice the night before, so the plan was to take a break between the last raking and the baling, feed the Buckmans, and then have some ice cream and pie.

We had always had pies, strawberry pie when in season, and made ice cream a few times a week during the summer, but this summer, the feeling was different, somehow. It felt like a party, a birthday party, maybe, over and over, with the Buckman kids somehow making our family happier, and things seem more special than they had, before. I could look over and see my father smiling as we rolled along. He would have been happy last summer, with the early start on the hay, the clear skies, and the machinery running without a hitch. Happy inside, but I don't think he would have smiled out where I could see it, before.

We baled the upper field that afternoon. With the Buckman kids, and the elevator that Mr. Morgan had given us, the routine was different, and we were able to get the whole upper field baled and in the barn, and still be able to milk the cows before they exploded. My father hooked the John Deere 14T to the tractor, then hooked a hay wagon behind that. We took Trish with us, and left Ellen, Tina and Susan at the house, cleaning up the kitchen, for a bit. The baler makes a slow pumping noise, as the flywheel swings the big tamper back and forth, with some clatter from the pick-up tines taking in the hay, but it's quiet enough for the folks on the wagon to be able to talk, and after we got our routine figured out, we could stack the bales and talk at the same time. My father drove slowly between the rows of dry, fluffed hay, the baler cleanly picking up a row and building tight, neatly tied bales as we went, pushing them back up the chute, and then into the hands of the kid in front of the wagon. That kid walked the bale back, and set it tight and square in the stack we were building, pounding the bale into place with our knees, while the next kid took their place, taking the next bale off. Four kids on the wagon was nice, giving us a little break in between each bale.

Baling hay was one of the very few times when my mother allowed the girls to wear pants, and dress for baling, not as a proper girl. It's hot, but the hay is sharp and sticky, and will wear a hole in your skin if you don't have some heavy cloth or leather to protect you. Trish was wearing her barn boots, of course, and the new gloves. She had borrowed a pair of my heavy jeans, with the waist cinched up tight with one of my old belts. She had on one of my long-sleeved shirts as well, the cuffs buttoned down, and her hair was tied up high, flopping from side to side as she moved on the trailer. She looked pretty great, really, with her freckles darker with the summer sun, and her smile just about killing me. Her eyes were lit up, and you could tell she was happy to be there, wearing her boots, and my clothes, and helping us put up the hay. I had to keep looking away, both to not look like an idiot, and to keep from stepping off the trailer into space. She winked at me from time to time, making it worse, and even said "Recess" a few times, real quite, so James and Roy couldn't hear her.

We talked some about lunch, and the strawberry pie that Trish loved so much, and how she thought my shirt smelled like me, even though it was a clean one that had been washed and ironed and put away in my closet. Trish always smelled like lemons, from still using the dish soap when she bathed, I guessed, and sometimes of the rose scented powder her mother had left behind. I asked her why her dad had wanted the trailer he bought, and the smile disappeared off her face for the first time since she had run up the path. I tried to apologize, but she shook her head.

"It's OK," she said. She walked past me, lugging the bale towards the back of the wagon, bouncing the weight of it on her knees as she went. When she came back, she said, "He's going to turn it into a club. The uncles can't go to the home farm anymore, after something bad happened up there. So my dad's going to bring the party down here, charge for the beer and liquor, and maybe even bring in dancing girls for bachelor parties some times." She looked at me, worried again that I would stop loving her if I found out what her dad was like.

"Like a bar?" I asked.

She nodded.

"Dancing girls? What kind of dancing girls?" I asked.

Trish grinned, and looked a little embarrassed. "They did that, some, up at the home farm. Paid girls from Barre to come up and dance around, naked, pretty much, while the uncles drank and swatted at them. It was pretty awful." She looked at my red face. "You don't want dancing girls," she said.

I took a deep breath, trying to clear my thoughts back up to where I thought they should be. "Nope," I said. I carried a bale to the back, which was getting high enough that I had to work to pitch the bale up where it fit, and step on another bale to pack this one in. Trish was just behind her brother, who was taking a bale off the chute. She stood with her back to me. "You look nice," I said.

She turned around, grinning again. "From behind?" she asked, then laughing as I tried to think of what to say.

We didn't talk about the trailer any more that day. I felt like I was more interested in it than I should be, and I didn't want Trish to think I was anything like those uncles of hers. We stacked the bales up, four high all across, nice and tight, and when the wagon was filled back, to front, Roy and James climbed up on top, and took another row of bales from Trish and me, stacking them along the middle, their weight holding the other bales in place for the bumpy ride back to the barn.

Dad set the full trailer right below the door to the barn loft, and lifted the elevator in place, running a yellow extension cord from inside the milk room. He left Roy and Trish and me to get the trailer unloaded, and those bales stacked right in the barn, while he took the second trailer back out to the field, with Susan, Tina, Ellen and James riding along on the back of it. My mom had brought out a half-gallon jar of lemonade, cold, from the fridge, and some paper cups, but we all just drank out of the jar. I turned on the elevator, and grinned, listening to the clack-clack-clack, with good memories of Mr. Morgan. I couldn't believe that the elevator was ours, and that we didn't have to pitch the bales up from the trailer to the loft. I climbed up the elevator like it was a ladder, showing off, a little I guess. Trish set a bale on it, and climbed onto the bale, and rode all the way up, her legs on either side, waving her hand in the air, and shouting "Yahoo!" like a cowboy riding a bronc. Roy sighed, looking at the two of us up in the loft, and then started loading the hay on, one bale after another. Trish and I were kissing for a while, "recess", you know, and there got to be quite a pile of hay bales jumbled up there on the board floor of the loft. I pulled away, while Trish grinned wildly, and I said, "We gotta get these stacked."

Trish shrugged, and said, "You're such a farmer." But she started hauling the bales over to the back wall, where we laid in row after row of tight bales.

The floor was clean, my dad having had me swept the whole thing out, with the old hay going down the chute to the cows, the dust rising up to where you could see a sunbeam through every crack in the barn boards. Roy was still faster than we were, even when "recess" was over, and he rode the last bale up, like his sister had. He looked at the pile of bales, and then at me. "You working up here?" he asked.

I blushed again, for maybe the fifth time that day, and said, "Loading's the easy part. We got to run them all the way across the barn, up here."

But Roy was grinning at me, not angry at all. "Trish," was all he said, shaking his head, and he picked up a bale and helped us put them all in place. With the elevator, we were able to get the wagon unloaded before my dad came back with the second one. We passed the lemonade around, sitting in the shade, on the grass beside the barn not saying anything. We were tired, but pretty happy. When we saw my dad bringing the tractor down from the high field, the hay all stacked high and tight, with the kids riding up on top, we lifted the elevator off, and pulled the wagon out of the way, so my dad could just pull in with the full one. He slid the full wagon into place, and Roy and I lifted the elevator back up, and flipped it on.

My dad motioned for us to climb up on the empty wagon, and Trish and Roy and I headed back up to the upper field, with James left to help with the elevator. We worked that way, swapping kids and wagons, until the whole upper field was baled up, and the hay all safe in the barn. When we were done, and my dad had checked the barn loft out, he parked the baler and the tractor in the shed. He offered to take us all down to the floating bridge for a swim. The girls ran upstairs, with Susan and Ellen finding suits for Trish and Tina. Roy put on some trunks of mine, and we all piled into the back of the farm truck, and headed to the bridge.

My dad parked up the hill a ways, and put his line in to fish while we swam. Ellen dived, with Tina watching how she did it, and trying to dive that way, too. Roy and me and James just jumped in, over and over, climbing up the side of the bridge, and hurling ourselves out into the water. Susan mostly floated a little way out from the bridge, and watched. Trish swam way out, by herself, to about the middle of the pond, then swam back, and then out again. I swam out to where she was, and found her floating on her back. She was just moving her feet a little, keeping herself afloat. She opened her eyes as I came up, and pushed the hair out of her eyes, looking at me. "I wish it could be this way, always," she said. She sounded really sad, and tired. I hadn't really heard her sound that way, before.

"It will be," I said, wanting her to feel better.

She smiled a tired smile. "I know," she said. "But sometimes I just don't think I can wait."

I couldn't think of anything to say, so I just treaded water, next to her, and then said, "I love you."

"I know," she said.

CHAPTER SEVENTEEN

The winter in Vermont, up on Bear Hill, is long and silent, with the world held in ice and snow, the days already darkening when a child gets off the school bus, and dark, again, in the early morning, when they wait, bundled up, beside the road, for the bus to come again. The cows took us from our warm beds before we were ready, and only the animal heat of their bodies, and the hot water bottle feel of their udders as we washed them off kept our fingers from freezing in the cold. Breath was a thing you could see in the winter, and peeing outside provided the chance to write your whole name in the snow, in necessary script that would remain for days, providing an early insight for our sisters that boys are, indeed, gross.

Summer in Vermont is brief, and precious, I think, because of that. It comes while the frozen shock of winter is still fresh, and comes suddenly, after a spring that breaks loose like an ice dam, the brooks crashing brown and thick with mud, overflowing their banks and stealing portions of the dirt roads as they fly down the mountainside. Summer comes one day, when the roads have dried back up, and the grass is not just green, but growing, and the sun on your skin can begin to bake away the winter ice deep in your soul. This summer, of course, came with the Buckman kids, and with Trish, like a summer sun, herself, reaching in with a laugh, to thaw and wake those parts of myself that I had not even known were inside me.

Second cutting came quickly. The garden was more green than brown, and the table was blessed with the fruits of my mother and the girl's garden labors. Spinach, broccoli, and lettuce, sweet peas, cherry tomatoes, tiny cucumbers, just right for pickles, these had all come as the hay again began to wave in the wind. My father took Roy and me and James out to the shed, and had us go over the haybine, the rake and the baler, offering only what guidance was needed, and actually complimenting our work when we were done. Roy, who had before seemed so proof against adults, soaked up my father's praise, and both James and I were a bit jealous. Roy cared more than we did, and tried his best to do things exactly as he had been directed, asking questions once, and then committing the answer to memory.

It seemed my father had bragged on the Buckman kids, in a letter to Mr. Morgan. Mr. Morgan and my father had corresponded almost weekly, with dad missing his friend, and Mr. Morgan unhappy in Boston, and longing for news of Vermont. My father had been uncertain as to whether he should mention the Buckman kids to Mr. Morgan, after what their father had done. I heard him talking quietly with my mother about it, while us four kids were stacking the wood my father had split earlier in the day, and he and my mother were sitting on the porch, drinking tall, wet glasses of ice tea.

"Why not?" my mother had asked, in response to my father's question.

"I don't want to remind him. To make him sad, or angry, again. He might rather not hear anything about it, at all," he replied.

My mother thought about that, looking down at the hat she was knitting, and tugging at something that seemed not right. "I doubt he's forgotten it for a day. But it isn't about the father, anyway. And he wouldn't blame the children for what their father did." She went back to the hat, one for my father, I believe, and I went back to stacking the firewood. She looked over at my father. "Mr. Morgan isn't an Old Testament kind of man," she added, teasing my father again with their old argument about the Bible.

He smiled back at her. "Maybe not," he said.

A package had come, from Boston, for my father. It was from Mr. Morgan, and about the size of a big shoe box, and all wrapped with brown paper, and tied with white string. There was a label glued on the front, with my father's name and address written in script, in black ink, and Mr. Morgan's name and address already printed on the label. We got packages, sometimes, before Christmas, one every year from a distant aunt, filled with broken cookies and itchy wool scarves, but this was the first package I remember getting in the summer time. When the mailman came, my father was already out by the ridge trail, cutting up a giant maple that had toppled in the spring winds. My mother looked at the box, and at the label, and then set it on the table. "Mr. Morgan has lovely handwriting," she said. "They used to teach it that way. My mother had a script that looked just like this."

I needed to get out and help with the tree, but I stopped by the table, looking at the box, with the printed label, and the colorful stamps, come all the way from Boston. I tried to picture Mr. Morgan living there, in what I knew was a big house, up north of the city, right beside the ocean. The label said Manchester, Mass. I had never seen the ocean. My father had said Mr. Morgan was unhappy, and missed being in Vermont. I couldn't understand that, if he lived in a big house right by the ocean. But James and I hurried out the door, and to the ridge trail, where my father was working on the tree, making firewood to keep us warn the next winter. The farm truck was parked beside him, and our job was to toss the wood our father cut up, into the back, and to keep the brush cleared away from where my father worked. I couldn't tell my father about the package, because the saw was so loud, so I just hauled wood and waited.

The Buckman kids came along the trail, just before we were going to take break for lunch. Their father had been keeping them working on the "bar" trailer, Roy said, scraping out the black mold from the sides, and using a can of tar to try and fix the leaks around the vents in the roof. The floor was soft where the leaks had been, too, and Roy said they laid sheets of plywood down, nailing them down right over the rotted floor. Two of the windows were broken, and plywood had been screwed over them as well, making the inside of the trailer pretty dark.

Trish said she hated the feel of the place, not just dark and stinky, from the mold, but ruined, somehow. Her father had taken the best couch from their own trailer, and set it up front, and put another couch across from it, as well as a table for cards. The first party was set for the weekend, with all the uncles coming up, but without the cousins, and some men her father knew were coming as well. Trish didn't look too happy about the "party".

My dad shut down the saw, and brushed the sawdust off his coveralls. "Hey, Mr. Landers," Trish said. "Sorry we're late. Dad had us working this morning."

My father smiled at her, and we all headed down the trail, leaving the truck and the saw up by the big maple, for the afternoon work.

Trish and Tina disappeared into the kitchen, to help my mother with lunch. Roy caught my eye, and we stayed on the porch when my father went in. He looked out at the barn, and then said quietly, "These parties are bad. You can't imagine. My dad's charging money for the uncles to come, and charging for drinks, just like a real bar. The uncles aren't going to like that. He invited some other men, too, guys he knows. And he has girls coming down from Barre. Three of them, he said. He's charging for that, too. I know there's going to be fights, but there might be worse than that, too." I would have gone off thinking about the dancing girls from Barre, but Roy's tone scared me.

"I'm going to bring the girls up to your barn, and have them spend the night there. I'll head back early, and see if I can bring them back to our trailer, if the party's done and everybody has left." He looked at me. "I don't want to sneak around your father, after everything he's done for us. And I don't want my dad getting mad at him, either." This last part cleared the dancing girls right from my mind. I didn't want Roy's dad mad at any of us. "I just don't know what else to do," Roy said. My mom came out and called us in to lunch. I didn't know what to say, anyway.

After lunch, the girls got the kitchen put away, and then my mom sent us all out side. I knew there was work to be done on the fallen maple, and thought that my mom wanted my dad to open the package from Mr. Morgan without mentioning it in front of the Buckman kids. Roy wanted to go scout out the hayloft in the barn, so Trish and me headed out to he barn. Trish was in her barn boots, of course. She didn't seem worried at all about the party her dad was throwing. She had a big smile on her face, and even teased her brother a little bit, calling him a worry wart. Roy looked at his sister, waiting by the ladder to climb up after us, and he smiled, for the first time that day. "Trish always manages to not worry about disaster. She leaves that up to me, I guess."

"It's just another bachelor party," she said. "They've had lots of them up at the home farm. Bunch of guys getting drunk, fighting, and pawing at the dancing girls. They've done it before."

Roy had climbed up the ladder, and was looking at the hay bales, stacked up high along the back of the barn. He climbed up the wall of bales, kicking his feet in between and trying to not pull the bales loose as he climbed up. I followed him, and Trish climbed up behind us. "This is different," Roy said. "The uncles aren't going to like having dad charge them for what has mostly been free before. And he has a bunch of guys coming that I don't even know. And you and Tina are older, now. Tina, especially."

Trish poked at her brother. "Tina and I get older at the same time. She's not getting any older than me."

Roy looked uncomfortable, but went on. "She looks older. More like a women, these days." He looked like he wished Trish could understand what he was saying, without him having to keep talking about it.

I had no clue what he was talking about. Trish looked confused, then irritated. "You mean boobs?" she asked. She colored up, and then poked at me, hard, in the ribs. "You're talking about me not having boobs, right in front

122

of my fiancée?" Trish said, starting to get loud. Roy looked at his sister, and waited for her to figure it out. Trish understood before I did. "You mean, you think the uncles, or the other guys, might see Tina like they do the dancing girls?" Roy nodded, and I started to understand what Roy was worried about. Trish looked like she suddenly understood, too. "You really think..." she started, then, gave it up. She thought that, too, I guessed. "So you're going to hide us up here, until it's over, and they all go home again?"

Roy shrugged. "Got a better idea?" he asked. "I can't fight off the whole trailer full of 'em. I don't even know who's going the show up. And I'd rather worry about it before hand, then not and get surprised. Dad will be pissed that we're gone, but I can't help that."

Trish had lost her smile. She looked stunned, like she had just seen the world differently, and that she didn't like what she saw, at all. She balled her hands up tight, and looked like she couldn't breath, and then she rocked up and down a little, and started to cry, quiet at first, then making a moaning noise that scared me, panting and rocking back and forth. I leaned up next to her, and tried to hold her, but she pushed me off, hard. "I'm OK," she said.

Roy looked at her. "It's who they are," he said. "We just have to know that, and figure out a way to stay safe."

What Roy was talking about, and what Trish had finally understood, was starting to get clear to me, and I felt like my lunch might come back up. I felt afraid, not just for Trish and Tina, and Roy, but afraid myself, to understand that there was evil in the world, not some abstract devil talked about in church, but real evil that would be camping just down the road from our house, threatening to spill out onto people I loved, Trish, and her brother and sister, and maybe our family, as well, with angry drunk men coming up the road, pounding on the door. This was made worse for me when I connected it to a Bible story where something like that happened. It was angels taking shelter in some man's house, while the other men in the city demanded he turn them over, for something I finally understood. The man had ended up sending his own daughters out, instead, to protect the angels. I couldn't understand it, when a boy in my Sunday school class had showed it to me, a big grin on his face, like he had with the naked verses of David. I had this crazy thought of my dad sending Susan and Ellen out to the crowd of drunk men, and then realized he would instead stand on the porch with his shotgun, and try to make the men go away. And then I saw the men, with guns of their own, and then, I was crying, right along with Trish.

Roy looked disgusted with both of us. "Crying won't help a whole lot," he said. "I think our best bet is to get up here, make kind of a hollow to hide in, up at the top. Even if they think of the barn, they'll be too drunk to climb up the hay, and if they did," Roy said, picking up a pitch fork from the spot on the wall where it hung, "I could keep them down with this." He was climbing back up to the top of the hay, with the pitchfork in his hand, not kidding at all, I realized. He was making a plan that involved stabbing his own father and his father's friends with a pitchfork, if he needed to. I thought back to Roy, when I barely knew him, finding the shady spot, and the tree roots, and calmly making a plan to destroy Danny Bowman. Then I understood something. In a world like the one the Buckman kids lived in, the adults around you, even your own father, were not there to keep you safe. In Roy's world, the adults were more of a threat than anything else, so it made sense for Roy to think and act the way he did. I went to sleep at night, trusting that my parents loved me, and the rest of us, and that we would all be safe in that love. Roy could only trust himself to think things out, and be ready to fight.

There was a stack of feed sacks downstairs, and Roy sent Trish and me to bring some up, to make the hay a little less prickly. Trish had stopped crying, and looked kind of hollow at this point, but she did as Roy said. I wiped my face on my sleeve, like a little kid, and followed her to bring up feed sacks. Trish and I didn't say anything. I was embarrassed at crying in front of her, and at not being strong, like her brother. And I guess she was embarrassed for me to see that her life was like, really, and to understand, finally, what it meant to be Trish Buckman. I remember her asking, before, if I would love her, even if her daddy was a crazy man. I stopped and pulled at her. She pulled back, then spun around, all angry at me. I ignored the angry part, and pulled her in close, petting some of the hay out of her hair. "I love you," I said. "I always will. We'll get married and have three kids, Luky, Puky and whoever, and make a nice house and keep them safe, and tuck them into bed every night, and make strawberry pie in the summer, and eat roast chicken and mashed potatoes, and love each other. Every day and every night." I told her this, like a story you might tell a little kid, scared from a nightmare.

Trish took a deep breath, and then hugged me back. "You better," she said. "If you ever stop loving me, I'll kill you."

It sounds awful, but then, it sounded right. I believed her. I knew that for some reason, Trish had taken one last chance on trusting love, and trusting another person, and that, for some reason, she had picked me at that last person to trust. I knew if I ruined that for her, she would pretty much be done. "I won't ever stop loving you," I said, which was true.

"I mean it," she said, handing me some feed sacks. She gave me a quick kiss. "Let's get this hiding place built before your folks come looking for us."

By the time Susan yelled into the barn, calling us back to the house, Roy had a hidden nest tucked up in the top of the hay, lined with feed sacks and an old army blanket I had taken from the chest in the milk house. The nest was about two bales deep, and three long, big enough for the Buckman kids to all fit inside, with a row of bales behind it that could be pulled over like a lid, hiding the nest as long as no one stepped on it. He was already trying to design a tunnel, with some boards on the top, making it even harder for him and his sisters to be found, but we were out of time for today. He kept the pitchfork up in the nest, just in case.

On the porch, my mother had made a jar of lemonade for us all, and my father had opened up the box from Boston. They sat in the rocking chairs, with the kids around them. My dad spoke slowly, carefully, like he had worked out what he wanted to say. "Our friend, Mr. Morgan, moved back to Boston," he started. I could see Trish tighten up. "I told him that you were helping us this summer, with hay, and with fire wood, and the garden. He liked that, and he sent something for each of the kids, including Roy, Tina and Trish." He reached into the box, and took out a gold foil wrapped orange, handing the first one to Tina, then Trish, the Roy, and then one to each of the rest of us. Seven golden oranges, each, it turned out, made of chocolate, with sections like a real orange you could break off and eat. "I'll expect each of you to write a thank you note, and I'll send the notes back to him, in my next letter. You can write the notes today. There's paper out on the table."

Trish was crying again, slow at first, then more, and my mother went to her, and held her, pressing her little blond head into my mother's dress. My mother didn't say anything, but she rocked a little back and forth, and Trish cried all the harder. Trish cried for a long time, with Tina looking over at her, like maybe she should do something about it. "It's OK," Roy said. "She's tired. We all are, pretty much." He broke of a piece of the orange, and had a tiny bite. "Wow," he said, breaking off a piece and handing it to Trish. "This is really good. You can taste a little orange in it." Trish ignored him, burrowing into my mother like she would never come out, and Tina finally took the chocolate from Roy's fingers.

My father tapped me on the shoulder. "You can write your note first," he said, and I went in, leaving Trish in my mother's arms, out on the porch, crying like she would never be able to stop.

She did stop, of course. We do stop, eventually, even if we have a world of things to cry for, and find a mother's arms to cry in, after being without that our whole life. But it took a while. My father finally shepherded the rest of us into the kitchen, with Roy being the last to come in. I saw him looking at his sister, maybe just looking out for her, yet again, but I think he might have been imagining what it would have been like, to be like Trish, to be able to just cry in my mother's arms, and to be held there, and comforted. These were things I knew he had given up on, probably a long time ago, but I could see that maybe he still wanted it as much as anyone else would. His eyes looked really soft, for a second there, and sad, and then they hardened back up, and he came in the screen door. "I guess you can only find chocolate like that in Boston," he said. "Nothing you can ever get around here."

CHAPTER EIGHTEEN

We worked on the old maple until suppertime, with Susan and Ellen and Tina helping my mom in the garden, putting in a second batch of spinach, and thinning the carrots out. Trish and Roy worked hard and steady, and the four of us kept up with my dad's chainsaw throughout the afternoon. We cut two full loads of wood by the end of the day, and had maybe another two loads still on the fallen tree. The maple was big enough that my dad's chain saw wouldn't get all the way through the main trunk, so we'd have to use the cross cut saw for the last part, an old two-man saw that had been the main wood maker back when my father was growing up. My father showed it to Trish and Roy when we got back, taking it off the wall of the shed, and letting them feel the weight, and see the teeth, filed sharp to cut in both directions. You could see that Trish and Roy wanted to give it a try. I'd used it before, with my dad, and was surprised at how well it worked, the weight of the saw riding on the wood and helping it dig in, and helping to keep the saw moving. Timing was everything with that saw. You had to work as a team.

We ended for supper, having parked the second load by the woodshed, and washed up with the hose. Roy jogged down the ridge trail, just to check on what was happening at the trailer. He came back a few minutes later, telling me and Trish that a few cars were there and you could already hear the men arguing. He had brought back a worn stuffed rabbit and two pillows, handing them to Trish and telling her to put them up in the nest. Trish blushed at the rabbit, looking at me to see if I was going to make fun of her, and then at her brother. She finally thanked him, held the rabbit tight to her chest, and disappeared up into the barn loft.

My dad had gathered the thank you notes up, and had them at his desk, where he planned to write Mr. Morgan a letter. My mother and the girls got dinner on the table, and my father's prayer asked God's blessing on "our family and our good friends gathered around our table", something that had been added the first time the Buckman kids stayed for a meal, and had been a standard since. I knew that Roy didn't think much about God, but he had said something about the prayers, that he appreciated my father bringing him and his sisters into our family that way. I wondered if God had just not noticed the Buckman kids before, and if their life would get better now that my father was reminding him to care about them a few times a day. If that were true, it seemed an odd way for God to go about looking after things.

There was rhubarb pie for desert, with Trish eating two big slices, then having another piece of her chocolate orange, which was about half gone. Susan had taken a tiny piece of her own orange, and was planning on saving the rest, James had eaten about half of his, and had to be made to finish his meat loaf. Ellen had shared her orange with Tina, explaining that the two of them both had the same two oranges. I had offered a slice of mine to Trish, who pushed it back to me, and then changed her mind and took it, saying it was about the best thing she had ever eaten. I promised her that when we were grown, I'd take her into Boston and she could buy a case of chocolate oranges every month or so. Roy had eaten a slice of his, and then folded the gold foil back, putting it in the fridge with the others. He liked it well enough, he said, but it bothered him that there were things like that, so good, and yet, most people would never have a chance to taste it.

The Buckman kids left after supper, heading down the ridge trail, stopping, I suspected at the old beech tree with our heart on it, and waiting there until the lights went out in our place, then heading back up and crawling into the nest in the loft, hoping to spend the night hidden there, without problems.

The parties started that night, a Friday, and went on, once or twice a week, into the summer. You could easily hear the yelling, and some bits of music, since the nights were warm enough that we slept with the windows open. There seemed to be cars and trucks driving down the road, coming from Northfields, Barre, and Montpelier, maybe. When you could hear some swear words, my mother came into our room and closed the windows, not saying a thing, except "Go back to sleep."

That night, in the hallway, I could hear her asking my dad if he thought the Buckman kids would be OK. "Roy has it covered," he answered. "They'll be fine." I wondered if he somehow knew about the nest in the barn loft. He left my mother to her bath, and sat by himself out on the front porch, working on his letter to Mr. Morgan. I wondered if he had his shotgun with him. I thought about Trish and Roy and Tina, out in the barn, hearing all the noise just down the hill, and wondered if they could sleep tonight. I could still hear some of the party, even with the window closed, but I couldn't hear the swear words any more. I could hear cars drive past, and my mother's voice, in the tub, praying, I would guess, since my dad was still out on the porch. I heard "Under your wings" twice, and knew that she was praying for the Buckman kids, reminding God again that he needed to keep an eye out for them. I added my prayers, picturing Trish and Roy and Tina all tucked safe under the wings of a great eagle, sleeping in a nest of hay, lined with feed sacks, with Trish clutching an old stuffed bunny, her mouth a little open and her hair all loose in her face. As I fell asleep, with that odd mix of how God was watching over them, and at the same time, me thinking of how pretty Trish was, all combined in my dreams.

My father looked tired that next morning. It was dark, of course, when we got up for the cows, but I could see his face in the kitchen light, drawn and a little puffy. I saw the shotgun, his Stevens double-barreled twelve, up on the top of the kitchen Hoosier, where it belonged, but I noticed a box of shells still on the kitchen table. Number one buck, not the bird-shot we used for turkey and partridge. Coyote loads, my father had called them. My father's letter to Mr. Morgan was done, and sitting on the table, with extra stamps glued on to cover the weight of the thank you notes. I pictured my dad out on the porch all night, writing his letter, his shotgun ready to protect those he had under his wings.

We did the cows, with a bit of light just starting up in the east as we sent them back to pasture. We cleaned up the milker, and put the milk in to cool. Then my father, who was usually silent in the morning, loudly told me and James that breakfast would be in a half hour or so, and that he thought my mother would be making an extra batch of pancakes and sausage, hoping that the Buckman kids came up early enough to have some. His voice was loud enough to carry, and James looked at him, trying to figure it out. I understood, though. Somehow, he knew the Buckman kids were up in the loft, and he was inviting them to breakfast.

When we were washed up, and in the kitchen, there was a soft knock at the door, just as the first batch of pancakes were getting to the table. Trish was there, with Roy and Tina behind her, most of the hay brushed out of her hair, and a tired smile on her face. "OK if we come early today?" she asked.

"Perfect timing," my mother answered. "I made too much batter, and we have a fresh box of sausage to get through. How was your night?"

"We did OK." Trish answered. "Ready to work today."

My mother poured out coffee for my dad, and laid her arm on his shoulder.

"You going to be OK today?" she asked.

He smiled at her, forking pancakes onto the kid's plates. "I'll be fine," he said. "I might do with a nap this afternoon, though." He smiled at her.

My mother brought a pan of sausages over to the table, and set the hot skillet on a cutting board. "Hot pan," she said, while the grease sizzled and some smoke still came up. She took the shotgun shells off the table, without a word, and set them back into the Hoosier, where they belonged. You could tell that James wanted to ask about the shells, but we didn't do that sort of thing. Roy was thinking about the shells, though, and about the wake up call for breakfast. When my father had ended the prayer before breakfast, Roy added, "Thank you, God, for those who look after us."

Trish eyed her brother, not used to him talking with God, but she didn't say anything. She ate a whole stack of pancakes, then a few more pieces off her sister's plate, then ate some extra pancakes that my father forked onto her plate. I didn't count the sausages she ate, but she caught me looking at her plate, and she sort of gave me a quick snarly look. She turned to my mom. "This is just so good," she said to my mother.

"You eat all you want, Trish," my mother said. "You could use a little meat on your bones." Then my mother looked at me, the hairbrush look, letting me know I was to not stare at the plates of our guests. I looked down at my own plate, but not before I saw Trish grinning that I had gotten myself in trouble.

The boys got a head start on unloading the farm truck, stacking the smaller rounds of maple, and rolling the big blocks out for my father and me to split. The girls joined us, after the kitchen was cleaned up. Trish whispered at me as she walked past, her arms filled with fire wood. "Toby got in trouble," she sang.

I grinned at her, a little annoyed, but mostly happy that she was feeling better. "I just never saw a person eat that much, before," I said. "Livestock, sure, bears and what not, just not a human being."

Trish gave me a swat with the firewood, grinning that great freckled smile as she walked past. "You be nice to me, or I'll tell your mama on you. She likes me."

"She does," I replied, smiling myself.

We got two more loads of the tree done that day, with Susan, Ellen and Tina helping my mom in the garden, and James, Roy and Trish and me working with my dad. We stopped for lunch, with Trish giving me the stink eye when I watched her eat, but my mom could see we were kidding, and she didn't say any more. Roy had run down the ridge after lunch, and came back, saying that there were still four cars parked in the road. He was worried about getting in trouble for being gone, and was hoping that his dad had been busy enough with the party to have not noticed. "But he'll figure it out at some point," Roy said, as much to himself as to me and Trish. "I'll just tell him we're sleeping up in the woods when he does that, that we're not going to stay in the trailer with all the yelling and fighting, again. Worst he can do is whip me, and we'll just do it next week, anyway. We can't stay there."

Trish looked worried. "I don't want you to be the one in trouble," she said. "Let's tell him I got scared, from the yelling and all, and that you took me and Tina up to the woods to get away from the noise. He'll like the idea of us sleeping on rocks." She turned to me. "Your dad seemed to know we were up in the loft. You didn't tell him, did you?"

I shook my head. "He just knows what goes on at the farm," I said. "He told my mom that Roy had it covered, so maybe he figured Roy would get you guys away from there."

Trish dumped the load of firewood she was carrying, and pulled my face over to hers by my ears, kissing me nicely for a bit. Then she pulled back, and said, "Were the shotgun shells about the party?"

I felt kind of bad about that, but I nodded. "I think so," I said. "I think he stayed up, on the porch last night, writing that letter, and just keeping an eye out. He was probably worried that someone would get drunk and come up to the house and try to cause trouble."

"They might," said Roy. "But he probably oughtn't to sit out there in the open like that, where they could just pick him off." Roy looked at me, as he said this last part, and he must have seen the blood drain out of my face. "Not that they would," he added, "but you ought to not let them get the jump on you. Better to stay inside, with the lights off, porch light on, maybe." You could see him working it out, how best to defend the house with a shotgun, against intoxicated attackers, likely led by his own father. "Maybe even camp out in the wood shed, where you could see the house, and have the drop on 'em if they came up." He looked again at me. "But they probably won't come up," he added, trying to sound more sure than I thought he was. "With us gone, they won't even think about us. It sounded like they were pretty busy last night, from all the ruckus."

Trish carried another load of wood from the truck to the shed. "Why would girls come all the way from Barre just to fight off a bunch of ugly, drunk men?

I can't imagine putting yourself there by choice."

Since I had watched Trish figure out why Roy had spirited her and Tina away last night, the excitement I had first felt about the dancing girls was gone now, replaced by something that just felt awful. "Money?" said Roy. "I guess they get paid, beforehand, and then extra tips, or whatever. That's the way it worked up at the home farm."

"Not enough money in the world for that," Trish said. I didn't say anything. I felt bad about having been excited by the idea of the dancing girls, before, and now the whole subject just made me feel bad, and scared for Trish, and Tina. "They doing it again, tonight?" she asked.

Roy shrugged. "I don't know. I can't ask him. We'll just have to wait and see what it looks like. The barn is OK, anyway."

"I'm glad it's summer," said Trish.

We got the wood done, except for the main trunk, just in time for dinner, with the wood shed looking a lot better than it had a few days before. Dinner was three bubbling chicken potpies, fresh rolls and butter, some asparagus and a big salad, all from the garden. Dessert was a chocolate layer cake, with sour cream frosting, my dad's favorite. My mom must have been thinking about him staying up all night to watch over us. The girls had made the cake, and were really proud of it. It came out perfect, three layers tall, and iced with little swirls like my mom always did. When the cake was served, Tina said, "I can't believe we made that. It looks like a picture from a magazine." After dinner, and after we had the kitchen cleaned up, Dad took us in the truck down to the bridge for a swim, with Trish joining me and Roy in cannonballing off the rail, all at the same time. My mother had shortened the straps of Trish's suit, making it fit her better. Trish liked that, and said, "She sewed it up, for me. Without me even asking."

It was dark by the time we got back to the farm, and the air was cooling off. Trish sat right next to me, our towels draped over us against the cool night air, and her warm skin goose bumpy next to mine. "You feel nice," she said, snuggling up against me.

Ellen was leaning up against Tina, too. "Getting cold," she said. "The water was warmer than the air is."

Roy was looking through the heavy wire screen over the back window, watching my father drive, with James siting up front on the worn out seat, beside him. "Your dad's gotta be tired," he said. "But he took us swimming, anyway."

I was thinking about how warm Trish's leg was, up against mine, but I thought about that. "He usually takes us for a swim after chores in the summer. Sometimes he swims, too, but usually he just sits on the bridge and watches, or fishes some. My mom comes swimming some, when it gets really hot, " I added.

"You've got a good dad," Roy said.

I nodded, and pulled Trish in nice and tight. "He sure likes you guys," I said. Roy didn't say any more, and Trish wanted to kiss some, now that it was getting dark.

I had kind of forgot about the conversation, until the truck finally stopped by the wood shed. "Well, we like him, too," said Roy.

Roy jogged down and scouted out the trailer, found it empty, and came back up and gathered the girls for the walk along the ridge back to their own room. Trish carried the rabbit and the pillows, and the Buckman kids headed back down the ridge. Trish turned and waved to me, just an outline against the sky, and then she disappeared into the woods. I waved back, and whispered "Tomorrow", as if she could hear me.

We usually skipped our baths when we had an evening swim, with my mom figuring that pond water was just as good as bath water. She got us into bed, and prayed with us, reminding God to pay attention to the Buckman kids, and then she closed the door, and went down the hall to the bathroom, where my father was drawing her a bath. I heard her laughing, and him laughing, too, like they were a young couple still in love, and pleased to be with each other, with the kids all put to bed. I thought some about the feel of Trish's skin next to mine in the farm truck, her shivers and mine from the cool air, and maybe from her being so close to me. The noise down the road had gone away, with the only sounds being the distant truck tires on the highway, and a train, probably down in Randolph. I heard a barred owl, calling out, and then it's mate answer, from a ways away. I had a mate, too, just down the hill, and we were going to get married, and have three kids, and buy a case of chocolate oranges every month, down in Boston. And Trish and I would sit at night, when the kids were put to bed, and laugh and talk, while she took her bath. With these pleasant thoughts, I fell asleep, and dreamed.

CHAPTER NINETEEN

The summer was looking like a good one. Second cutting was coming on, the hay nice and smooth after the first cut, and getting tall enough to start to moving with the breeze. The garden was having one of the best years ever, with the extra hands of Tina and Trish helping out. My mother had put the whole garden plot into use this summer, including the third she usually kept fallow, planted in clover as a cover crop, rotating that third from year to year. With the Buckman kids eating up at our house, the extra garden was a good thing. My father kept back more milk and cream, and took an extra pig from his brother, already done and packaged. We had the big freezer half full of pork, and then, one of the cows broke a leg in a rusted culvert, so we butchered her as well, renting space in a freezer down in town. We probably ate better that summer than we usually did, which is saying something. People took food pretty seriously back then, farmers, especially, and my mother was set on raising strong, healthy, and well-behaved children.

Trish and Tina studied how my mother cooked, and were given credit, along with my sisters, for most of the desserts that came our way. Ice cream and lemonade used up twenty-five pound bags of sugar. We ate and we ate, and if we hadn't been working so hard, we all would have gotten fat. Trish and I got to spend time together, almost every day. I saw her with my family, I saw her working with my mother, and working beside me and her brother, when she could. I saw her swimming at the floating bridge, cannonballing off the rail, or swimming out to the middle of the pond, and I saw her at the end of the day, walking down the ridge trail, with her brother and sister, heading back to the trailer, and whatever waited for her there.

Trish came up to the farm with her face bruised from time to time, and her lip split, twice. My mother eyed the handprints on Trish, and on Tina, in silence, but you could tell she was angry about the treatment the girls got. She never slapped any of us in the face, believing, as she said to my father, "that God had provided a better place to discipline children." She put crushed ice in a hand towel for Trish to put on her lip, but said nothing other than, "That must hurt." Trish was embarrassed by the whole thing, sometimes trying to joke it off, but mostly saying nothing, either. I felt my anger at her father a little stronger each time Trish had been hit, and scared myself sometimes with fantasies of shooting him with my father's shotgun.

Trish didn't want to hear anything from me about it, and Roy had only said, "I'm doing the best I can," clearly feeling like I was blaming him for not having protected Trish. "He's drunk and mean, and she's mouthy, and the trailer is small. It's better than it was, 'cause we're up here all the time, now." I told him I wished it really was all the time, and that they didn't have to go back. He just shook his head, like he did when he thought I'd said something that was too stupid to comment on. So we didn't talk about it much.

I had a chance to look at the "bar" trailer one Sunday morning, when my father had to slow down from all the cars still parked half out in the road. The cars were still there after a noisy Saturday night, while we went to church, on Sunday morning. The "bar" trailer was big, almost as big as the single wide that the family lived in, with the hitch sticking out into the road, and dug a little down into the ground, trying for level I guessed, the wheels up on boards, and the sloping back end hanging out over the creek. It was made of aluminum, once shiny, maybe, but now corroded to a dull grey with streaks of black running down the sides. There were a few tiny windows, up along the top, and a round window in the door, like the porthole on a ship. You could see where a padlock had been bolted on the door. I thought of how dark it must be inside. It said "Spartan" on the front, which was the brand of the trailer, I guess. The name reminded me of a story we had heard in school, the story of a boy from Sparta who kept a stolen fox hidden under his shirt, even thought it clawed him up and bit him. He was tough, like the other Spartans, and that story reminded me of Roy, and Trish, too, I guess. It seemed a fitting name for the trailer, although Trish's dad had hung a sign over the door that said "Trail's End", the name a real bar would have, I guessed.

Neither my father nor my mother said anything as we pulled off to the other side, easing past the cars parked raggedly along the road. But my mother looked out her window, her face tight like it got when she was angry about something. As we pulled onto the pavement of Route 12, my father said, "Cummings is going to hit all that with his plow, this winter, and knock it all back into the creek. He won't stand for things being parked in the road when he has to plow."

We had left the Buckman kids up in the loft, pretending to be asleep. Roy wouldn't let them all come in for breakfast on Sundays, since we weren't working that morning. Roy felt like that was too much like just grabbing a free meal. My father figured this out after the first Sunday morning, in which he had made his now usual announcement about breakfast, only to have the extra biscuits my mother had made left to cool on the counter, the Buckmans having been a no-show. My father and my mother had talked about inviting the Buckman kids to church with us, but had felt stuck about asking their dad for permission to take the kids. Nobody wanted to talk with him, but they also didn't want to draw his attention to the obvious fact that his kids spent more time with our family than they did back in their own trailer. Trish didn't want to go to church with us, anyway. She said she felt bad dressed up, and worse if she looked trashy and the other girls were all fancy. She said she sang like a bullfrog. Roy would have liked to go, I think, but he never said anything about it. After church, when we got back, the Buckman kids were there at our house, usually weeding the garden, or maybe Roy or Trish splitting wood, and the other's stacking it into the woodshed. Trish would tease me about my tie, and my mother would call the Buckman girls in to help with lunch, usually feeding them the left over breakfast first while they all cooked.

It was just after church on one Sunday that my mother heard about Trish's mother being dead. Mrs. Partlow was a nurse at the Central Vermont Hospital, and she had been there the night before when the Barre ambulance crew brought the body in. I had seen Mrs. Partlow talking with my mother, her finger jabbing the air, and her face angry and disgusted. My mother had gone pale, and I had that response I always did, wondering if I had done something wrong, and that Mrs. Partlow was telling my mother about it. My mother took out her little notebook from her purse, and wrote down some things. She was quite on the way out to the car, having whispered to my dad before she gathered the kids in for the trip home.

She explained once we were on the road. "Mrs. Partlow was working at the emergency room last night when the ambulance brought a woman in, a woman who had died the day before, she thought. The woman had been drinking, and had gotten sick, and choked to death. Carla Buckman was the woman's name, from Barre, and she thought that Carla might be the Buckman's mother. I think Tina told me her mother was named Carla, and that she lived in Barre." She wiped at her eyes, and took a breath. "We're going to have to ask the kids if that was their mom, when we get home. They won't know about it, yet.

We'll have to tell them." She made an odd little noise, and put her face in her hands, crying, I thought.

The Buckman kids were in the garden when we got home, Trish grinning at me with her dirty face, tugging at an imaginary tie, and ready to start making fun of me. But she saw my mom, and stopped. She was still kneeling in the dirt when my mom got out to the garden, stepping right into the damp soil in her good church shoes, kneeling down in the dirt beside Trish and Tina, pulling them in while she talked. Roy stood off to the side, listening, and then leaning in to hear. His face was blank, like stone, again. I walked out and stood a few feet away, not sure what to do. Trish and Tina were crying by then, leaning against my mom hard enough to tip her over onto the ground, where she just sat there in her best dress, the girls burying their faces in her chest, while she held them and rocked and cried along with them. Roy looked at his sisters, then over at me, and turned and headed over to the hose to wash up. I started to follow him, but he held his hand up, telling me to back off, and then carefully washed the dirt from his hands and feet. He stood, looking out over the valley with that stone cold look, and then said, really quiet, "Trish always thought that maybe she'd come back for us. I guess not."

I didn't know what to say. I said, "I'm sorry," and Roy looked back at me, shaking his head.

"Yeah. Me, too," he said. "She wouldn't have come back, anyway, though." He wiped angrily at his face. We stood there, watching his sisters push into my mother's lap, still sobbing and clinging to her. I saw that look again in Roy, and I thought Roy wished he was there in my mother's lap, too, then, it went away. "You mom's good with the girls," he said.

My father came up beside us, and watched my mom comfort the girls for a bit. Then he turned to us, and said, "I've got a quick errand down in town. You boys want to come along?" We both nodded, although I couldn't figure out what my dad needed to do in Randolph. All the stores were closed, it being Sunday, and he just visited with our church friends that morning. He still had his Bible in his hand, so I knew he hadn't left it at church. But we followed him back to the car, after he leaned over and said something to my mom, and we drove back down the dirt road towards Randolph. Roy looked out the window at the two trailers, and the piles of scrap metal, which seemed to be falling down into the creek. He put his hand up to the glass, his fingers curled a little. I could see his lips moving as we drove past, but I couldn't hear what he said. His face was reflected in the window, though, and I could see his eyes were on fire, and I guessed he was blaming his father for his mother's death.

We were quiet all the way into town. We usually were, when we rode in the car. Our parents might talk some, but the kids were quiet, pretty much. But this quiet felt different, heavy and dark, and dangerous, and the trip seemed to take forever. I wondered at how unhappiness could change the way time seemed to run, and I wondered what would happen next with the Buckman kids, and how Trish would be when we got back. I wondered why my dad needed to go back into town, and then I wondered what we were going to have for lunch.

We pulled back up to the church, empty, now, I guessed, and my dad left us in the car while he went to the door, and then walked in. I knew Reverend Sykes might still be there. He lived next door, in a little house that came with the job, and he was usually at the church, working on sermons, counseling parishioners or trying to fix the heat or the windows. Roy didn't ask about my dad, but he finally did say, "This where you go to church?" I nodded. "Looks nice," he said. I thought about that. The Baptist church was pretty big, but not fancy at all, the congregation preferring to send money off to the Lottie Moon offering, in Africa, or somewhere, rather than spend the collection plate on fancy windows or carpets.

"The people are nice, most of 'em," I answered. "Reverend Sykes is really old, but he's a good preacher. My mom and my dad both like him, even though they argue some on the sermons."

Roy just nodded, and we waited in silence, until my father came back out the door, with Reverend Sykes beside him. The Reverend looked out to the car, and gave us a little wave. We waved back, although I'll bet he couldn't see us very well through the glass. My father got into the car, and only said, "Let's go home and see about lunch." He drove almost all the way to the dirt, and then added, "Reverend Sykes is a good man."

It was twenty minutes down to town, when the roads were good, and twenty back, and I guessed we had parked in the church lot for another twenty minutes or so. When we got home, the garden was empty, and the front door was open, to help the heat from the kitchen get out. I could smell fried chicken, and when we went in, we found the girls and my mother, all in aprons and working on the meal. Biscuits were in the oven, and Tina was working on a big bowl of mashed potatoes. Ellen and Susan were snapping green beans and Trish was cutting up carrots for the salad. My mom gave my dad a big, long hug, trying to keep her floured hands off my dad's brown wool suit coat.

James was sitting at the table, looking irritated that we had gone to town without him, but he didn't say anything.

Trish gave me a tired smile, and put her hand up to where a tie would have been, and then rubbed at her eye with her elbow, trying to keep her hands away from her face. The kitchen was hot, with three of the four burners of the stove still going, and the oven hot from the biscuits, green beans now boiling, and a pot of coffee on, and you could see the sweat on the girls' faces as they worked. I went to stand beside Trish, and leaned into her and whispered, "I love you."

She looked like she would have punched me, if she hadn't been trying to keep her hands clean for the salad. "Stop!" she said. "I just barely stopped crying enough to make the salad. You're going to get me going again." She rubbed the fresh tears with her elbow, then, softened. "I love you, too," she said. "Leave me alone." She started in on a tomato, cutting thin slices that she laid across the bowl of lettuce and carrots. "I don't know what we would have done without you all," she added. She finished the first tomato, and picked up another. "I guess we would have got through, somehow. We always do, I guess." She picked up a third tomato, taking the stem out, and starting to slice it. "Your dad sure keeps the knives sharp. Your mom says a ripe tomato is the test of a sharp knife." She cut off a few more slices, then, turned to me. "You go do whatever you boys do. We're almost done here. Tina and Ellen made a peach pie, and your mom is going to have you boys churn up ice cream to go with it. Then we can go down to the bridge and swim some, I guess." She gave my shoulder a quick kiss, and sort of shoved me on with her forehead.

We washed up, and sat at the table, while the girls brought out a platter of fried chicken, a basket of biscuits, wrapped in a dish towel to keep the heat in, a bowl of green beans, dressed with bacon, a pitcher of iced tea, and another of milk. We sat for the prayer, waiting for my father to speak. It was different today. My dad sounded uncertain, like he was working hard to say the right thing. "Lord," he started, "We ask your blessings on this food, the bounty of your good earth, and on our family and loved ones gathered here." There was a pause, and I could tell that the Buckman kids were hearing that part about being loved. "We can't always understand what happens in our lives, and how your plan for us is made and carried out. But we can feel your love for us, in times of sadness and sorrow, a comfort to us, even when we can't understand. Lord, hold these young children in your arms, and comfort them as they cry for the loss of their mother. Take their mother into your love, and find her a safe place there with you."

My dad stopped, but we hadn't had the amen yet, so I opened an eye up just a crack, and saw him crying, tears falling onto his clasped hands. Trish looked at him, openly, her mouth a little open, the way she did sometimes. Roy had his eyes closed, and then I saw my mother, looking at me, not angry, but still sad. I closed my eyes, again, and we waited. Finally my dad just said, "Amen", and we all said "amen", too, and then we started passing the food and filling our plates. I was hungry, even with everything that had happened. I felt kind of bad about that, until I saw Trish going back for seconds on the chicken and potatoes, and then taking yet another crispy thigh off the platter. She saw me looking, again, and glared at me, but just because she was kidding me.

We had pie, and ice cream, and we got the dishes done and the kitchen cleaned up, and then my dad took us all swimming at the bridge. Mom went along this time, taking her Bible and a folding chair, and sitting in the shade beside the water, watching us dive and swim. My dad sat on the ground next to her, holding her hand, some, and I could see them talking. Trish swam out into the middle of the pond, and rolled over on her back, just floating there. I swam out to her, but she just gave me a quick kiss and sent me back, saying that she wanted to be alone for a bit. Tina was diving with Ellen again, and Roy was trying to learn how to dive, too, while Susan watched him, treading water a little ways out from the bridge. James was catching crawdads, so I joined him, and we started keeping the big ones for supper.

We got through the day, and back to the house, in time for the cows, and a cold dinner of left over chicken and biscuits. I hadn't had much time that day with Trish. She had stayed pretty close to my mom, helping in the kitchen again, and then sitting with her, while my dad and us boys did the evening milking. She and my mom were on the couch when we came back in, my mom reading her Bible, and Trish just leaning up against her. Ellen and Tina were sitting at the kitchen table, talking low, their hands tight together on the tabletop. My mom had made some hot chocolate, even though it was summer, and there was still some in the pitcher when we came in. We washed up at the sink, and Roy gathered his sisters up, and brought them to the door, thanking my parents. Then they went out on the porch, closed the door, and slipped off into the night. It was dark, with only a sliver of a moon' and clouds covering even that most of the time. I could barely see the Buckman kids, little dark shapes, heading off into the dark, back to the trailer, but I watched, anyway,

141

trying to imagine Trish stopping by our tree, and putting her hand up on our heart.

"Bedtime," my mother said, and James and I headed upstairs. I was tired from the swim, and tired from all the feelings that day, and filled to the brim with lunch, and now dinner. The hot chocolate made me tired, too, I think, and when I fell into bed, I could barely move enough to push the covers aside, it being one of those hot nights. But I didn't fall asleep right away. I thought about Trish, of course, but I also thought about her mother, and what it might be like to leave your kids with a man like Mr. Buckman, and then to die, up in Barre, and never see your kids safe or grown up. I prayed for her, that night, after I had prayed for Trish, and Roy and Tina, and my parents. I hadn't cried that day, though most everyone else had. I could hear Ellen still crying some, across the wall, and Susan whispering for her to be quiet. James was asleep, and I lay there, listening for my own mother's voice, but I couldn't hear anything. She and my dad must have stayed downstairs to talk. I tried not to think about the fact that mothers could die, and leave their children behind, alone.

CHAPTER TWENTY

It might be the hard stuff that helps you grow up some. I felt like loving Trish had changed me into someone older, but seeing her so hurt, and not being able to do much to help, that changed me, too. Roy was harder these days, and he said even less than he had, although he still shadowed my father with the farm chores, asking a few questions, and committing the answers to memory. Tina stayed glued to Ellen, whispering with her when she talked at all. And I think my brother and sisters were shaken some, the same way I was, thinking maybe parents might not be forever.

Trish was still happy to see me, but some of the spark seemed gone from her eyes, her smile seemed tired and thin, and her playfulness disappeared. She stayed closer to my mother now, leaning into her, even scooting her chair around to sit closer to her at the table. When there was a choice about working with me and my dad, or staying in the kitchen or garden to help my mother, Trish was with my mom. I missed her, and I wondered if she would ever go back to being the way she was, before. She snuck in a kiss for me, from time to time, but the kisses were different, too, brief and sad, somehow, more like remembering something than discovering something. Trish still ate everything she could, and my mother kept putting extra food on her plate, but Trish stayed "skinny as a rail", as my mother put it. I didn't understand her sadness, thinking her mom had left Trish and her brother and sister, over a year before, leaving them with their father. I didn't know how to ask her about that, so I asked Roy. He looked at me, the way he often did, and then he said, "Her being dead means it can't get better. Trish kept thinking she might come back for us. Tina, too, I guess. It means that her leaving us, leaving us with him, and then never seeing us, except on the street, by accident, and then drinking herself to death, well, that's as good as it's going to get. Ever. That's what's wrong with Trish. No hope, at this point." Roy looked down at his hands, calloused and marked up some by the work on the farm, tough hands, with scars across the knuckles, and a big, round burn mark on the back of his right hand. Not the hands you would expect to see on a twelve year old. Then he looked up at me, with a bitter smile. "I never expected anything different. But I feel bad for Trish, and Tina."

My dad's visit with Reverend Sykes had been to see if we could hold a funeral for their mom, at the church, and then bury her in the church cemetery, which was usually for members of First Baptist. Reverend Sykes agreed to do it, if there weren't other plans by the Buckman family. There weren't other plans, it turned out, with the boyfriend in Barre disappearing, and Mr. Buckman, visited by my father and Reverend Sykes, staggering to the door, cursing the mother of his children, his children, and the two men standing outside the trailer door.

I had already been to two funerals, one for my grandfather, back when I was little enough to be carried, and the other for one of our deacons, a friend of my father's, a man who had slid his truck off the road, and down fifty feet or so into the creek, two winters before. They left the truck there all winter, the snow making it impossible to get it out. We drove past it every time we went to town. The deacon, Mr. Hadley, was about my parent's age, and left behind five children and a pale wife, who looked pretty close to death herself. They moved away, right after the funeral, back to Massachusetts, moving in with grandparents. I never saw them again.

My mother brought Trish and Tina upstairs on Monday afternoon, and had them try on dresses, some from Susan and Ellen, and some she had borrowed from her friends at church. When they decided on the right ones, Trish came downstairs, wearing shiny black shoes, with straps across the black socks, and a pretty black dress, pleated, and coming to just below her knees. There was some lace at the neck, and on the sleeves, and maybe twenty shiny black buttons up the back. My mother had brushed Trish's hair out, and braided it in a single thick braid down her back, tied with a black ribbon. "Your mother bought us shoes and black ribbons down in town. Tina's dress is blue, but it's so dark you'll think it was black. Your mother said I look nice."

I looked at her, and she slowly turned around, her hands down at her sides, then she faced me again, and made a little curtsey. She still looked sad. "You look beautiful," I said. And she did. She reminded me of the little girl on the cover of *The Secret Garden*. Smaller, somehow, in her sadness, than she used to be. I gave her a shy hug. She smelled like mothballs a bit, the dress having been stored in someone's attic.

Trish hugged me back, sudden and fierce and hard. "I'll get better," she said. "I know I'm no fun any more. I'm sorry." This brought tears to my eyes.

144

I tried to say something, but I couldn't get anything out. I held her, tight, and we stayed that way for a bit, until we heard my mother on the stairs.

Roy borrowed a suit from one of my cousins, and mom got him a black tie, and a white shirt. Mom bought him shoes, too, and some black socks. He had tried it all on upstairs, but I didn't see him in it until the day of the funeral, Wednesday. We got to the church at nine in the morning, the cows done, and then everyone scrubbed until we were all red and sore. I had on my regular Sunday jacket and tie, since we all had church clothes, and didn't have to wear black. First Baptist was pretty much all there by nine thirty, the church filled up, even though none of these people had known Trish's mom. They knew my dad, though, and Reverend Sykes had put the word out that the congregation was expected to come. There was a big, polished box, where Trish's mother was, in front of the church, and the pianist, Mrs. Berry, was there, already practicing when we came in. Trish and Tina walked towards the casket, with Roy following them. The girls put their hand on the dark, polished wood. I stayed back, not sure of what to do. Roy put a hand on Trish's shoulder, and another on Tina's, and the three of them just stood there for a while. My mother joined them, and stood behind them, her head bowed. Reverend Sykes came in from the back, and went right to the three Buckman kids, laying his hand on Trish's head, then Tina's then Roy's, taking his time, blessing them each, and handing them, I knew, into the loving arms of the Lord. Trish glowed afterwards, like something had come inside her and lit her up, and even Roy looked less dark.

Our family sat in front, with the casket right there, flowers laid on the top, and in big vases at either end. Reverend Sykes went up in the pulpit. He nodded to Mrs. Berry, who started up with the piano part of My Redeemer, running it through one whole verse while the congregation settled, and then Reverend Sykes lead the singing, the choir members sitting in the pews, without their usual robes. We sang two hymns, with my mother opening the books for the Buckman kids, who didn't know the words, but tried to follow along as best they could. My mother had Trish tucked under one arm, and Tina under the other, and her hand on Roy's shoulder. I noticed he didn't pull away.

Reverend Sykes preached about love, the love of a mother for her children, and the love of God for every one of us, no exceptions. My mother would have said it was a New Testament sermon, full of redemption and blessings, and not a word of blame or punishment in it. Mr. Sykes called Trish's mother a "sister in Christ", and then went on to say that Christ's love reached out and touched everyone, churched and un-churched, alike. My mother smiled, proud of the Reverend for risking the ire of his congregation in order to sooth the hearts of the Buckman kids. Universal salvation, my mother called it, not a usual thing for the Baptists, but it was a good thing, my mother thought. We sang two more hymns, then Reverend Sykes came down and, while the congregation stood, he lead a prayer of blessing on the Buckman kids and their mother, stressing the love that bound them together, and the love of God that would see them into each other's arms in paradise. He placed his hand on each of their heads again, and then stood behind the casket, with his hands on the wood, willing a blessing to their mother. After the prayer, my mother moved the Buckman kids up by the casket, and stood with them as the congregation filed past, the men and boys shaking Roy's hand, and the ladies hugging them, one after another.

When we went outside, there was a backhoe parked off to the side of the cemetery, and a fresh hole in the ground, draped with a green canvas. The deacons carried the casket out of the church, with Roy invited to walk along side, but he stayed with his sisters, just behind, with my parents and us following. The Buckman kids were quiet, not crying, but worn out, pretty much, by then. The Reverend stood beside the casket, his hands on it again, and prayed, and then it was lowered into the hole, the ropes underneath being let down by the deacons, who strained against the weight. They dropped the ropes in, and then the Buckman kids were given a rose from the vase beside the grave, and asked to toss them in as well. Trish tore a petal off hers, and then threw the rest of the rose in, holding the petal in her hand. We had another prayer, and then we filed back into the church, for the lunch that was served after the funeral. As we walked back to the church, I could hear the backhoe fire up, with one of the deacons in the seat, still in his suit, and start moving over to fill in the grave.

In the basement of the church, the long tables were set up, with food already there, in casserole dishes and trays, with paper plates and napkins. The two big coffee pots were plugged in and hot, and I knew there would be iced tea and milk in the refrigerator, my father having brought a thirty pound can of fresh milk already cooled. My mother had brought some rolls, but she said we weren't expected to bring food, the funeral being for our family. Trish had been there, and Tina, too, when she said that, back at the house, and I saw Trish's eyes get shiny. She was holding onto my mom's hand, but she held it tighter, I could tell, from my mom's face.

We all ate, filling our plates first, and sitting at the table with Reverend Sykes, who quietly tended to his food, having already said what he had to say. My mother picked up the empty plates from in front of the Buckman kids, and went back to the tables, and filled each plate again. I watched the Buckman kids, not just Trish. Roy had been touched more in the last hour than he probably had in his entire life. His face looked troubled, but less like stone than it had in a while. Trish glowed like sunlight, and Tina did too, some. I didn't know if it was the love of the congregation, in the prayers, the songs, the blessings, and the food, or the love of God that Reverend Sykes had called down in the Buckman kids, but they were all different, all better, than they had been before the service.

We had moved onto the pies when two of the deacons came for my father, whispering to him, and pulling him up from his chair, the three men going up stairs as quickly as they could without running. Reverend Sykes looked up, but stayed at the table, and simply asked for the sugar for his coffee. The deacons were there to handle things, and Reverend Sykes had already led the congregation to a better place. Sunday School took place in the basement, and the nursery was here as well, so the floor above us was pretty well insulated. We could hear one voice, loud, but indistinct, and then silence. Our father and the two deacons stayed upstairs, though, and after a while, my mother packed up the food that was on my father's plate in some foil, and cut him a big piece of cherry pie, his favorite, and wrapped that up in foil, as well. The women swept and cleaned the basement, putting everything away, and when it was done, we all went upstairs. My father and the other two deacons were sitting in the back seats, by the door, but there was no sign of what might have gone on.

We all piled into the car, and quietly headed back up the hill to the farm. We got out of our fancy clothes, and still almost too full to move, settled in the kitchen and the parlor, reading. We had a few hours before the evening milking. The girls all headed upstairs with my mother. She came down alone, saying she had put the girls down for a nap, putting Trish and Tina in the boy's bed, with everyone being as tired as they were. We were to stay downstairs and let them sleep. I wondered if Trish and Tina had ever been put down for a nap before. My father had settled into his chair with a farm journal, and Roy asked him, "Was that my dad upstairs, at the church?"

My father folded the journal back up, and set it on the table beside him.

He nodded. "I think he might have been drinking," my father said. "He was angry, and said some things. We asked him to leave, and he did, finally." My father stopped, trying to think of what to say. "I'm sure he's upset at your mother's death," he finally added.

Roy sighed. "I thought he might come and try to stir things up. At least he was late." Roy sat down on the couch, next to me, and pulled out the checkerboard from the drawer in the table. "I wonder if he'll still be up when we get home."

My father smoothed out the paper with his hand. "Are you safe, there? You, and your sisters?"

Roy finished setting up his checkers, then, nudged me, reminding me that I should go first. "Pretty much. If it's just him, we're OK, most of the time." Roy paused, and I could see that he was thinking about saying more, but he nudged me again, and he put his attention to the game.

I could see my father still worrying about his question, and not feeling reassured by Roy's answer. "Well, you're always welcome, up here. Day, or night. Any time," my father added.

"I know", said Roy. "We appreciate that." Roy settled into the game, and then beat me four out of four.

My father sat for a bit, with his journal un-read. Then he put the paper away, and went to his desk, and started on a letter. I guessed that he was writing to Mr. Morgan. Roy goaded me into playing a fifth game, and then beat me at that, too. "You got to stay on the wall, Toby, where you're safe," he said. "Just like anything else." I was annoyed that Roy kept beating me, since I had just introduced him to the game the week before, but I played, anyway. I would have lost, even if I had been focused on the game, because Roy was a lot smarter than I was, but I was distracted. I kept going back to Mr. Buckman at the church, trying to cause a problem. I was wrestling with something, and it finally occurred to me that I didn't see how any of this could work out. That what we were doing could only last so long, before something bad happened. That having a young boy be responsible for keeping his sisters safe was really impossible, and that it was only a matter of time before something really bad happened.

CHAPTER TWENTY-ONE

One night, while another bachelor party raged just down the hill, and while the Buckman kids were all tucked into the nest that they had made in the hay loft, one of the dancing girls had come running up the road, way in the middle of the night, pounding on our door and crying. My dad had gone downstairs, opened the door, and found the half-dressed girl, sobbing on the porch. He called my mother down. The girl was so loud that all of us were awake, wondering what was going on. My father stuck his head in the room, and simply said, "Go back to sleep."

She was still there for breakfast, having been put to sleep on the couch, her makeup smudged, and her hair a mess, dressed in one of my mother's nightgowns and robes, looking a little sick and confused, and trying to drink a cup of coffee. The Buckman kids had been on the porch, right after we were done with the milking, Trish's soft knock bringing my mother to the door. My mother simply introduced all of us to her as Cindy, and said she was going to have breakfast with us, then, my dad was going to give her a ride back up to Barre. Roy, James and I shook her hand, a thin, cold, lifeless little thing. We didn't ask anything, of course, and we all got through breakfast as if she were a silent cousin just stopping by for a quick visit.

When breakfast was over, my mother took her upstairs, and gave her a shirt, and then my dad drove up to Barre with her. The girls were doing the dishes, Roy and I playing another game of checkers, with James watching, trying to point out my mistakes. My mother had still said nothing about the girl, but only cautioned the girls to make sure things were dry before they were put away. I looked up at my mom. "That was one of your best shirts," I said.

My mother gave me a warning look. "I didn't know that you were supposed to keep track of my shirts," she said. "Let James play checkers, and you go sweep the porch. You have too much time on your hands." I could see Trish smirking at me. She loved it when I got in trouble.

I went outside, and swept the porch off, starting at the back, after moving the chairs up. The porch floor was made with narrow boards, and the dirt got into the cracks between. You had to sweep it a certain way to make it look right, and I knew my mother would look it over when she came outside. When I was done, the girls were just finishing up the kitchen, and James was getting a checker lesson from Roy. My mother took us all out to the garden, so we could weed while we waited for my dad to get back. Later, Trish had told me that she recognized the early visitor as one of the girls that came for the bachelor parties. "Sometimes they run out," Trish said. "But why would they come back?" she added. I couldn't think of any answer. I wondered if the girl would come back, again. I was sure my mother had talked to her.

July brought the real Vermont summer, days of hot sun, and cool, star-filled evenings. The water at the bridge was warm, for the top couple of feet, anyway, and we all went there, my mother, too, almost every evening, after the hay and dinner, and then the milking. Swimming was the perfect end to a hot summer day spent in the hay fields, or in the garden. The Buckman kids were up to our farm almost every day, and stayed in the loft on the nights of bachelor parties. Roy threw himself into the work, showing off for dad, James thought, but I didn't see that. Roy wanted something in his life that he could best, something that made him feel at least a little in control of his life. Since Peacemaker had been shot, and since Trail's End had opened, Roy had a hunted look on his face, much of the time.

We were pitching bales from the second cutting, perfect hay, clean and fresh, springy enough to give the bales a little bounce, with no dust at all. We were stacked this hay in the front of the loft, for Mr. Morgan to truck down to the Woodstock farm. We were in the upper field, with Trish down in the garden with my mom and the other girls, and Roy, James and I, the boys, up on the wagon. The baler made a slow, steady thump, thump, thump, like the heart beat of a whale, and the tractor ran at half throttle, my dad leaning off a bit to the right, keeping an eye on the windrow of hay moving beside him as he drove. The sky was blue, and there was no hurry to get the hay in today. My father had a smile on his face.

Roy was working under clouds, though, it seemed. I could see him working something out, without the confidence he usually had when approaching a difficult task. I lugged yet another bale past him, bumping it on my knees, just for fun, really. "You OK?" I asked.

"Peachy keen," he said, moving up to take the next bale. "Why wouldn't I be?" He pulled a bale off the chute, and James stepped up.

Roy was giving me that look, again, but I had grown used to him thinking I was stupid, and it really didn't bother me any more. "You seem worried. I don't know..."

James moved past us, dragging the bale to the back. Roy helped him get it up and stacked. I carried another bale back.

Roy looked at me as he passed, and said, "Ok. I can't figure how it's going to work out. For the girls and me." He pulled a bale off the chute, letting it bounce from the twine. His gloves, new this season, already were worn, like mine, dark with sweat and dirt, and lines formed in the fingers from the twine. The sun was high, straight overhead, and Roy's face was hidden in the shadow of a Red Sox cap he wore. "We've always had to keep moving. Our dad keeps messing things up, so we move. But it never made any difference, before." James moved up to the chute. "His bar is getting too big for folks to ignore it," Roy said. "And the guys that come up for the bachelor parties are showing up during the week, drinking and playing cards and whatever. But it means I can't trust that the girls are OK down there, even if there's not a party."

The scene at the trailer was getting pretty big, I thought, as I pulled another bale off the chute. There had been cars parked all along the road, almost all the way up to the bottom of our lower field. The noise kept up until the sky was starting to get light. My parents were unhappy with it all, but had said nothing, not wanting to upset the way things were, I guessed. The local sheriff, known as Sheriff Joe, had one of the cars parked down there, sometimes, not to stop things, not to police anything, but just being there for the dancing girls, I guessed, or the liquor or card games. Being out in the country, Sheriff Joe was pretty much all we had for law enforcement, the state troopers reserved for car accidents and big crimes, and the Randolph police just staying inside the town limits. The local sheriff wasn't going to shut the Trail's End down. It felt like a powder keg, just waiting to go off.

I hated to think that the kind of men who came for the parties were now just stopping by the trailer, when maybe Trish, or Tina would be there. I could see why Roy was worried. Now I was, too. Then I thought about the "It never made any difference, before," part of what Roy had said. I should have felt how hard losing our family might be for Roy and his sisters, but instead I was stuck thinking about how hard it would be on me if they moved away. Even though Trish was spending more time with my mother these days than she was with me, I still got to see her, and be with her some, almost every day. We hadn't really had that much time with just the two of us, but seeing Trish, even just across the table, eating bits off her sister's plate, that was my favorite part of the day. And Roy was the other favorite part. Roy tried to spend some checker time with James, and fished with him some, when he could, but Roy was my best friend. We both knew that. The first one I had ever had, and I couldn't think about giving that up. And if Tina went away, Ellen would miss her as much as I would miss Trish.

I hauled another bale back, having needed a poke from Roy to remember that the bale almost falling out of the chute was mine. If you dropped a bale, the tractor kept on going, and you had to jump off the wagon, and run back, hauling the bale back to the moving tractor, and get the bale, and yourself, back on board. I tried to imagine my parents letting the Buckman kids move away, and I couldn't do it. I didn't see that they had any say, any legal right, about where the kids lived, or how they lived, really, but my mother was tough, tougher than my father, not in terms of muscle, but in terms of will. She didn't seem to want much, but what she wanted, she got. And I knew she wanted Trish and the Buckman kids safe, and happy.

While I stewed on all of this, we somehow got the rest of the high field baled, riding wagon after wagon back to the barn, running the bales of fresh hay up Mr. Morgan's escalator, and then stacking the fresh bales away, safe, in the loft of the barn. It was close to milking time, so after my dad got the tractor and baler cleaned off and back in the shed, and after he had helped Roy and me drag the escalator up into the loft, we went right to the cows. They were ready, lined up by the gate, and looking forward to some grain and a bit of hay, after a day of sun and fresh pasture. We were just done, and washing up, when Trish came out to the barn, and called us all in for dinner. My mother was braiding Trish's hair these days, every day, sometimes even twice a day, even though I knew Trish could do it herself. Tonight, her hair was in two pigtails, with blue ribbons tied on the ends. She looked happy, and then even happier to see me. She came into the barn, and stayed with me, not talking much, but standing beside me, the two of us managing to be the last to turn off the lights and walk back up to the house, behind our brothers and my dad. We held hands and kissed a little, with her kissing my nose again, and then kissing each of my eyes. Her hand was warm tonight, tight in mine, and her fingers always moving a little, reminding me that I had a living creature there, in my hand, loving me. By the time we were on the porch, taking off our barn boots, I had stopped worrying about the future, the Trail's End crowd, and the possibility of the Buckman kids moving away. I was just full of happy, with Trish.

Dinner was pork chops, with applesauce from last fall, hot rolls and butter, green beans, again, and some slaw that Ellen and Tina had made, under my mother's eye, with shredded carrots mixed in with the cabbage, and raisins dotting the top. For dessert, Susan had made a pound cake, with lemon icing drizzled over the top, and then the whole thing dusted with powdered sugar. I watched Trish eat, happy to see her feeding herself so well, both at the table, and with my mother, the starved parts of her finally getting fed. She caught me watching her, and got snarly at first, but then she saw something different in my eyes, and blushed, looking down at her plate, then back up into my eyes. Her eyes opened up like flowers, loving me, right there at the table. She made a little kissing thing with her lips. I saw my mother watching us, smiling and happy, too, that we loved each other. I felt like Trish was coming back to me.

THE BUCKMAN KIDS

CHAPTER TWENTY-TWO

With the second cutting in, the days were getting shorter, and my dad and the boys began to focus on firewood. We needed around ten cords to get through the winter. There was an oil furnace, but oil had to be bought, and I don't remember the big steel tank in the basement ever being filled while I was growing up. The farm had over one hundred and sixty acres, and about a third of that was in woods, and we could just about pull ten cords out from the falls, alone. Maple was my dad's favorite, with yellow birch a close second, with cherry, ash and white birch being cut when they fell. My father tried to have a full wood shed, ten cords worth, cut the summer before, and another ten cords of green wood stacked under tin roofing sheets, seasoning for the next winter. The summer before, his hand had been stepped on in the barn, and he would have fallen behind, but for the deacons coming out on three Saturdays, cutting wood with him. He had done the same sort of thing for them. First Baptist was that way. Farm injuries were common, and farming needed to happen, anyway, hay needing to be cut, cows needing to be milked, whether the farmer was hurt or not. I was used to the church helping each other out. But burying the Buckman kid's mother was the first time I had seen the church help out a stranger.

We had been to the grave at least once a week, since the funeral. Mom took the girls with her, all four, when she went into town, shopping for what we couldn't raise, sometimes stopping for ice cream, and then stopping at the church, to visit the grave. When I saw it on Sundays, there were always flowers on the new laid turf, which was as green as the rest of the grass, being kept watered from the church faucet. Trish had ended up eating the rose petal she had saved, unsure as to where to keep it, and not wanting to lose it. Although Roy stayed dark and quiet, Trish seemed to come back, a little, over the next weeks, grinning at me sometimes, almost like she used to.

One morning, at breakfast, a morning after another party had raged down at the Trail's End, my mother asked Trish how she had slept. Trish had looked embarrassed, and happy, and had said that she slept all comfy and snug.

My mother replied, oddly, that she would have not the people she loved be sleeping on feed sacks. My mother went on frying the potatoes, and Trish gave her a hug, and then went to help with the table. Later, Trish told me that when the Buckman kids had snuck up to the barn loft to sleep that night, they had found their feed sack nest remade into two nests, each with a real mattress, sheets, blankets and pillows. Roy had a twin bed, and the girls, a double. There were flashlights for each bed, and pajamas. I didn't know how my mother found out about the old nest, or how she got the heavy mattresses up into the loft, and up to the top of the hay. My dad must have helped, but he never said anything about it, when I asked him, other than to say it would be best to keep my mother informed next time.

My father and us boys worked on firewood, hauling down-falls and some fresh cuts out of the woods with the tractor, down to the lot next to the wood shed, where my father bucked them up into blocks with his chain saw, then split them up with an eight-pound maul, setting each block on a huge round of maple, set on gravel, out in front of the wood shed. Us boys would gather and then stack the splits he struck off, trying to stay out of the path of the swinging maul and the flying wood. He explained as he swung, taking the time to show us where the wood wanted to split, and how to take a ring of splits off a big round, rather than just burying the maul square in the middle. I listened this time as my father explained, and my brother, Roy and I tried splitting wood, with mixed success. My father gave us the ash to practice on at first, which was an easy splitter, compared to the maple. The maul, eight pounds when we started, seemed to weigh twenty or more after a few swings, and the axe was just too light to do any good. My father brought home a smaller, six pound maul from the feed store, and Roy and I began to have some success, even with the maple, with James taking his turn when he wanted. My father moved from close supervision and instruction, to silent observation, and occasion approval, to finally leaving us in the woodlot and heading off to the machine shed or the barn for other projects.

My mother and the girls stayed mostly in the garden, moving from the early greens and salad goods to the beans and peas, and then finally to the root crops. They canned almost every day, turning the kitchen into a steam bath, with the big canner boiling away on the stove, surrounded by tall pots of boiling water. Susan had always hated canning, for the heat and the steam and the occasional burns, but Trish and Tina were excited. They chatted quietly as they washed and cut the vegetables, taken from the garden earlier that day, to be later put away in the basement, that afternoon, safely trapped in glass. The girls had cleaned out the basement, sweeping and scouring the shelves, the barrels, and the gravel floor, cleaning the cobwebs off the ceiling and the light bulbs, and sweeping the steps. Trish had taken me down there for a tour one afternoon, wanting to show off their work. My mother sent Ellen along as well, suggesting that she show us the crocks that lined one wall, but we all knew Ellen was there as an observer, a chaperone, to keep me and Trish in line.

That didn't seem to slow Trish down at all. Once we were down the stairs, Trish led me to a rack of barrels, for potatoes and apples, leaned me up against a barrel, and then pulled my face to hers, holding me by my ears, and kissed me long and deep, while Ellen first watched, then blushed and turned away, straightening some jars. It only took a minute, maybe two, but I was back to being lost and confused, and happily out of breath. "I missed you!" Trish whispered. I missed Trish, too, but couldn't say anything, my mouth suddenly pressed against hers, again, and my brain pretty much scrambled, anyway. Ellen finally made a coughing sound, and then suggested that we head back up the stairs before my mother poked her head down.

We worked hard in the day, long, full days when we were bringing in hay, but always we stopped for lunch, and then dinner, and made it to the bridge for swimming on all the days it didn't rain. The heavy heat of July was starting to fade, and the water was getting a bit cooler. The summer had come, and was starting to go, with school on the horizon. We put in a third cutting of hay, thinner than some years, but with our big second cutting, the barn had hay enough for selling some two thousand bales, my father figured, in addition to the eight hundred bales Mr. Morgan had reserved.

One evening, my mother suggested that we go to the drive-in movie, south of Randolph, with a picnic supper. They were showing a musical, I think, which my mother felt would be appropriate for children, and there would be cartoons as well, before the show. There was a concessions stand where they sold cokes and popcorn. We always tried to go once a summer, if we could. The owner charged by the carload, so people tend to pack the car with kids and then spread out onto a blanket once they were parked. We would get a bargain this time, with seven kids packed into the car. We rode down the hill after dinner, with Susan, Tina and myself filling the back seat, with James in my lap, Trish in Tina's, and Ellen sitting on Susan. Roy rode up front, between my parents. There was another party starting up at the

Trail's End, with cars and pickups parked all along the road, and a group of men standing outside the trailer, smoking, a few with bottles of beer, staring at our car as we went past. I saw Sheriff Joe, with a bottle of beer in his hand, laughing and pushing at the man standing next to him. We had to drive slow, because there were cars parked on both sides of the road, with only a little room left to drive between them. The men stared at my mother, right through the car window, and somebody pointed and said something, and the others laughed. I could see my mother's neck color up, and she moved her elbow up to lock the door. My father was silent, but his jaw muscle was moving, the way it did when he got angry.

Trish nudged me, from Tina's lap. "That's our dad, the one by the door, in the brown hat." I looked, in spite of myself, and saw a small man, his face whiskered lightly, his hair oiled back. He looked at the car, not with lust, like the other men, but at the back seat, with anger. Trish mouthed something at him as we drove past, and he pushed away from the other men, and moved towards the car. My father held the steering wheel tightly in his hands, and pushed the car to speed up just a bit, moving tightly between the other cars and out of reach of Mr. Buckman. I could see Trish turned around, looking out the back window. "He's standing," she said. "Better take a picture."

Roy sighed. "That's what I mean by mouthy. She'd poke a bear with a stick," he added.

My mother and father were still upset, I could tell. As we pulled onto the pavement, finally past the line of cars parked by the ditch, my mother said, "If he's your father, Trish, you should show some respect. Regardless of…" She didn't finish her sentence. My father worked the car through the gears, and the back seat of the car was silent.

I could see Trish, her eyes wet, like she was crying, but her mouth was angry. She loved my mother, and wanted my mother to love her, I knew. But she said, "Him jumping my mother doesn't make him my father. He don't act like he's a father to me, or to Tina, either." Tina moved her hand to cover Trish's mouth, and Trish pushed the hand away. "You know it as well as I do," she said to her sister. "You know how he is. He acts just like the uncles." She muttered something so quiet I couldn't hear, even though I was sitting right beside her. Tears were flowing out of her eyes, and Tina held her tightly, either out of love, or as a restraint. "I don't claim him anymore," she said, into the quiet car. "Ever again."

I was still shocked by what Trish had said. She had answered back at my mother, something that we didn't do. And what she had said was terrible, but her saying it wasn't the terrible part. The color had gone out of my mother's face, and not just from hearing the word "jumped". There was more there than just the words Trish had said, I could tell. But my mother didn't correct her, or ask my father to pull the car over, so she could take Trish outside, as she would have done with one of us. It wasn't because she didn't see Trish as her daughter, deserving of her correction as well as the more gentle parts of love. Trish had already made it into the same hairbrush circle that my siblings and I lived in, as Trish had proudly announced to me a week or so before.

My father kept one hand on the wheel, and reached for my mother's shoulder with the other. Only then could I see that my mother was crying, silently, her hands clenched up by her chest, and her body shaking just ever so slightly. We drove that way for a bit, almost into town, with Trish feeling like she had done something awful, and my mother crying, too, up in the front seat. "Pull over, please," my mother said. My father pulled the car off to the side of the road. My mother got out of the car, and called to Trish to climb out as well, which took her a little bit, with James in the way. Trish went, closing the door behind her, probably expecting to be spanked right there by the road. But my mother took Trish into her arms and held her tightly, swaying some, back and forth, both of them crying openly, my mother saying something to Trish, and Trish finally nodding and saying something back.

The movie that night was something about hot air balloons and fancy cars. The cartoons were Roadrunner, usually my favorite, and my dad sent me and Roy up to the concession stand for two paper buckets of buttered popcorn, something we usually didn't do. But none of seemed to matter to me. It was as if I wasn't even there. I didn't laugh at the cartoons, and I didn't try to follow the movie. I didn't even eat much of the popcorn, which led Trish, still tear streaked, to announce that she was eating my portion. My mother sat quietly, not in the car where she usually sat with my father, but instead, we all sat on the blanket, outside, swatting at a few mosquitoes, my mother sitting with Trish tucked in between her knees, and Tina by her side, her arms holding both of the Buckman girls tight, as if she would never let them go.

CHAPTER TWENTY-THREE

Trish no longer was bathing in the creek. The Buckman kids were either swimming, or taking a bath in our tub these days. My mother ran a bath for the girls, then a second bath for the boys, with me giving Roy first dibs on the clean water, and James and I following up after. The girls had jockeyed for position, according to Trish, with Trish and Susan finally getting the first bath, and Ellen and Tina following up in their sudsy water. Since the creek no longer played a part in the Buckman hygiene, when Trish first reported that the creek had gone dry, we didn't think much about it. We were into late summer, with school set to start in a few weeks, and the hill tended to dry out some that time of year, anyway. Trish must have mentioned it to my mother. My mother thought about it, and then said something to my father, that evening at dinner.

"Dry?" he asked, like maybe he hadn't heard correctly.

"All dried up. Not so much as a trickle. It's been low all summer, but it finally just stopped," Trish said, kind of butting in, but it was her news, I guess, and my parents had seemed to loosen up a bit on the goal of quiet children at the table. We chatted at the table pretty easy now, kids and parents, not talking over each other, my mother made sure of that, but not silent, either. It felt nice.

"I never knew that creek to go dry," my father replied. He took another piece of roast, and then forked a piece onto Trish's plate as well. "Even in the dry years, and this year hasn't been that dry." He eyed the plates around the table, and suggested more roast to the other kids. "Beavers, I'll bet," he finally said. "You kids can go exploring tomorrow, after lunch. Head up the creek and see if you find a beaver dam. I suspect you will."

Roy and James and Trish and I headed out that next day, staying clear of the Buckman trailer, and finding the creek back behind the high pasture. It was dry, just like Trish said, and the moss on some of the rocks had become black and brittle. I flipped a few stones over, and found the ground beneath them dry as well. We headed up the creek bed, which now seemed a little like a rough cobblestone road, winding up beneath the trees, up and up, into a deep saddle between the two ridges of Bear Hill. We were up on State Forest land at this point, up near where the fire tower was, set with a few picnic tables and some charcoal grills. We had come up here twice already this summer, hiking up the ridge trail, when we were tired of swimming, climbing the eighty odd steps of the steel tower, and looking out over the land, in all directions. You could see all the way to the White Mountains over in New Hampshire, down to Killington, and up to Camel's Hump, where the bomber had crashed a few years before.

I was already thinking about climbing the tower when Roy called out, "Beaver dam. Just like your dad said." I looked up. Roy had stopped, and stood completely still, his hand back, warning us to go slow. "They're out. The whole family. Three little ones, too, all bringing twigs back". I quietly moved up beside Roy, Trish's hand now in mine, and we looked out over the brand new pond. The water was huge, and black, being mostly in the shade. The new pond looking almost as big as the pond by the bridge, where we swam. Living trees emerged from the water, like islands. The dam was about six feet high, and stretched all the way across the little valley where the creek had run before, maybe a hundred feet, or more. It was built from branches and twigs and mud, the ends gnawed down to rough points, with the stumps similarly pointed, about a foot high, all around where the pond now lay. In the glassy-still water, we could see two shiny wet heads, a little like dogs swimming, followed by three smaller ones, smoothly tracking vees as they brought smaller twigs up towards a mound of bigger sticks and mud, set in the middle of the water.

Trish squeezed my hand, and whispered, "It's a whole family!" We stood without moving, holding our breath, watching the family bring in what must have been food for the winter, diving down near the mound, and coming back up again without the stick they had carried. The beaver family then tracked silently back through the water to the brush at the high end of the pond, climbed heavily out onto the mud, and used their teeth to snip off another twig, carrying it back to the mound, again, and again. We watched until we were tired of standing, then, we carefully sat where we could watch some more. "That one there is Toby," whispered Trish, pointing to one of the baby beavers who had dropped his stick, and was circling back for it.

I had never stopped to think that a pond could be made like that. I had been up this mountain plenty of times, hiking up to the fire tower, or looking for mushrooms with my mother. The saddle where the water now was had been boggy before, mostly filled with blackberries and fiddleheads. The creek was small, up here, but I guessed that if you added up all the water it carried for a month or so, you could build a pretty big pond. I guessed the thorny bushes were still there, out of sight, rotting, probably, under the water. I wondered what my dad would think about the beaver pond, and if we could maybe swim in it next summer.

"Marty, Arty and Farty," Trish said, squeezing my hand, again. "Farty takes after his dad," she added. She had snuggled down between my knees, and she tipped her had back against my chest, looking up at me. "You look a lot better upside down," she said, and then she did that thing with her lips, asking for a kiss. I bent over and kissed her, her nose now up against my chin. I looked down at her neck, and the way the lines of her throat merged into the lines her collarbones made. Her neck was less freckled, and less tan then the rest of her. I kissed her pointy chin, then her nose. Trish sighed and closed her eyes, and pointed her lips back up at me, again.

James made a farting sound, and said, "Toby is Farty," but we ignored him. We sat that way for a while, Roy watching the beavers work, James digging in the dirt where he sat, and my neck getting sore from bending over. "Let's leave them alone," Roy finally said. "They're putting up food for the winter. Imagine eating sticks every day."

We headed around the pond, trying to be quiet, and then climbed up towards the fire tower, silent as we walked. There was no one at the little park on the top of the hill. There was a swing set, nice and high, and we tried the swings for a bit, Roy pushing hard to get as high as he could, and Trish and I trying to keep our swings side by side, but getting off kilter over and over. We tried holding hands while we swung, but we almost fell off that way.

We gave up on the swings, and climbed the tower, holding onto the rails with both hands. There is a little wall around the top platform, maybe three feet high, and a pitched roof, all made out of metal, punched here and there with holes from deer rifles. Kids had written stuff on the inside, and there was a little heart, on the south side, facing down the hill towards our farm, where Trish and I had scratched away the grey paint and made a heart with our initials in it. Trish touched that heart as she came up the stairs, then stood, looking out over the valley. Randolph was there, church steeples and all, right by the White, and then Bethel, then Royalton. A ways past Royalton was White River Junction, where you could see black ribbon of the Connecticut

River, taking the water from the White and carrying it all the way down to the Atlantic ocean, right by New York City, I knew.

There was a map in our classroom that Mrs. Ferris kept rolled down, on the back wall, by the coat-room. It showed the whole United States. You could see Randolph, Vermont, right there, and Montpelier, with its little star, and then the whole rest of the country stretching out in different directions. Trish liked that map, and she liked to stand there, her finger tracing out where New York was, and California, and Texas, and all the places she had heard about. Trish wanted to travel, before our three kids were born, just her and me, she said, all round the country, and maybe over to Italy or something. She wanted a map, just like the big one we had in school, and hoped to put pins in it, whenever we have visited somewhere. "Then we can go back and visit the best places, with the kids. After we've already seen it, ourselves," she had said.

I thought she was thinking about New York, but she pointed out to the south, and asked me, "Where is Boston?"

You could see Mount Monadnock from the fire tower, and I was pretty sure Boston was behind it, hidden, somewhere, by the ocean. I pointed it out, and then she said, "That's where Mr. Morgan lives, now?" I said he lived up north of Boston, in a town called Manchester, but that he lived close enough to go shopping in Boston, and go to the museums there. Trish put her head right by mine, so she could look out over my finger, as I pointed. "I feel bad for him, " she said. "And he's so nice to us."

Mr. Morgan had heard about Mrs. Buckman's death, from my father, and had sent another package, with chocolate oranges for each of the kids, and three leather bound copies of the New Testament, each inscribed in his neat hand, with the names of the Buckman kids, and the date of their mother's death. He had added a line. "I hope you find some comfort here, in your time of sorrow". He listed five verses he specifically wanted the Buckman kids to read. All three little bibles were kept at our house, "kept safe", as Trish said. Trish and Roy spent some time reading through them, usually when my mother was reading her Bible, as well. Mr. Morgan's weekly letters to my father always inquired after the Buckman kids, and my father kept him up to date in his letters back.

You could see the back pasture, behind Mr. Morgan's old place. I pointed it out to Trish. His horse barn was hidden by the trees. "Boston's a long ways away, isn't it?" she said.

I nodded. "Not as far as New York. Maybe five hours? My mother went there once, with her parents. Boston. I don't remember why." We stood there, on the top of the tower. There were a few pines right around the tower, and we were higher then they were. You could look down onto the top of the pine tree, small and tight at the point, showing the lighter green of the new growth, and the little cones, all hidden from the ground. Even the swing set looked small.

Trish leaned back up against me, and I held her tight. Her shoulder blades were a little sharp against my chest, but I liked the way she felt. "Do you think he'll come back up here?" she asked.

I was confused. "Who?" I asked.

"Mr. Morgan," answered Trish, sounding a little annoyed. "Who do you think?"

"Maybe," I said. "He's buying that hay in the front of the loft. He might come up. I don't know." I didn't want to tell Trish about what my father had told me.

She waited for something more, but I was quiet. "I hope he does," Trish said. "I'd like to thank him. And say we're sorry."

Roy had been standing beside us, looking out towards Camel's Hump, away from Boston. James was trying to tell Roy the names of all the mountains, some of which I think he was just making up. "Sorry for what?" asked Roy. "We didn't shoot his damn horse." Roy sounded angry, which surprised me. Roy didn't get angry very often.

Trish was surprised, too. She started to say something to her brother, then stopped, and set her hand back on my shoulder. We stood that way for a while, then, still quiet, made our way carefully down the metal steps, onto solid ground once more, then headed down the ridge trial to our house. About half way there, Roy said, "We didn't pick him to be our father. All we can do is to make it until we're old enough to be out on our own. Tina will be eighteen in five years, and then maybe we can get a place of our own. We just need to make it until then. Feeling bad about what he does doesn't help." We didn't say anything back, but just kept on walking. "Five years," Roy said, again, to himself, I thought.

My mother was in the garden when we got back, with Susan, Ellen and Tina working beside her, gathering some early potatoes, and pulling up yellow onions, which I knew she would dry for a few days on the porch, then braid together into strings. My father was splitting wood, and we went to spell him, getting the six-pound maul from the shed. He didn't ask about the beaver dam, and we didn't think to mention it. We were thinking about how long five years seemed, and how impossible it seemed to keep things together for that long.

CHAPTER TWENTY-FOUR

As the nights grew colder, my mother had begun to talk about clearing out the parlor, a room that had been kept for company since my father was a boy. It had always been furnished with two ancient, carved leather chairs, and a dark brown horsehair couch, with a high, curved back, and carved arms. The couch was a fancy thing, really, for our farmhouse, and it was scratchy, I remembered, from the few times I had been allowed to sit there. In between, there was a low table, which my mother regularly dusted, including the two figurines, young ladies in fancy ballroom dresses, dancing, it seemed, and between them, a cut glass bowl. The bowl and figurines had once belonged to my grandmother, and the bowl had wooden fruit stacked in it, apples, pears and plums, carved to look like the real thing, and painted in faded colors that might have once looked real. Pictures of my grandparents, looking dour and ancient, hung on the walls. It was not a friendly room. The parlor was small, maybe ten by twelve feet, the size of my parent's room, which was next door to it. The two bigger rooms downstairs were on the front of the house, the kitchen and the dining room, with windows that looked out down the valley. The two back rooms each had a tiny window, looking north, with a storm window over it, trapping the moisture in the winter and fogging whatever view you might have had.

My mother's plan was to move the boys, the boys now being my brother and I, and Roy, downstairs, into what had always been the parlor, and have the four girls take over the attic room, two to a side. Bunk beds and a twin would fill the space in the parlor once occupied by the scratchy couch, the carved chairs, and the fancy table. She had asked my father to offer the parlor furniture to his brother, who might want it for it's family history, but there was some discussion in my uncle's house about taking the furniture that was yet to be resolved. My father deferred to my mother's planning in this, as he did with most things. He was planning on building the bunk beds, and had gone so far as to order a sheet of plans from the back of his farm journal.

Before we heard back from my uncle about the couch, and before my father had bought the wood for the bunk beds, an aluminum step van pulled up at the house, with "Emmon's Furniture" painted on the side. The driver came to the door with a purchase order, with our address printed on it. Mr. Morgan had ordered bunk beds, and a twin, mattresses, pillows, sheets, blankets and pillowcases, as well as two nightstands and lamps, having called a furniture store in Burlington, and arranged to have it all delivered to our house. He explained this in a letter to my father, which came later that day, but I remember at the time the confusion the delivery caused.

My parents talked while the two men waited by the van, then my father and the men carried our old couch and chairs, and the table, out to the machine shed, setting them up on the workshop floor. My father draped sheets over them, and then put a tarp over the sheet. The new beds were brought into the parlor and set up, with the tables placed beside them, under my mother's directions. It was the only furniture that ever came into our house, when I was a child. My mother had Susan and Ellen make the beds, using the new sheets and blankets. The blankets were dark green, thick and soft, made from lamb's wool, my mother said, and the pillows were filled with goose down. "This must be how they sleep in Boston," Susan said, irritated at the luxury suddenly bestowed on the boys, but quiet enough for my mother to not hear her. James was thrilled, and demanded to sleep on the top bunk. I gave Roy the single, of course.

We moved into our new room that night, with the girls happily taking over the attic room. Susan and Ellen changed the sheets in my old bed, making things ready for the Buckmans. Trish brought the pillows and her stuffed rabbit in from the barn loft. Roy and I brought the mattresses from the loft over to the machine shed, and put them under the tarp, on the couch. Roy put the pitchfork back downstairs as well, and we filled the nest hole in with hay bales, not wanting to leave a trap for us to fall into, later. Roy pulled his Savage gun out from under the hay, and a box of .22 shells. I hadn't known he had brought it up to the barn. "Do you think you dad will let me keep this inside?" he asked.

I nodded. I wondered if he had brought the gun up to defend his sisters, and decided he probably had. When Roy showed the gun to my father, my father look it carefully, making sure it was unloaded, and then sighted down the barrel. "Savage makes a good gun," he said. He opened and closed the gun a few times. "Nice and tight. Nice thing about the smaller calibers, they don't beat the breech up too bad." He handed the gun back to Roy. "Do you want to clean it up, some?" Roy nodded, and my father got out his gun cleaning kit, a small wooden box filled with solvents, oils, swabs, metal rods and a black plastic handle. I loved the smell of the kit, a mix of Hoppes Number 9 and Remington gun oil, and the turpentine scent of the gun stock oil my father used to keep the wood in good condition.

My father set some newspapers up on the kitchen table, and selected the right swabs for .22 and the .410, and set to work, showing Roy what to do, and then having Roy do the actual work. I watched, burning up with envy, wishing I had my own gun to clean, and to keep and shoot. Roy offered me his gun from time to time, letting me scrub and swab and oil, and my father must have seen what was going on. "I guess it's time we got Toby a rifle of his own. You two could go get us some partridge, maybe, or a turkey, this fall. We'll have to down to Snowsville and see what Mr. Buska has in stock. That Savage is a good choice. He might have one."

My jealousy washed away with a flood of happiness. Roy grinned over at me, but didn't say anything to me. "If I could go with you, I need to get a box of .410," he said. "All I have is a half box of .22 at this point."

My father nodded. My mother was watching him, listening to the conversation. I could see him check with her, a little later than she would have wanted, but I think the "boys and guns" category was his, and I think both of them respected that. "You be careful," was all she said.

The water at the bridge had gotten cold enough in the past week that the tourists and adults no longer swam. The kids always made it a point of honor to swim until school started, which would be the following week, not wanting to waste a single day of our summer. We cannonballed in, but we pretty much cannonballed back out again, clinging to the bridge, gasping for breath and laughing. The color was already up in a few of the trees, and there were nights when a sweater felt good. The house was cool, except the kitchen. We lingered there, in the warmth, sitting at the table, or even standing beside the cook stove. My father wouldn't fire up the wood stove until the middle of October, but the windows were closed at night, and my mother ran the baths hotter in the evening. The summer was almost over.

My father did run the heat in the car, that next Sunday morning. We were all in the car, nine of us, heading down to First Baptist Church. Trish had asked my father if they could go with us, the night before, with Roy standing beside her, obviously wanting to go as well. My mother had been looking at my father, when he had turned to look at her, and somehow she silently communicated that she would like for them to come with us as well. I watched her eyes to see how she did it, but I couldn't see anything. My father nodded. Tina and Ellen were putting the last of the supper dishes away, standing so close as to be bumping into each other as they dried the dishes and put them behind the glass cabinet doors. Trish grinned when he gave his permission, and gave him a hug, hard and quick, not at all like the hugs she gave my mom. Roy smiled a little, and went back to the table, where I was setting up the checker pieces, since the loser sets up the board. Roy beat me, every game, even when he seemed distracted by something, or when he was using our game as a teaching moment for James. But I liked Roy, and kept playing, anyway.

We got to church early, as we usually did, the barn dirt scrubbed off and our bellies filled with a big breakfast. As we entered the building, it was a little cold, and I could see Trish remembering the other time she had been here. She walked up front, and stood pretty much where her mother's casket had been, looking a little confused. She put her hands out in the air, as if there might be something she could rest them on. I walked over and stood beside her. "She was here," Trish said, and I nodded. Trish's eyes were shiny with tears, but she was smiling. "This is a good place," she said, turning away, and going to help my mother with the alter flowers.

Our Sunday School lesson was a story about honesty, I think, but it was nothing I could remember, even five minutes after it was over. Mrs. Tucker was our teacher, an older woman who was hard of hearing. That might have influenced her teaching style, because she said pretty much the same things over and over, getting louder and trying to drive her point home, pointing at each of us in turn with her finger. Trish sat with the girls, Mrs. Tucker keeping a boy's side and a girl's side in her class. I watched Trish, to see if she would look at me, but she didn't. Trish kept her eyes on Mrs. Tucker, nodding from time to time. Trish looked pretty great, and I wished that she'd look over at me. She was wearing a light blue dress she had borrowed from Ellen, who sat beside her, chewing at a fingernail and tapping the toes of her shoes together, listening to the little click they made. Roy sat beside me, his fingers laced together and his hands on his knees, perfectly still. Susan and Tina were in the older girl's class.

There was always a break between Sunday School and church, with the basement tables serving up coffee for the adults, and Tang for the kids. There were boxes of powdered sugar donuts and some Oreos as well, and the congregation stood around and talked politely with each other, before settling down to hear Reverend Sykes. I knew that Trish loved those powdered sugar donuts, and palmed three into one hand, while taking the allowed two in the other. This technically wasn't stealing, since all the kids did it, the boys, anyways. If caught, you could say you had gotten the extras for your sister and brother, handing out the extra donuts to the smirking faces of your siblings. Trish had picked up two donuts and a paper cup of Tang, and was standing off to the side, near the stairs in the back. She was talking with Ellen, who was watching Tina across the basement.

I offered her my handful of donuts, but she pushed my hand down. "We're only supposed to take two!" she hissed. Trish looked around, like she thought we were going to get caught, then, she took a donut out of my hand and popped it into her mouth, whole. "This is church!" she hissed, again. She took another donut. "Didn't you even listen to Mrs. Tucker?" she said, her mouth still full of the last donut, while she took another. "'Honest in the eyes of the Lord' is what she said. If you hadn't been staring at me, you would have heard her." Trish smiled at me, her lips frosted in powdered sugar. Her voice had softened. "I look nice, don't I?" I nodded. She did. "Do we sit together, at the regular church thing?" she asked. I nodded again, my mouth full of donut, although Trish seemed happy to talk around her donuts as best she could. "I want to sit next to your mom," she said, "like we did, before." She looked sad, right then, her mouth still working on the last donut. "She's nice," she said, dabbing at her eyes and getting powdered sugar up on her cheeks. "Maybe we can have recess later, this afternoon," she added. She finished off the last donut, her two and my five gone, now. She took a sip of Tang. "This stuff is really good!" she said. I told her about the powdered sugar up on her cheeks, and she blushed, showing the powder off even more. She took a napkin and thought about dipping it in her Tang, but decided not to at the last minute, and wet it with her tongue, instead. She dabbed at her face with the damp napkin, reminding me of a cat, then grinned at me, all mischievous, suddenly. "Do I look OK?" she asked.

"You look beautiful," I said. Trish blushed again, and grinned. "Church, dressed all pretty, with donuts, then lunch with you guys, then recess," she said happily. "I love it."

Reverend Sykes sermon was about the woman who had touched the robe of Jesus, and was healed, even though she was sneaky about it, and didn't even ask. I knew the story already, because my mother had a print of it happening in the big Bible she had gotten from her parents. It was a really nice picture, from a painting done a long time ago, I think, and it showed Jesus looking startled, maybe even confused, feeling that something had happened, while the woman was down near the ground, reaching through a bunch of legs to touch the hem of his robe. You can see that the woman is lit up inside, the way Trish gets, and there is what looks like a spark of light right where her finger touches the robe. Reverend Sykes told us that this was proof of the power that was in Jesus, the power of love, so strong it could sneak out and heal people just by touching his robe. Reverend Sykes demonstrated this by reaching his finger out towards the pulpit, slow and careful, and I thought for a second there I saw a spark flash between him and the pulpit, when he got real close. "Just like that!" the Reverend said.

Trish was up on the edge of her pew, leaning in towards the Reverend's words, still bumped up close to my mom, and holding one of her hands. Trish's face looked just a little like the face of the woman in the picture, not her hair or her nose or anything, but her eyes, maybe, all excited and charged, eager, and lit up, somehow. I wondered at that. It was just another sermon, to me. I usually day dreamed through the sermons, planning out the day after church. I had been thinking about recess, of course, and wondering how cold the water would be in the pond. But something about watching Trish listen to Reverend Sykes reminded me of Roy listening to my father, and then it hit me. I had been missing most of what went on in my life, not listening, not paying attention, just drifting along. Roy had woken me up to that fact, around my dad, and now Trish seemed to be doing the same thing for church. Trish and Roy both talked about how much our family had helped them, but I knew it was the other way around. I thought about our family, now happily talking around the table, my parents teaching the Buckman kids things I thought we already knew, about making hay, or splitting wood, or cooking or working in the garden. We had a second chance, now, to do it over, and do it better, this time. It was all different, now. I knew that Trish had given me a future, with three kids and a loving wife, and that she had brought something to life in me that I never knew before. But the Buckman kids had changed our whole family, changing how my parents were, and how I was, with them, and woken us all up, somehow.

CHAPTER TWENTY-FIVE

There was a radio in the kitchen, a Zenith Eight, I think. It was ivory colored, and had an FM band, but it was usually tuned to the AM station we listened to for the weather. It was already on when I made it to the kitchen on Friday morning, the last day of summer vacation. There a scratchy voice was telling my father what to expect for the day. This morning, I was shushed, even though I hadn't said anything. My father was standing by the counter, where the radio was on, and he was listening to a storm warning. Heavy rains and wind were predicted for the afternoon and the night, and early the next day, as well. Flooding was expected in the valley, and wind damage likely throughout the central Vermont region. Hail was a possibility, the man said. When the local news came on, my father switched the radio off. "Sounds like a big one," he said. He took the coffee that my mother offered, smiling at her.

"Gardens in, all but the potatoes, and they won't care about the hail," she said. "Hay's all in, too. Good thing it wasn't a couple of weeks ago."

My father nodded. "Good thing we live on top of a mountain. We'll get the rest of the split wood up under cover, and close the shed up. Bring the cows in early, I guess. They won't mind the rain, but the hail will make them break the fences. We'll be OK," he said.

Roy was up early, too, joining us in the barn for the morning milking. We got it done, and came back in for breakfast, with the girls all up at that point, and a bowl of hot biscuits just getting set on the table. Trish smiled a sleepy smile at me. I smiled back. I wanted to go to Snowsville, and look for a rifle today, but I knew to not ask my dad about it. Nagging wasn't something that worked out well, and I didn't want to put my new gun at risk by sounding pushy. School was starting up next week, though, and I wanted to get the gun before that. Once school started, I'd be busy during the week, and the Snowsville store was only open Saturday mornings on the weekend. I fretted as I sat at the table.

Trish was already finishing on a second biscuit, loaded up with butter and molasses. "Can I sit out on the porch?" she asked. "When the storm comes?"

My mother put a third biscuit on Trish's plate. "We'll see," she said.

Trish grinned at me. "I love a good rain storm." She looked out the window. It was still dark, with only the faintest grey showing in the east. "You can almost feel something coming," she said. Her biscuit paused, half way to her mouth, her eyes suddenly serious, maybe worried. It was quiet, outside, and the rain hadn't even started yet, but I knew what she meant. It was like something was waiting, just out of sight. I forgot about the trip to Snowsville. Everyone at the table was quiet, with only the sound of the wind, just starting to pick up outside.

My mother moved to snug the kitchen window shut. She looked worried, as well. "I think you can stay inside tonight, if it's going to be stormy."

Trish nodded, and moved the biscuit back up to her mouth, but she didn't take a bite. She looked towards the window, out into the moving shadows, looking past the porch, and on down the road, to where her father's trailers sat, silent and dark. She shivered, and tried to smile. "Inside sounds good to me," she said.

"Weather man said noon, but it feels like it might start before then," my father said. "We might as well get things under cover, first thing, and make sure things are snug. Then maybe we can head down to Snowsville, and see what they have for rifles." He was looking right at me, when he said this last part, like he knew what I'd been thinking. I grinned, and Roy asked if he could go along. My dad nodded. "Let's get it all done, and be back here before things start to happen," he said.

By the time we were in the car, headed down the hill, the storm was really starting to pick up. It was late in the afternoon, with my father having to work a bit on one of the shed doors to get it to close nicely and hang right. I was excited about my rifle, but I couldn't shake the feeling that something bad was coming our way. When we got to the Buckman trailers, there were already a half dozen cars and trucks parked along the side of the road. Mr. Buckman was on the porch of the house trailer, talking with a man at the foot of the steps. He stared at us as we drove past, turning as we went by, and then leaning out from the porch to keep us in his vision. My father drove slowly. With the sky already getting dark, and half the road taken up by parked and parking cars, he wanted to be careful. But I wished he would hurry up and get out of Mr. Buckman's range. That man scared me, and when I saw him, the hatred I felt for him scared me, too. I turned to look out the back window, and wished I hadn't. Mr. Buckman was standing in the road, pointing a finger at the back of our car, and shouting something. We couldn't hear him, with the windows rolled up, and the wind blowing, but I could feel it, just the same. It was like we had driven right past the center of the storm, the place where all the darkness and worry was coming from.

Roy sat quietly, staring down at his hands. He rubbed a finger on the round scar on the back of his hand. His eyes were half closed, but I could hear his breathing, fast and hard, like he'd been running. He must have felt me looking at him. He tried to smile at me, and said, "Good thing Trish isn't here. She would have tried to pick a fight with him." My father just kept driving, slow and steady, working the car through the gears, and onto the paved road, taking the right up the Brookfield gulf, and finally into the parking lot beside the Snowsville General Store.

I tried to forget about Mr. Buckman, and to get excited about finally getting a rifle. The Snowsville store had been there since my father was a kid. There was a huge pot bellied stove, a Live Oak, I believe, with wood chairs set around it. The stove was cold, though, Mr. Buska being on the same wood heat schedule that my father was. To the left were rows of rifles and shotguns, with the glass cases in front filled with pistols and revolvers, and some holsters, as well. There were boxes of ammunition stacked beneath the long guns. There was clothing, heavy jeans, wool socks, some flannel shirts, and thick jackets, on shelves in the middle of the store, and a few rows of canned food, and two glass door refrigerators along the back, filled with soda and beer. A braided rag rug was on the floor in front of the wood stove, and two huge mastiffs lay on the rug, their giant heads lifted up over hand sized paws, their eyes watching us carefully. Mr. Buska was behind the counter, smiling as he recognized my father.

My father explained about the need for me to have a gun, and mentioned both the lever action .22 I had planned on for so long, and the Savage .22/.410. Mr. Buska nodded, and said it was time I got a start, and lifted some guns down off the rack. He opened the breech of each one, and then set them on plastic pads, printed with the word Remington, and a scene of dogs and duck hunting. There was a Winchester lever action .22, with a dark walnut stock, and a brass saddle ring, just like a cowboy gun would have. Beside it was a Remington bolt action, with an octagonal barrel, heavy and long, hard to carry, I guessed, but accurate and worth the weight, Mr. Buska countered. It had a small scope mounted on it, and Mr. Buska let me look through its, pointing the rifle at a stuffed bobcat mounted on one of the top shelves. I could feel myself getting excited, and starting to forget about Mr. Buckman. There was a Savage, as well, in .22 on the top, and twenty gauge, below, but not one in .410. Mr. Buska argued on behalf of the larger shell, pointing out the turkeys and geese could run after being hit with a .410, but not a twenty. It was heavier than Roy's gun, and longer, too. Buska took down a pump twenty, and a double barreled twenty as well, and then two more .22s, one a Browning automatic, and the other a Winchester pump. The counter was filled with long guns, and I picked them up, one after another, lost in the possibilities, and the pain of having to choose, while the storm built outside. All the guns were used, but in nice shape, the pump .22 being the roughest. The Browning was twice the cost of the other guns, so I pushed it aside. My father wasn't a fan of automatic rifles, anyway, believing them to be less reliable than a gun that let you chamber your own shell. I wanted them all, but decided on the Winchester lever action, with the brass saddle ring. I moved the lever back and forth, and Buska slid a piece of paper into the breech, and had me look down the barrel, the white paper casting enough light for me to see the perfect grooves all the way up the inside. "Not sure that one's ever even been shot," he said. "It came in oiled and clean, from an estate. Can't go wrong with a Winchester."

Mr. Buska nodded to my father, who turned to me. "Is that the one?" my father asked.

I nodded, and said, "Yes, sir." I sighted it again, picturing me and Roy bagging partridge after partridge up the creek.

Mr. Buska put the other rifles back on the rack, and took down a brick of .22 ammo. He also got a box of .410, for Roy. My father was looking at the revolvers beneath the glass top, but when Mr. Buska asked if he would like to see one, my father shook his head. "No need for a hand gun," he said. "Just the .22 and the ammo for today." The rain had started up solid, pounding on the tin roof of the porch out front, and making the street look like boiling water. My father paid Mr. Buska, who offered us a plastic trash bag to cover the gun while we made our dash to the car.

It was dark enough on the ride home that my father pulled on the lights, the dim beams showing the torrent of rain pouring down onto the road. When we went past the Buckman trailers, there were lights on in The Trail's End, and another dozen cars were parked along the road. "Something big, tonight," Roy said. I turned and looked out the back window, forgetting my new rifle for a moment, but there was no one to be seen, only the rain and the black sky, now showing a few flashes of lightening in the south. "Put your rifle on the porch, Toby," my father said. "No need to get it wet. And don't load it in the house. I'll go over my expectations with you after we get the cows done."

My father made his way out to the barn, leaning into the wind, while Roy and I ran to bring in the cows. The lightening flashes in the south were getting closer, and I could see the shadows of the cows, pressed up against the gate. It was a dark now, at four o'clock, as dark as it usually was for the evening milking. I thought maybe the cows were confused by the darkness, but when we opened the gate, they pressed into the barn in a rush that I knew was from fear, not a need to be milked. After the milking, we left the cows in the barn. Roy and I ran to the porch, watching for my dad, a little worried as the wind whipped up higher and higher, and the deafening thunder rolled up the valley. There was a closer flash of lightening, and only a split second after the flash, the crash of thunder split the sky, making me jump back, in spite of myself. We saw my father running for the house. He bounded up the steps, and pushed us through the door, into the warm kitchen, where my mother saw us, surprised, and relieved. She hugged my dad, then sent Roy and me to change. She had a kettle of water on the stove, and a pot of coffee already made.

Trish was at the kitchen table, and the rest of the girls were in the living room, huddled together on the couch, under a quilt, reading. The front widow was fogged, and when I wiped off the glass, I could see a sheet of water pouring off the porch roof, like a waterfall, and in the lightening flashes, the water pooling in the yard, and spilling down the drive to the road. Trish was beside me, taking my hand in hers. "I was scared for you," she said. Then she grinned. "I'm glad we're not sleeping in the barn, tonight. Did you get your gun?" I nodded to the plastic bag on the table, but her eyes kept going to the window, watching the storm. "I've been scared all day long. Scared of the storm, I guess, I don't know. But it's good to have you all home."

I left my gun on the table while I put on dry clothes, then took it out of the plastic and showed it to Trish and my mom. They tried to look interested, but I could tell that the storm was what they were thinking about. It was dark enough now that we could only see outside when the lightening flashed, with the whole world lit up in blinding white. Trish and I stood by the window, holding hands and looking out. You could feel the wind on the glass of the window, the pane shaking and moving back and forth, like it might break. The window was latched shut, tight, I thought, but a little water leaked in and made a puddle on the sill. My mom dried it up with a tea towel, then, she sent us kids to check the other windows, to make sure they were latched, and dry them if they needed it.

Trish and I were standing right by the living room window, checking to see that it was dry, when the lightening flashed, and we saw a face there, on the other side of the glass. We both fell back and I yelled. It was black again, outside, and we couldn't see anything. Then there was a pounding at the door, and screaming from the porch, and my father moved to open it. I started to tell him not to, but then the door was open, and three soaked girls poured in, off the porch. They were crying, and one of them had the top of her dress half torn off. They tried to talk, but all they could do was to cry, and look back at the door, like they were scared something had followed them. My father looked out into the storm, then closed and locked the door. My mother was up, handing dishtowels to the girls, and sending Susan upstairs for bath towels and a sweater. Trish was crying now, too. I tired to comfort her, but she pushed me away and ran to my mother, who held onto her with one hand, and tried to help the girls get dry with the other. There was another flash of lightening, right in the barnyard, it seemed, and then all the lights in the house went out.

My father moved through the darkened kitchen to the middle drawer, and took out two flashlights. He handed one to me, and told me to check all the outlets, switches and lights in the house, upstairs and down. "Look for smoke," he said, "or something that's burned. That was lightening on the pole, and it might set a fire here, in the house. Don't touch anything," he added. "Run!" He gave me a push, as he moved towards the Hoosier, and I headed off into the dark house. All I wanted to do was to stay in the kitchen with my parents, but I went, like he told me. I found Roy in our room, his Savage in his arms, and the box of .410 open on the bed beside him. He was standing in the corner, where he could see out into the living room and the kitchen, and the front door. I didn't say anything, but checked the electrical things, and then headed upstairs. I could still hear the girls from down the road in the kitchen, crying, but softer now, and I could hear my mother, calm and comforting, saying soft things over and over.

When I came back down the stairs, my mother had lit the lanterns, and my father had his Stevens cradled in his arms, sitting in one of the kitchen chairs, looking straight at the door. Roy was still in our room, his eyes trained on the door as well. "He's going to come up here," Roy said. "He's going to want the girls back, and he'll want us back, too, Trish and Tina, anyways, once he gets here." Roy said it like he knew it was true, and I didn't doubt him. It was hard to imagine something that was more scary than the storm, but now I could. "He'll know they came up here. And with the storm, he'll know that we're not out in the woods. His crowd will be wanting their money back, with the girls gone, and he won't want to give it to them. He'll come up here."

I thought about that. Roy was dead calm, like he had been, when he was waiting for Danny Bowman. My dad looked calm, too, focused on the door, the shotgun held loose in his hands like he might not need it. But he had the box of 12 gauge shells open on the table beside him, and I could see the safety was slid up and off, the little red button just showing in the lantern light. I was anything but calm, almost crying, still, and my breath came in painful gasps. I was scared, scared to death, and I felt ashamed that I wasn't more like my father, or like Roy.

Roy looked at me, then, put his eyes back on the door. "He won't come for a while. He'll wait for the rain to slow down some. He's probably trying to get the crowd to have another drink while they wait. It's OK, for now." He was trying to comfort me, and that made me feel even worse.

I could see my mother and the wet girls all standing together, and then my mother decided to bring them all upstairs, to the girls room. She lit another lantern, and shepherded the three strangers, and Tina, Ellen and Susan up. Trish turned loose of her, and ran to me. "I'm sorry!" she said. "I'm so sorry!" She dropped to the floor beside me, and hung her head, saying something soft, over and over. It was hard to hear, with the rain and wind whipping up outside, but I finally heard that Trish was praying, asking God to keep us safe. I held onto her hand, and prayed with her, not out loud, but asking God to keep us under his wings.

The thunder was so loud that you could feel it more than you could hear it. It came right with the lightening, now that the storm was over us, the glass in the windows rattling like they were going to break. Roy had moved up next to the window, watching out into the yard every time the lightening flashed, trying to see the shadow of his father coming up road.

Suddenly something like thunder, only louder, and constant, sounded outside, shaking the whole house, the pictures shaking on the walls, and the box of shells rattling and moving slowly across the table. It was too loud to yell, too loud to think. There was a shaking and a rumble, louder, and then, impossibly, even louder, and louder, still. The lightening flashed, and even the thunder was drowned out by the constant roaring sound. But in the flash of light, I could see the far edge of the low field seem to melt and turn to liquid, like the world itself had come undone and was flowing away down the mountain. Another flash showed the giant maple trees along the creek tumbling into the risen tide, the field itself washing away, and the creek larger and larger, as big as the Connecticut, it seemed.

Almost as quickly as it came, the roar softened, then, went away. When it was gone, the storm slowed, and then died. The barn was still standing, and the wind was still fierce, but the rain tapered off, and the lightening moved on up the mountain, towards Northfield. My ears rang like I had been too near the shotgun going off, and I looked at my father in the faint lamplight, trying to see if maybe he had fired the gun. Roy was up on his toes, still staring at the door, but he had a confused look on his face, not the focus he shown, before. Trish was still on the floor next to me, but now she was praying, "Thank you, Lord! Thank you!" She looked up at me, smiling through her tears, and I could swear she glowed in the dark, there on her knees, one hand in mine, and the other holding the leather Bible that Mr. Morgan had sent up from Boston.

None of what I had seen or heard made any sense. I felt like I might throw up, or that I might pass out. I stayed, holding onto Trish, and my father stayed, watching the door, with Roy still watching it from the side, but I could tell that something was different. That the thing we had felt was coming, that bad, scary thing, had come, and now, it had gone.

CHAPTER TWENTY-SIX

I woke up to the smell of pancakes. I was in my own bed, under the soft, green blankets, my head settled into a goose down pillow. I was in my underwear, and not my pajamas, and I realized my father must have carried me in and put me to bed. Or maybe my mother. I hoped that Trish hadn't been there to see it. Then I remembered Trish on the floor, filled with joy and light and thanking God for having sent an impossible flood through our farm. I didn't know what was real and what was a dream. There was a little light showing outside the window, which meant we were late to milking. I climbed out of bed, and then reached up and shook James awake. The bed that Roy slept in was empty, and still made from the day before. I had an awful thought that Roy's father had come up in the middle of the night and taken Roy, and Trish, and Tina back down the road, to the bachelor party. That didn't seem right, either, and I couldn't imagine my parents letting them go, but I shot out into the kitchen, my shirt still in my hand, and my pants barely on.

My mother was dimly lit by a kerosene lamp, there at the stove, a big bowl of pancake batter on the counter beside her, and a stack of pancakes already growing on the platter. "Where's Trish?" I said.

My mother looked up at me, tired, and she said, "Get dressed. We have company." She nodded towards my parent's bedroom, which didn't make sense, either. James was falling asleep standing next to me, leaning into me, and I shook him awake, again. "Your father and Roy are already out in the barn. You two can go help, now that you're up." She looked at me, and her face softened. "Trish and the other girls are upstairs, still sleeping. It was a long night. So hush, and go help your father."

I got my clothes fixed, and headed out onto the porch. James and I put on our boots, and headed out into the darkness. There was a hint of light in the east, enough to show the trees black against that part of the sky, but not enough to see anything else. We knew the way, though, and the barn was lit, softly this morning, the power still being off, and my father doing the milking by lantern light, the way his father had, before.

"Just in time", my father said, handing me and James our buckets and rags. The cows were quietly eating the first of the summer hay, having been put in early last night because of the storm. James and I got busy cleaning udders. Roy was bringing in flakes of hay from a bale he had broken. He looked tired, and I wondered if he had slept at all. I suddenly remembered my new gun, and then wondered if that had been a part of a dream, too. James was half asleep again, so I shook him awake, and put my attention on the cows.

When we were done, and the milk was in the cooler, my father fired up the generator that ran the milk house, and then flipped on the light. It flickered in the unsteady power, but the compressor on the cooler was chugging away, cooling down the morning's milk. The house was mostly dark, with only lantern light showing in the kitchen window, but as we walked outside, there was enough light in the sky that I could see the telephone pole in the driveway, splintered and broken, with wires laying on the ground. My father shook James awake, again, and told us to stay away from the wires, that when the power came back, the wires might be dangerous. He turned and looked down the hill, and I looked, too. The bottom corner of our lower field was gone, just like I had remembered, and where the creek had been, there was a huge cut in the land, as wide as the barn, and about as deep, from what I could see. It looked fresh and raw, with trees dropped over the edge, their roots up in the air, and big stones showing half out of the mud and gravel. "Land's changed," my father said. "You don't see that, too often. We'll go look, after breakfast. We'll have to fix the fences, too, I guess. Cows don't have much sense. Then I've got to take those girls back up to Barre."

Roy was looking at the cut in our land, too, and his eyes went on down the road, towards where I knew his trailer was. James was leaning up against Roy, tired of being shoved and shaken by me, I guess. Roy looked over at me. "It's done, I guess. Trish thinks so, anyway." He smiled at my sleepy brother, and guided him along the path to the house. We washed up at the hose, and slipped our boots off. My mother had a second lantern lit, but there was some light in the sky at this point, too, and the kitchen was well lit. I could see three girls, the girls from Barre, I guessed, sitting at the table, looking shy and sleepy, still dressed in my mother's robes and pajamas. Tina, Ellen and Susan were sitting with them, uneasy in their company, and Trish was helping my mother, frying bacon in the big skillet, dressed in the same clothes she had worn the day before. Her hair was brushed, though, and she turned to smile as me as we came in. Her face was lit, brighter than the lantern that burned beside her, like

I had imagined it to be last night. "Two pounds of bacon," she said, happily. "And four times the regular recipe for pancakes, whatever you call that." She shook a loose piece of hair out of her eyes. "We're OK, now," she said. "God came."

She turned back to the bacon, flipping strips over while the grease splattered and popped. My mother poured my father a cup of coffee, and set the big platter of pancakes on the table. "Start with two," she said. "There's more coming."

I got the jug of syrup and set it on the table, and then we stopped for my father to say grace. "Thank you, Lord for your gifts and your loving care, for the comfort you bring in the darkest hour, and the beauty you show us at the light of day. Bless those around our table, and keep them safe, under your wings, and guide them along your path, to a life of goodness and love."

Trish added something. "Thank you, God, for looking after us, last night, and for making us safe. Amen."

We all said "Amen", and my father started forking out pancakes, two to a plate, while Trish scooped the bacon onto a pad of paper towels, then brought it to the table as well. "Start with two," she said, echoing my mother. "There's more coming." She went back to the stove, and laid out more bacon, the cold fat melting on the hot pan, and starting to sizzle. My mother shooed Trish to the table, taking over the last of the pancakes and bacon. Trish sat down next to my mother's chair, where she usually sat, and filled her plate. My father tossed another pancake on the two she had, saying "Cook's tax", and handed her the syrup.

Trish was half way through her pancakes, and done with her bacon, when my mother filled the platter again with both, and sat down to eat with us. It was quiet at the table, the Barre girls being shy, and everyone being tired, and the food good enough that you just wanted to pay attention to eating. But Trish couldn't keep still. "I saw Him, last night, walking right down the creek, taking all the water with him. He was as big as one of those maples, bigger, maybe, and he was wearing a barn coat and black boots, just like ours, only really big. He didn't look that old. And he had the beaver family in one of his hands, and the little ones were looking down over the edge of His fingers, at all the water rushing below. And He smiled at me, right as He walked past, and said, "It's going to be OK, Trish. It's going to be good.""

Trish teared up at this point, happy tears, but it was all a little scary.

Nobody said anything. I knew Trish was talking about seeing God, and it seemed weird that she had him dressed like a dairy farmer, almost disrespectful, or something. I waited for my mother to say something, but she didn't, and my father didn't say anything either. Trish looked around, then she blushed, and said, "Well, He did."

My mother reached around and pulled Trish over to her. "You're a lucky girl, to have seen Him," she said.

Trish smiled through her tears. "I know," she said. "I know I am."

We made our way through all the pancakes, with my mother sending Susan to mix and fry another batch, and all the bacon, as well. My father made another pot of coffee, the girls from Barre being coffee drinkers, it turned out, and still we sat there at the table. Trish got up and fried some eggs, taking two, herself, and we got half way into the morning with everyone still at the table, talking a bit, now, about the storm, and the cattle, and the land that had washed away. I remember that morning as being the start of something, or maybe the end of something. I know that everything was different afterwards, and I remember being amazed that the twelve of us, my family, the Buckman kids and the three girls from Barre, were all sitting at the table, crowded together, eating pancakes and bacon and eggs, drinking coffee and milk, and telling stories about the storm.

What we didn't talk about was the Trail's End, and Mr. Buckman's single wide, which we all knew were no longer there by the little creek. Looking at the huge canyon that had been made in our field, it didn't take much imagination to see that things would have changed down stream. Maybe we stayed at the table so long just to put off the trip down the road, to look and see what was left. My mother stayed at the house with the visitors, getting them bathed and dressed and ready for the drive back to the city, while my father and the rest of us walked down the driveway, and then down Bear Hill Road, towards where the trailers had been.

We stopped about half way, where you could see the road break off, the new canyon taking the road right out, and some of the mountain on the other side of the road. As we walked up closer, all we could see was dirt and gravel, and torn trees, with the little creek now flowing again, some thirty feet below where it had been, brown and thick with mud, but starting to clear. There were a few beaver-chewed sticks along the side, and Trish reached down over the edge, with my father holding onto her, and picked one up, holding it and wondering at the little teeth marks in the wood. "This is how He did it," she said. "He worked on it all summer. He must have started the first time I asked him to."

I looked at the raw cut where the land had been, where the road had been, where the two trailers had been, and where all the men had been, that night, before. Now all of it was gone, swept away, broken into tiny pieces, as we would learn, by the force of the water and stones and trees. I thought back to my prayer, and I thought that maybe it had started then. Trish and I worked it out, later, with her pointing out that the creek had dried up a few weeks after she had first prayed, but that it must have taken the beavers a while to walk over to where they were supposed to build the dam, and then to built it up high enough to stop the water. She thought the timing was just right, and I had no reason to argue with her.

I had grown up worshiping God, going to church every Sunday, praying before every meal, yet God had always been something vague to me, Someone talked about, but not seen, and certainly not seen walking down the creek, wearing barn clothes and pushing a flood down onto a trailer full of men, while a handful of beavers looked down through His fingers and watched. I tried to point this out, once, to Trish, and she just nodded, and said, "So you were wrong. That's OK. I never would have thought about God that way, either, until I saw him. Most people have to live by faith, I guess. I'm lucky."

And she was. Trish stayed happy, even in the hard times, always feeling like she was one of the luckiest people on the planet, blessed in every way. The spark came back into her eyes, and never left. She grinned when she woke up, and grinned again when it was time for us to go to bed. The glow that had been so bright in her that night might have dimmed a little, but it never went away, and I could always find her in a crowd by looking for the light.

The only way to get to town now was to drive up the mountain, then cross over the bridge to Stone Road, and drive through Randolph Center, then down to Randolph. We drove that way, the next day, getting to church a few minutes earlier than we needed to, my father being uncertain as to how long the drive would take. The Buckman kids were used to the church at this point, and Roy went with my father to help get things ready. Trish stayed with my mother.

People at church were talking about the storm, and about the flood that had swept down Bear Hill. A couple of the kids asked me if I had seen it, and I told them a little, but I didn't say anything about the trailers or the men washed away. That news would come out, later, with pictures in the paper showing bits of car and trailer found all the way down in Bethel, some sixteen miles downstream. The biggest pieces weren't that big, and there was never an exact number for the men who were lost. Mr. Buckman was there, or course, and all the Buckman uncles, and the sheriff, and some men from Barre, and Montpelier, and Northfield, and even as far away as White River Junction. The Trail's End was a popular place, it seemed, and aptly named, it turned out, for the men who had gone there, that night.

Reverend Sykes stuck to his planned sermon, resisting the temptation to respond to the flood. He preached on faith that day, as he had planned to, faith like a candle in the darkness, and the power of faith to move mountains. Trish sat beside my mother, a little powdered sugar on her lips. She listened closely to the sermon, and she nodded at the moving mountains part. She had seen the mountain moved, and her faith was the kind that came from seeing God at work in the world. An easy faith, she said. No work involved.

Mr. Morgan saw the news of the flood, at his big house down there, in Boston, and he tried to call my father, that afternoon. When his call couldn't get through, he worried enough about us to get in his car and drive the five hours from Manchester to Brookfield, and finding the road gone, then driving up around through Randolph Center, and crossing the bridge to get to our house. He drove up just as we were having a late afternoon apple pie, the Barre girls delivered back to the city, right after they had lunch with us. Mr. Morgan was driving his city car, long and black and shiny, and he was wearing city clothes, too, having been to Mass early that morning before heading out. My mother cut him a big piece of pie, and introduced him to the Buckman kids. They thanked him for the gifts, and the beds in the boy's room. Mr. Morgan was unusually quiet, looking at the Buckman kids, and then looking out the window, like there might be some sort of answer for his questions out there. After pie and coffee, Mr. Morgan and my father went for a walk. Mr. Morgan borrowed a coat from my dad, and the two of them walked up the hill, to look at the place where the flood had come, and then they walked up the road, past our house, and were gone for a long time. They might have walked over to Mr. Morgan's house, which was only a half-mile or so, up the hill, and then down towards the bridge a little.

It was getting dark by the time they came back, with the air of men who had decided something. They shook hands, and Mr. Morgan came in the house long enough to thank my mother again, for the pie, and to say goodbye to all of us, for the night. He was going to spend a few days at his house, up the road, he said, and make some plans. I wondered if he were going to bring the brood mares back up from Woodstock, and if the hay we had for him would go to his barn here. We got the milking done, my father obviously happy to have Mr. Morgan back in town, and then we headed in for a light dinner. My mother sent the girls up for their baths, with a lamp, and a reminder that the first day of school was tomorrow, and that she would check them to be sure they were clean. Roy and I played checkers, while James watched, and tried to give me hints about what moves I should make. My father took my mother out for a walk, with one of the barn lanterns for light. When they came back, Ellen was just calling us up for our baths.

I was dead tired when I climbed into bed, and fell asleep l listening to my mother and father, in the bathroom, whispering and laughing.

CHAPTER TWENTY-SEVEN

School started that Monday, with the school bus showing up a good thirty minutes late, Mr. Beller not having had a chance to figure out a new route yet, now that the road was gone. He sent me down to the Campbell's, to have them run up the road to our place, where Mr. Beller would turn the bus around in our drive. My mother watched from the porch, with my dad helping guide Mr. Beller to stay out of the ditch at the side of the drive. My mother had bought new clothes for all of us, from the J.C. Penny's, down in Lebanon, and she had buzzed the boy's hair, and trimmed the stray ends off the girls. We had on our new school shoes, tight and stiff and hard to wear, after the summer freedom of running barefoot most of the time. We had notebooks, pencils, and a note for Mr. White, letting him know that the Buckman kids would be staying with us for a bit. The ride on the bus was quiet, and a little confusing, since we were going up the hill, instead of down it, but we got there, just the same, only close to an hour late. Mr. Beller told us that he would get the new schedule figured out today, and send it home with each of us, so we could know what time to meet the bus tomorrow morning. Mr. White was standing by the door, making eye contact with the kids he thought might be trouble makers. He did this every year, on the first day, and the boys thought it was a badge of honor to get the evil eye from Mr. White on the first day of school. I thought he would stare at Roy, but instead, he reached out and took Roy's hand, and said, "I'm sorry about your father, son."

I could see that Roy wasn't expecting this, either, and Roy answered, "We're sorry about him, too, sir," which made Trish snort until Tina gagged her sister and pushed her on into the school. Nobody teased the Buckman kids about their dad, remembering what happened last year with Danny Bowman, or maybe scared to think that a kid's parents could both die. We got through the day, with cinnamon rolls baked by the girls Sunday night, just for our school lunches. Trish ate half of Tina's, and all of mine, as well as her own. Trish and I had recess, which was great, while Roy sat near us, reading. The three of us still owned the spot under the big maple. When we got on the bus,

Mr. Beller had the schedule worked out, and reminded us to be on time, or be left behind.

When we got home, Mr. Morgan's black car was in the driveway. We found him inside, sitting at the kitchen table, dressed in what he thought were his country clothes, tall leather boots, thick wool pants, and a wool jacket with leather patches on the elbows and the shoulder. My mother asked us all to stay, and we sat as best we could, with Trish perched on my mother's lap, and Ellen and Tina sharing a chair. Roy stood by the door. There was a half tray of cinnamon rolls on the table, and pitcher of milk for the kids. We were all quite, sensing, the way kids can, that something was about to happen to us.

My mother started. "Trish, Roy, Ellen? With your father dead, and your mother gone, we need to think about where you can live, and who can take care of you." Trish smiled and snuggled back against my mother. My mother went on. "We love having you here. You feel like a part of our family, already." Trish smiled, her eyes half closed. "But we can't adopt you, even though we'd like to." Trish popped her eyes open, and tried to shoot out of my mother's lap, but my mother tightened her grip and held her in place. "Listen now, Trish. If we adopt you, that makes Toby your brother. Not your sweetheart." She let this sink in. "I didn't think you would want that. Not you, Trish, or Toby, either." You could see Trish going over this in her head. "Stop squirming. I'm not finished." My mother's voice had the tiniest bit of hairbrush in it, and Trish settled immediately. "Mr. Morgan would like to be the guardian for the three of you, to watch over you, help with your expenses, and help you make good decisions in terms of your education and your future. He can't adopt you, because that would involve his wife, and she feels she has already raised all the children she is going to raise. But he can offer you a home, and his support, until you are grown and able to make a life on your own. He would rely on me to continue to serve in a motherly role with all three of you, in terms of guidance, and discipline. And hugs. Children need a mother, and I would continue to be that to each of you, as best I can. If you would like that," she added. "While you would live with Mr. Morgan, in his home, here in Brookfield, I would hope that you would visit here on a regular basis, whenever you want, to help with the garden or haying, or just to talk, and that you would stay here when Mr. Morgan needs to be in Boston, for example." My mother scooted Trish around a bit, and looked into her eyes. "It's a big decision, for all of you, and Mr. Morgan only wants to do this if it's something that all of you want to have happen." She kissed the top of Trish's head. "I want you to think about it, and I want you all to talk about it. Ask whatever questions you might have, and then make a decision. There's no hurry. But you need to think about it."

Mr. Morgan looked embarrassed in the silence that followed. "I'm a little old to be much of a father, but I think I'd be a good guardian. I'd like the chance to try, anyway." He sat at the table, his eyes on his coffee. None of the Buckman kids looked happy at the idea. I think all the kids had been thinking that they would just keep living with us, and they didn't know anything about Mr. Morgan. And that business about Trish being my sister, if my parents adopted her…well, I guess that's true, but it seemed like being a sister would have had to come first, in order for it to count. I felt like me and Trish had already made each other our future, and that where she lived wouldn't change that. Tina was holding Ellen as tight as my mother held Trish. Only Roy stood alone, over by the window, looking unhappy and a little lost.

Mr. Morgan got up, and rinsed his coffee cup out in the sink. "Well, maybe this was a bad idea. I'm sorry, if it was." He set the cup by the sink, and moved towards the door. "Let me know. We can move that hay over whenever you have the time. The brood mares are coming back up this week, and we'll need some good hay for them." He looked sadly around the room, and made his way to the door. My father held the door for him, then, followed him out. We were all stuck there, no one wanting to say anything, or even to move, for some reason. Finally, Susan got up to put the cinnamon rolls and the milk away.

James put his hand over the roll on his plate, and then picked it up and started eating it. "Mr. Morgan is really nice," he said. "And his house is huge. All fancy on the inside. And I think he's lonely, living there with himself for company, and the cleaning lady, sometimes. I think maybe that's why he talks so much, when we're putting the hay up with him. He doesn't really have anybody else to talk to." James started in on his cinnamon roll, and everyone else stayed quiet. Trish was crying, just a bit, and I was glad that Mr. Morgan had already left, so he didn't have to see it. I knew it wasn't about him, but just the Buckman kids having thought that they would be adopted by my folks.

By the time the next morning came, and the cows were milked, and we were all sitting down to breakfast, Roy said that he and his sisters had talked about it last night, and that they would like to talk with Mr. Morgan, maybe when they got home from school. Trish nodded at my mom, but she didn't say anything, and she didn't seem too happy. My mother moved over and took her in her arms, holding her tight, then tipped Trish's head back and looked right at her. "I'll always be your mother, Trish, just as much as you need. You don't have to worry about that."

Trish nodded, and then tugged towards the breakfast on the table, where Susan had just put a bowl of hot biscuits down. "I know that. It just takes a while to get used to things changing, again." She took a couple of biscuits, broke them open, and filled them with butter and honey. When the first one was gone, she said, "I know it's going to be OK." She said that with the certainty of someone who really does know, and I guess she did.

And it was OK, with only a few of the ripples you might expect when growing up. Mr. Morgan and all of us went to the courthouse, the next week, over in Chelsea, and got the papers signed that made him the legal guardian of the Buckman kids. My father put the Buckmans into his car, that afternoon, along with Roy's books, and Trish's rabbit, and an old leather suitcase filled with their clothing. The Buckman kids left their barn boots there on the porch, saying they'd be back to work, right after school, pretty much every day. We said goodbye out in the yard, filled up with lunch from a restaurant down in town, where Trish had ordered both a hamburger and the fried chicken. Roy got in the car last, after seeing his sisters into the back seat. He sat next to Mr. Morgan. He turned and waved through the window, just a little wave, and then the car pulled away and drove slowly up the hill.

Ellen was crying as the car went out the driveway, and ran up to her room and threw herself on the bed. My mother let her cry for a time, then, called her back downstairs to help with the laundry. We kept the rooms the way they were, since the Buckmans would be coming up for overnights any time Mr. Morgan went back to Boston. That night, after our baths, James and I were in the boy's room, with James up on the top bunk. He leaned over and called my name. "Do you think Trish really saw God?" he asked.

I was tired, and worn down, inside and out. I'd thought about it, though, and I'd talked with Trish a little, too. "Yep," I said. "I think she did."

"Wearing barn boots and everything? God?" asked James.

"I think so. No reason God has to run around in a robe all the time." I rolled over and tried to fall asleep. I could hear James moving around some, and then he was quiet, his breathing slowed down like it did when he fell asleep. I lay there in the dark, trying to picture what Trish had seen. I'd asked her what God was like, and she'd just said, "Friendly. You could tell he liked the beavers." I wondered if my parents would have seen that night as evidence of an Old Testament God, or a New Testament God. I was sure they had talked about it, my mother teasing my father for his ideas, and loving him all the more because of them. I fell asleep, and I dreamed about walking through the woods, high up on the ridge, with Trish. She was old, and so was I. We walked slow, watching where we stepped, like Reverend Sikes did. The beech tree was bigger, but it still had our heart carved on it. The farm was in good shape, down below, the fences tight, and the fields newly mown. And there were kids, I knew, all grown up, with kids of their own, at this point. I didn't know their names. But I knew that Trish had been right, all along. It was OK, and better than OK, really. It was pretty great.

NOTE FROM
THE AUTHOR

Word-of-mouth is crucial for any author to succeed.

If you enjoyed The Buckman Kids, please leave a review online - anywhere you are able. Even if it's just a sentence or two.

It would make all the difference and would be very much appreciated.

Thanks!

Gary

THE BUCKMAN KIDS

ABOUT THE AUTHOR

Gary D. Hillard lives just up the road from the Lander's place.

His life's work with other people's children, and raising four of his own, gave him some ideas about the lives of kids.

He remembers growing up in the early 1960s, and how things worked back then, as well.

Hillard writes every morning, and spends the rest of his time drinking tea.

THE BUCKMAN KIDS

OTHER BOOKS BY GARY D. HILLARD

Betts' Best

Book One of the Betts Trilogy

Betts' Best introduces us to Betts, a quiet and curious seven-year-old already bruised and battered by the chaos in her life. After a life of abuse, a whirlwind of failed foster homes and a locked psychiatric unit, Betts finds herself in a kinship placement with her shy uncle, Ames, a wounded vet, living in a cabin on Bear Hill, trying to keep his own demons from the Sand Wars at bay. Zoey is the young social worker who believed in this placement, and who falls in love, first with Betts, then with Ames.

Family, school, and friendship are all hard, as Betts slowly adjusts to her new family, and the magic of the Vermont woods. The center of Betts' universe is a tiny cabin near the top of Bear Hill, deep in the Vermont mountains. Travel with Betts and her family, up twisting dirt roads, through the Vermont seasons, to a special place of long views, cold springs, wood heat, poverty, resilience, and love, deep into the hearts of the Vermont people.

Find Betts' Best at Local Independent Bookstores

or

Online at Amazon and B&N

Made in the USA
Monee, IL
07 February 2021